I0619041

ORDER OF THE WORLD

ROHIT DHARUPTA

Rohit Dharupta

Rohit Dharupta

"For my wife Richa and son Aahan."

Rohit Dharupta

Rohit Dharupta

Contents

Winter

"Sleepy pavement. Lazy sidewalk.
Morning snow crust cracking under his little feet.
My son shines in the sunshine."

Chapter One

I was standing there, right in front of him, motionless and clueless, unable to utter a word. My eyes could not spot anything beyond him amid the deep mist, and my ears heard nothing more than my incessant breathing in the dead silence.

Taking off his long hat, thereby exposing his bald, shiny head, the man with a noticeably long nose, dressed in black overalls, began to speak. "Hello, Mandira. I am Jack. It is my pleasure to talk to you," he said with a smile, gently placing the fancy black hat back on his head.

I acknowledged his greeting by nodding but then kept gazing at him sheepishly, wondering what to say or ask.

Assuming the expression of a wise man about to say something important, Jack continued in his deep voice that echoed from every corner, "Before I disclose the reason for making your acquaintance, I want to say that you are no ordinary woman, and this meeting is extremely important and absolutely necessary."

He paused as if to collect his thoughts and continued, "You see, Mandira, I want to draw your attention towards something precious, like a gift. A gift that we have but do not appreciate, that we know but do not cherish, that we notice but do not value.

"You must be wondering what that is. That gift, my dear lady, is the gift of life. The world that we live in is a treasure, and it is our responsibility to protect and preserve it."

I kept looking at him intently, trying in my head to break down the words of wisdom that this noble-looking man was showering.

"The reason I am telling you all this, Mandira, is that I need a favor…"

BANG.

Suddenly the mist intensified, and Jack's figure turned hazy. His voice sounded faint and distant as he said, "A huge favor indeed."

BANG.

Jack disappeared in the dense fog, and his grand-sounding voice became inaudible.

It was then that I woke up.

"Mandy, what's up? Are you awake? Hey, Caesar! Don't you jump on the couch, stupid!"

It was 6 a.m. by the clock, and Viren was back after walking Caesar. He let him loose in the living room and approached the bedroom door.

"Mandy! What happened?" asked Viren, pressing against my hand as he sat beside me on the bed. "Did you have that dream again?"

I nodded my head.

"Man, five days in a row! Now I am jealous of this guy. I'm sure you haven't seen me that many times in your dreams!"

"C'mon, he's an old man."

"That's worse. An old and mute model is hogging the limelight in your dreams," Viren joked.

"He spoke for the first time."

"Really? What did he say?"

"I don't know. He said it was necessary to talk to me. He was telling me something about life."

"About life? Like what?"

"Like, it's important to value life. Life is a precious gift."

"Oh, he said life is a gift? A precious gift, eh! Did he also give you the address of the gift shop?"

"Why can't you be serious for once? Dreams can have meanings, Viru!" I returned, slightly vexed.

"What, serious for your silly old dream man, who says life is a precious gift? I'll tell you what it means. It means either you worry too much about your life or want a gift on your birthday."

"No, it does not. And I don't need a birthday gift. Not from you."

"Yeah, yeah, why would you when you already have one. The precious gift of life!" Viren chuckled.

"And why can't you remove your shoes at the entrance? What is that shoe rack for?" I returned in haste, unsure if it indeed was the roaming about in shoes that bothered me or his bantering.

As Viren left to take off his shoes, Caesar approached with playful excitement, as usual, breathing heavily and wagging his tail.

"Women. Always schooling their husbands. Why don't you teach some manners to this stupid dog?" Viren said, leaning against the bedroom doorjamb, shoeless this time.

"Why, what did he do?"

Viren told me how that morning, as he had walked Caesar to Mount Mary Hills, he had pooped twice on the way, once while ascending and then again when descending. Viren, who had run short of plastic bags after cleaning up the first time, decided to leave the waste behind the second time, unaware that a peace officer was quietly following him. Viren was caught red-handed for sparing his hands from the effort and had been fined.

"I wonder if these cops are going jobless. Who the hell drives around at 5 a.m. in the freaking minus fifteen degrees cold, looking out for people who leave their dogs' shit behind?" said Viren, visibly displeased.

I could not control my laughter. I noticed a twinkle in Caesar's eyes, who momentarily blinked (or perhaps winked), as if mischief was dancing in his head. I always wondered if Caesar teased Viren like this on purpose.

5

"You're laughing? His shit has cost me two hundred dollars. What am I, a stupid man working hard in the office to pay not only for his food, but also his shit? Had it not been for Ryan, I tell you, I would have given him back to that shelter long ago. And where are your sleeping beauties? Are they dreaming too? Reva!" Viren shouted, as usual, keeping up with his habit of announcing his arrival every morning, "I tell you, life is really a gift for all of you. Ryan! Revs!"

"Down here in the kitchen, Dad! I made you honey lemon water," returned Reva.

"Oh, my good girl. I tell you, Revs, you are the only one who cares for me in this house. You are my precious gift," mumbled Viren as he advanced towards the kitchen.

"Caesar, my dear! Go and get Ryan. It's time to wake up," I said, and Caesar immediately sprinted off for an attempt to wake Ryan, which, I knew, would not be his first that morning, but definitely his most resolute this time around, after my command.

Caesar. A grey and brown German Shepherd that we adopted from the dog shelter when he was merely two years old, when Ryan was six. Mrs. Danielle Silver from the dog shelter had told us the terrifying rescue story of Caesar, whose pregnant mother, a stray dog, had wandered off into the jungle on one of those cold winter mornings. Attacked by a wild bear, she instantly succumbed to injuries, delivering three puppies on the spot, out of which only Caesar had survived.

I remember not being able to sleep for two nights after hearing the story, thinking about how poor Caesar was deprived of his mother's love. I had always felt ever since that I had not two but three kids.

Caesar got the credit of being the first living creature whom teary-eyed Ryan had hugged tightly, a rare display of emotions and proximity we witnessed that left us with overwhelming joy. Ryan spends most of his time with Caesar, hugging, wrestling, pulling his tail, opening his mouth with his bare hands, and doing all other annoying things—a luxury perhaps only Ryan could afford—that Caesar didn't seem to mind.

Viren's behavior towards Caesar could be described as seasonal (and I am not speaking metaphorically), which may be attributed to his walking him to Mount Mary Hills every morning. It ranged from fair in spring, bearable in summer, complaining in fall, to irritable in winter; something that could also be said for his mood in general.

As for Reva, well, she cared for Caesar as little as she did for those mundane picture-frames in her bedroom.

I rose from the bed, wobbled a little as I reached out for my sandals, turned off the lamp at the side table (that Viru had turned on upon arrival), and drew the curtains. The darkness had not yet paved the way to the morning light, though the white blanket of fresh snow along with the illuminated streets managed to diminish the usual gloom.

Thanks to the low visibility, the fresh falling snow flurries could be discovered only in the illuminated field of view of the solitary lampposts on the street and in the headlights of scarcely moving vehicles on the road.

The snow removal had entered its last leg by now, with the smaller plow truck scraping the sidewalks while the heavier one on the roadway was busy plowing, spreading salt for de-icing, and pushing the heaps of snow to the sides. Despite the thick white covering formed by the accumulation of dense flurries, the city of Abbynton never stopped, thanks to the tough men working through the whole night in the freezing cold.

Looking through the crystal-clear windowpane, my lips moved to bring a soft smile to my face upon seeing a familiar figure jogging, who perhaps did not miss a single day without conquering Mount Mary Hills. The girl who Viren jokingly called "the fittest girl in North America."

In the next moment, my mouth dropped open and my brows raised, switching my expression from amused to bemused, as I felt something or someone right in the middle of the street. No sooner than I felt the sensation, it went away.

"What was that? Was there someone on the street looking at me?" I said to myself. I thought about that momentary figure that was now nowhere to be seen. "Was it a shadow of a tree or a lamp post? But, it's gone now. Is it something in my head? Could it be some mental image formed in my head because of my dream?" I pondered over that for some time.

It was now 7 a.m. Viren left for the office after ranting about the weather and complaining several times about his rough start to the morning by making the frequent use of his favorite prefix expression— "I tell you…"

Reva, as usual, was at the breakfast table pouring cornflakes into her bowl, all set for school. She rarely asked me for any help. I sometimes wondered, *How and when did my twelve-year-old become self-sufficient and organized?*

I wished the same could be said for the boy who, as usual, was still in bed. Caesar, who, like an expert taskmaster, had sprinted off enthusiastically to execute the waking-up task that I had assigned to him an hour ago, soon caved in to the temptation of Ryan's cuddling and cozy, warm bedding. He was now lying beside Ryan, snoring in sync with him.

I couldn't remember seeing Ryan wake up by himself, ever. In the absence of external intervention, he could perhaps sleep for a whole day or even more. Out of curiosity, I had once let him go on for sixteen straight hours over a weekend before I got worried and woke him up in the afternoon.

The school bus would arrive in another twenty minutes. It was time to literally drag Ryan out of the comfort of his bed and drop him under the wet shock of the shower, the only place where Caesar would not accompany him.

It would not end in the shower, though; I also had to force him into performing ablution, getting dressed, and having breakfast. With his disinterest in everything in general and the reluctance to get ready in particular, it was an uphill task to get him out of the house in such a short span of time.

Finally, with a desperate attempt on my part and a half-hearted one from Ryan, together with welcome support from Reva, I was able to get them both to board the school bus that had already been waiting at the door for about two minutes.

As always, Caesar displayed affection for his favorite buddy by sprinting behind the bus, following it almost half a kilometer before returning.

Chapter Two

"Hi, Mandira!" shouted Sebastian from the other end as I descended the escalator.

"Hi, good morning, Seb!" I returned as I approached nearer.

"Very good morning, dear lady. Good to see you again."

"How are you today?"

"Could not be better. I get to see and meet wonderful people like you."

"Nice to hear that, but aren't you cold?" I asked, noticing the old, rugged cloak he wore that had a few holes and a torn seam right under one of his arms.

"It is cold, but not enough to kill me. Believe me, I have witnessed worse than this and survived, Mandira."

"Yes, but it's freezing this morning. It's been snowing all night."

"Snow is beautiful, Mandira. Snow is nothing but God's way of filling brightness in our life."

"How lovely. Perhaps the best definition of snow I have ever heard. Snow is nothing but God's way of filling brightness in our life! That's a good one," I said with a smile, "but don't go outside, stay at home." Then, checking myself, I added, "I mean, stay indoors, don't get wet."

"Yes, yes, I get it, my dear. Don't worry, I take good care of myself. This winter, I am putting up at Victoria Hospital. The hospital authorities provide shelter at night, a warm and cozy hall in the basement for the people living on the streets. It turns out our hospitals don't only cure but care too. It's incredible, Mandira, how we humans display passion at work and compassion at heart."

"Wow, I am glad to hear that. Here, take this!" I took out the paper box from my bag and handed it to him.

"Ah, lovely! I think of food, and here you are. You are very kind, young lady!" returned Seb, as his wrinkled, sagacious face lit with joy.

"See you then!"

"Oh, by the way, those brown balls of sugar you gave me yesterday were delicious."

"That's called gulab jamun, an Indian sweet," I returned, giggling. "Brown balls of sugar! Never heard that before. You're funny."

"Goodbye, dear lady, and thank you very much."

Sebastian. A good-humored, gentle, and jolly homeless old man. Every morning when I went to the dimly lit Saint Thomas Subway Station, I would find him standing at the other side of the escalator, glowing even in those tattered rags.

Every day, just like today, he laughed off any adversity. I never saw him begging for money or asking for anything or complaining about his misery. In fact, I don't even think that the question of misery presented itself to his mind in light of his state of affairs.

Initially, I thought it to be a façade of positivity that he wore on his face to amuse people, but then for how long can anyone with an empty stomach and deprived living put up a brave front?

This quality of being so content though having so little, was kind of mesmerizing to me. My initial curiosity to observe soon turned into a habit to visit him, and I don't remember when I started bringing food for him, which he always accepted graciously.

The act of helping someone is not selfless when you seek help in return. The best part is that you don't even know about the help you seek or the favor you're getting in return. I realized that the pleasure I derived was not from helping poor Sebastian, but from merely seeing him, hoping that his cheerfulness and optimism would rub off on me, and it did.

I needed a dose of positivity on a morning like this one before arriving at the place I was heading. And he never seized to drop those gems in the form of one-liners that cheered me up on most occasions.

How else would I have known that snow was not just a natural phenomenon caused due to moisture in the atmosphere under low temperatures, but also God's way of filling brightness in our life?

If this man, who had nothing, had nothing to complain about, then why did I, who had so much, have so much to complain about?

I probably would not bring food regularly for any grumpy old man who pitied his life and begged for money or food.

The subway station was sparsely occupied. I punched my metro card and walked the steps down to the platform. The large monitors suspended from the ceiling displayed local news and the time left for the next metro train to arrive.

There was a familiar face of a lean teenage girl with short hair, sleepy eyes, and a large backpack who walked clumsily, going up to almost every person asking the same question monotonously, "Could you spare me a dollar?"

She was as formal about her question as she was casual about people's responses, which were mostly unfavorable. An apt mind reader, she did not even wait for an answer from some people. However, she waited a little longer for some, even after the negative response, perhaps sensing something positive in their body language.

Sitting on the bench, I thought about Jack, the man with the long hat and conspicuous nose, who I had seen in my dreams and could not get out of my head.

Those dreams felt like a video of a strange man emerging out of bizarre mist, being played every night, each time for a longer duration than before, with sharper picture resolution and better sound quality.

How was it possible to dream about the same mysterious man for five nights in a row, somebody who I had never seen or met in my life? How was it that I remembered every detail of these dreams vividly, including his name and whatever he said? That had never happened to me before, or perhaps to anybody, for that matter.

Why did I feel that he wanted to tell me something important? Was I going to see him every night in my dreams and remember the following morning? Did this really mean something? Was I putting a lot of thought into something unimportant and trivial?

The metro arrived at the stipulated time predicted by the monitor, and I, along with my fellow passengers, entered the door that slid open in front of me.

As I stepped in, I felt as if somebody with a long hat and an overcoat entered the adjacent door of the same coach. Bewildered, I scanned every person who entered and those already stood and seated in coach to try to catch a glimpse of someone dressed in black in a similar outfit. Then I anxiously looked out through the door (that was again sliding, this time to shut) and the windows to check if anyone was left behind.

The metro started to move. I did not find who I was looking for. Then I wondered, *Who am I looking for? And why? Why am I stressing so much about a random person in my dream, who perhaps does not even exist and who I imagine around me?*

It was like watching a horror movie and then freaking out in the dark, fearing the same horror scene might unfold around you. Yes, that was it. That was the only way to explain this strange feeling of being followed.

My dream impacted my imagination so much that I sensed or vaguely visualized a fictitious person in flashes. That could only be an outcome of my overthinking.

Like I always did under the circumstances of uncertainty, I pacified myself by concocting more examples in my imagination in favor of what I wanted to believe, and against what I did not want to consider.

It was 10:30 a.m. when I changed from the orange to the green line at the central station. I got off at McMurphy Metro Station fifteen minutes later.

The patches and stacks of snow on the sidewalks and the corners of the street shone brightly under the brilliant round sun in the clear sky, producing the illusion of millions of tiny illuminating white pearls and gems scattered over a rich fertile mine in no particular fashion.

I walked two blocks further along the street to finally arrive at the clinic for my appointment with Estelle Silver. I hoped today I would not break down in front of Estelle as I had done in my previous visits.

What is the greatest delight and distress in a mother's life? The delight is watching her child grow well and hit every developmental milestone successfully. Her distress, however, is in witnessing the other way around. The effect of these overwhelming feelings is equal but opposite.

For instance, when we flip a coin and wait for the outcome assigned to each side of the coin, whether or not our desired one, it produces an effect that is equal in capacity but opposite in nature. The difference, though, is that the effect of the outcome of the coin depends upon the degree of significance or consequence attributed to its sides.

The mother's heart, on the contrary, knows no such boundaries, and the degree of her delight and distress cannot be manipulated.

"Hi, Mandira. Nice to see you again. How is Ryan doing?" asked Estelle upon greeting.

"Well, Estelle, looking through a mother's lens, my opinion of my son will always be clear and biased," I returned, and she smiled. After a brief pause, I continued, "So, have you completed your assessment?"

"I did. That is the reason I requested an appointment with you. As we discussed in our previous meeting, I visited Ryan's school last week for observation. I also spoke to his teachers and received their feedback."

"I see. And what's the feedback?"

"Well, Ryan does not interact with his peers. He does not have a friend in the class. The class teacher said that he hardly talks to anyone and barely manages to complete his work."

"But he does speak."

"He does, but very little and only when prompted. The teacher says he seems to be daydreaming all the time, hardly paying attention." Estelle paused, perhaps expecting me to say something in Ryan's defense, but I remained silent.

"Look, Mandira. I know Ryan has potential, and we just need to push him to get the best out of him."

"Ok, so what next?" I asked, trying to avoid discussing details of Ryan's limitation.

"There are two areas we need to focus on: social interaction and communication. We need to encourage him to talk more and express himself. I will introduce a new program in his therapy to target those areas."

I did not shed any tears. It was the only thing I felt glad about in my meeting with Estelle, the psycho-educator and Ryan's therapist.

Lately, I had learned to mask the "hows" and "whys" appearing in my mind and only let the "whats" get through. "What is to be done next?" would be the only question that occupied my mind.

The questions of "why only him (or me)?" and "how could it be possible?" no longer presented themselves as often now as they did back in those days. It took several months of denial before I accepted that Ryan was different.

It took me many more months to realize that different was not an abnormal occurrence. Different was simply an uncommon occurrence.

Call it the irony of statistics; the higher factor of an occurrence always enjoys a favorable opinion than the significance that the lower factor draws in the ratio. For instance, a joke would not qualify as funny due to the ratio of 1:9 if only one out of ten laughed. If, however, the same joke garners nine out of ten favorable reactions from another audience, it would be perceived as funny by a ratio of 9:1. So, a joke being funny is not determined by its quality but simply by virtue of the number of people reacting to it.

I thought about Estelle's conclusion about training Ryan in social skills. I sometimes wondered if we really needed to train him to be like everybody else. *Why not let him be the way he is?* But then, was our society mature enough to let everyone be the way they were? I didn't think so. So, was it Ryan who needed to be trained, or the society that we lived in?

Then I gave up thinking of the big question (about what was right and what was wrong) and focused on the rather small question: what was practical. All I could think was, *If I can't train our society to accept everyone, let's continue to train Ryan to be like everyone in society.*

Chapter Three

"Britney! Come over here, sweetheart! Your mom called me. She will be late." Standing at my front door, I called to Britney as she got off her school bus.

"Hi, Mrs. Sharma," she said as she approached. "How are you?"

"I'm good, darling. Your mom is stuck in a meeting. She will be back in an hour."

"One hour! Oh, what will I do?"

"Why, you can play with Ryan. He should be home soon."

"Oh, Ryan does not play with me. He doesn't talk to me. I don't think he loves me anymore!"

"I'm sorry, what? He doesn't love you? Do you mean to say *like you*?" I asked, amused by the young girl's casual utterance of the word "love."

"Yeah, like, love, it's the same thing. That's what Mom says."

"What does your mom say?"

"Mom was telling Aunt Nicole yesterday that Daddy doesn't talk to her. She said, 'I don't think he loves me anymore.'"

I was a bit perplexed at the innocence of an eight-year-old trying to figure out the complexity of relationships with the simplicity of a delicate mind. I fell short of words.

"But sweetie, Ryan does like you. He's just diffident."

"Diffident? What does diffident mean?"

"Diffident means…shy. It means that Ryan likes you but does not tell you about it."

"Oh, really? So, do you mean to say my Daddy is also diffident?"

I realized I had no simple answer to the question of love between her parents that bothered her curious little mind.

"Well, maybe. But you know, dear, your Daddy loves you a lot. He visits you over the weekends, right?"

"Yes. But he is not coming on Sunday. Mom said he has to work. Mrs. Sharma, do you think Mr. Sharma loves you?"

"Umm…yes," I replied with a pause. I had not thought about that in a while. And the question had not presented itself to me before with any hesitation.

"Oh. Last Sunday, Daddy took me to Woods Park. So many rides there! Then we had ice cream. I like vanilla. It's yummy. I like chocolate ice cream, too. Mrs. Sharma, do you know what an affair is?" The little chatterbox went on with her unconnected questions and non-stop blabbering.

Britney Hayden was my neighbor Elena Hayden's daughter, a year younger than Ryan, and the most bubbly and talkative child in the neighborhood. She had always been very fond of Ryan.

She must have been around five years old when she started blaming him every time she got hurt while playing. Once, when I was chatting with Elena, Britney was playing and running around in the yard. We witnessed her tumbling down and crying. When Elena asked what had happened, she said Ryan had pushed her. Ryan was nowhere near her. In fact, he was in the house at that time. It was only then Elena realized that Ryan had perhaps never pushed Britney.

Britney, for some reason, believed that one could only tumble or fall when somebody pushed them and that somebody in her case would always be Ryan, whether or not he was around.

Ryan, reticent as he was, would not have defended himself even if he were around. Elena even apologized to me after this unexpected revelation as she had hitherto believed in Britney's bluff, even though she had never seen Ryan pushing her.

Britney's curiosity knew no bounds. She always bombarded me—or anyone, for that matter—with her never-ending questions.

When she was merely three years old, she would come over and ask two types of questions. One, "What is this?" and two, "What are you doing?" A series of whys followed these questions.

She would begin with her adorable lisping, "Mithes Thalma, what you doing?"

"I am cooking."

"Why you cooking?"

"Because Ryan and Reva want to eat."

"Why Ryan and Reva want to eat?"

"Because they are hungry"

"Why they hungry?"

And this went on.

I think over the years, with the information gathered through the zillions of questions and sequential follow-up questions, she knew everything about everyone in my household, except Ryan.

Ryan was the mysterious boy she still did not know much as he barely spoke to her, thus fueling her curiosity. Perhaps Britney's lack of conception in Ryan's case explained her fondness towards him.

Lately, after Elena's separation from her husband (and Britney's Dad) Jim, her questions had revolved around relationships, and they were ones that I found difficult to answer.

I wished Ryan were inquisitive. Not as much as Britney, but even a tenth of her curiosity would suffice. He never bothered to ask a question or care for an answer.

My train of thought broke as I saw the school bus arriving on the street. Britney, by my side, was still chattering, now something about her friends at the school.

Caesar, who had already hastened across the street twice before, was now ecstatic to see the bus that was about to halt. Wagging his tail profusely, he darted back and forth between the bus stop and the doorstep where Britney and I were standing, as if demanding from us the reciprocation of his excitement. He then sprinted back to receive his dearest buddy, who got off the bus holding hands with Reva.

As they approached nearer, Reva greeted Britney and me. Britney reciprocated and continued to chatter, now comparing the size of her school bus with theirs.

Ryan glanced at Britney but did not return her greeting. Caesar rushed around, desperate for Ryan's attention, and we all went in.

Britney continued to amuse and occupy us with her childish prattle, occasionally addressing Ryan too without getting bothered and discouraged by his lack of response and overall involvement in what she probably considered a necessary conversation.

Sitting at the table, Ryan gazed at her the whole time, often appearing interested but holding back from taking part in the chitchat.

Elena arrived about an hour later to fetch her daughter.

*

At the dinner table, Viru was uncharacteristically jovial, not complaining or even mentioning his favorite "I tell you..." expression. He was cordial with kids and abstained from shouting at Caesar.

There was a small table for Caesar adjoining the dining table that we had put in about two years ago on Ryan's insistence, as he would not eat without Caesar joining by his side. Like a faithful sidekick, Caesar would always wait patiently at the table for his little master to start eating before he did. Except for Ryan, he would not care whether anyone else in the family ate or not.

"So, how's my son doing in school? Everything good?" Viru asked, and Ryan reluctantly nodded his head.

"Revs, darling, what about your dance classes? Learned any new moves?"

"I don't know, Dad. We hardly get a chance to dance. Miss Anne is so funny. She says, 'Watch me,' and then keeps dancing all the time. And in the end, she says 'You all did a great job.'"

"Ha ha, she is funny indeed. Wow, this vegetable dish is so delicious. Your mommy can give the chefs of the city a run for their money."

"Alright. What is it? You can drop the bomb now," I said, expecting something unpleasant.

"Why, I'm just appreciating the good cuisine."

"I know you appreciate things when you're guilty of something, so stop beating around the bush and tell us what we are going to miss now?"

"Well, I mean it. I think a little praise goes a long way, and I will miss your food during my business trip to New Jersey."

"There you are. It's not your praise that goes a long way, but you do. And how long is this trip?"

"Two weeks."

"When?"

"Around Christmas."

"What?"

"And New Year."

"Are you kidding me? Will we be alone during Christmas and New Year? This cannot happen, Mister Viru. No."

"Mandy, dear, listen to me, please. It's work."

"What work? Who works during the holidays? Why is your company so strange?"

"It's a high priority project delivery that must be done before Christmas, and we have to stay back at the customer's premises to ensure a smooth transition to the operations team during Christmas and New Year."

"And only you were chosen for this noble work?"

"Not me alone. We have a team of five people. This is a big assignment."

"This is not done."

I remained vocal in displaying my displeasure, whereas Daddy's girl adopted a somewhat mellower tone and implored him not to go. Ryan did what he always did in such situations, fixating his beautiful shiny eyes upon each of us from time to time as we spoke.

Caesar continued to enjoy his supper with satisfied gulping sounds. He clearly had no idea what we were talking about, and even if he did, he would not have cared as his slight association to Viru was only bound by the walks to Mount Mary Hills in the morning.

Caesar's relationship with Ryan and his Dad was so contrasting that what rocked in Ryan's case could only be termed as rocky in that of Viru's.

To make up for his absence or appease all three of us at the least, Viru came up with a proposal of a fun weekend going downtown that involved watching the pre-Christmas parade followed by shopping and some lunch in the kids' favorite restaurant.

Reva, my twelve-year-old, was a sorted and happy child. Any activity or celebration that involved large gatherings would be her favorite pastime, and for that reason, the Christmas parade easily fitted into her fun Saturday.

Ryan did not show interest in any activity, but he loved, rather longed, to eat outside the house. He did not mind eating the veggies and salads in the restaurants that he disliked at home, where he would take the cucumber and lettuce out of his sandwiches, thereby giving an opportunity to Viru to comment on my presentation.

As for shopping, I loved it like women in general. I would still not call it an even bargain, but *hell ya!* Viru, for a change, was offering to shop for me, the offer that he only reserved for birthdays or anniversaries.

The following morning, we headed to downtown Abbynton for the fun weekend as promised by Viru, who made it sound like a very lucrative deal in lieu of his absence during the holidays.

For the first time, I had no recollection of my dream the prior night, after a spell of consistent and inexplicable dreams of five previous nights in a row, and I did not know how to feel about it. One part of me was relieved that something strange that bothered me had stopped occurring, while the other part felt uneasy that the stopping was another strange occurrence.

Though there was a week left until Christmas, the holiday fever had already kicked in, visible on the lazy, relaxed faces of passersby and colorful decorations in the streets. It was a warm and sunny Saturday with a few patches of snow here and there on the sidewalks, prevented from melting due to the shaded areas.

My view on weather is subjective, as zero degrees would not usually qualify for warm weather. Still, after hitting minus twenty just two days before, weather at zero felt like summer. When you hit the extreme, every measurement becomes relative to it.

Riverdale Street was alive with a flock of people ranging from kids to the elderly standing on both sides of the street, occupying every inch of the sidewalks. While the infants in the colorful layers of warm clothing found comfort in their strollers parked at the edge of the road beside their moms, the older ones rested on the shoulders of their Dads, getting a field of view even better than the tall folks. Many children stood at the shoulder of the road, some of them sitting on the little folding chairs that their foresighted moms brought from home for them.

Reva paced ahead as if guiding us through the cheerful crowd to find a comfortable spot (that seemed an almost impossible task) to watch the parade that was due to commence shortly.

I held Ryan's hand, and he walked with his usual reluctance, enhanced by the discomfort of the proximity of people.

Viru, uninterested as usual, lagged behind, as if only tagging along to fulfill his promise.

With so many people occupying the narrow sidewalk on both sides of the street, it was not possible for us to walk together. After leading us for the next three blocks, Reva finally found what could barely qualify for a spot and waited for us to catch up.

"Hey Viren...wow, look at you, spending quality time with your family!" I heard a female voice addressing Viru and turned back to see who she was.

"Oh, hi, Anu. How are you?" returned Viru.

"I'm good. So? Kids excited for the parade? Hi, Mandira!"

I returned a superficial smile only for the sake of courtesy.

"Yes, the kids have been very keen since this morning. They can't wait. You here for the parade?" asked Viru.

"Not really. DK has asked me to collect the bouquets for G&L folks. I only realized about the Christmas parade when I arrived downtown and noticed the crowd on the street."

"Oh, I see."

"So, all set for next week?"

"Yes, kind of."

"Ok then, see you in New Jersey. I will be there on Thursday."

"Bye."

"Wait, what did she say? Is she also going to New Jersey?" I asked Viru as soon as Anu left.

"Yes, she is the part of the team that is visiting the G&L customer."

"Why didn't you tell me before that she was also going?" I returned in vexation.

"You did not ask me. I told you about the business trip with people from the office."

"Yes, but you did not say you were going with her."

"Mandy, I am not going with her, there is a team of people, and she is one of them. I'm not the one who decides this. Anyway, she's in the sales division and will be there with her boss DK for only two days to meet the officials while the rest of us are going for two weeks."

"Yes, but you could have told me that she is going, but you did not."

"C'mon, Mandy. I also did not tell you that Sylvain, Peter, Jack, and Octavia are going because you did not ask me. They are just my colleagues, and so is she. I cannot stop anyone from going on a business trip. You have to start trusting me."

"Yes, yes. Her going must be a coincidence, just like many of them in the past."

"Mandy, please don't start again and in front of kids. If you do not trust me, why don't we all go together to New Jersey?"

"What, go together? Don't you know Ryan gets anxious with a change in his routine? How can he manage a change of place?"

Anu was Viru's rumored girlfriend from the office before we got married. Viru never admitted having any relationship with her. He would say, "Why would I marry you if I'd had an affair with anyone else?"

But then we did not have an affair, either. Our marriage was more of an affair of two families who had plotted to bring their young ones together through Sunday potlucks, dinners, and many other get-togethers.

I must admit, though, we liked each other, and Viru would go out of his way to impress me during our family gatherings as well as our meetings and he pursued me even when I occasionally played hard to get one. But it did not feel like an affair, as our families were always involved, approved of, and even encouraged our relationship.

Viru always maintained that he and Anu were just colleagues. But I could tell with the way that woman looked at my husband that she did not think so. Back in India, in those office parties, I had sneaked up on him when gossiping with his colleagues, engaging in what they call "men's talk," as they bantered with Viru, mentioning Anu, and he would blush pink and flush crimson like a teenage boy.

And then, within a year of us moving to Abbynton in Canada, she moved here too, which, as per Viru, was just an opportunity for which the company selected her, just like they did in his case. I mean, what are the odds of such a coincidence?

And then, one year back, I heard from a mutual friend (because Viru would never talk to me about her) that she had separated from her boyfriend. Since then, I had worried about all the coincidences that seemed to happen more frequently nowadays, like working on the same projects and going on the same business trips.

I was mad at Viru for two reasons. One, that Anu was also going to New Jersey, and two, that he did not tell me. Though I was more upset about the former, I could only blame Viru for the latter as my argument of him being responsible for her joining the business trip would not fly.

Now, I don't want to sound like a suspicious wife, but the thought of my husband and the woman I hated being present at a distant place during the holiday period, when I could not be there, was enough to make me feel insecure.

Viru knew I was upset, and standing next to me, he kept looking at my face now and then, as he always did in such situations, waiting for me to look back and hoping I would smile at him, but I didn't do either those things.

Reva, holding Ryan's hand, was now ahead of the crowd right at the front, standing at the edge of the sidewalk, from where they could witness all the action on the street without any obstruction.

The action had begun as the sounds of music and people on the microphone were audible now, but the participants and the entourage were still about two blocks away, not visible on the street from where we stood.

Soon, we spotted the traffic control policemen riding their bikes slowly along the road, gently directing overexcited people crossing the edge of the sidewalk to stay clear of the road, who took their former spots as soon as the policemen rode on.

The stage was set for a remarkable show. At first arrived some twenty-five or thirty cheerful young girls disguised as butterflies, dressed in the colors of the rainbow, floating and fluttering in sync, dancing to the tunes of music played in a vehicle behind them which was decorated to look like a giant red sledge.

Then came the young boys dressed as elves in green and red walking casually, offering Christmas candies to the delighted kids.

Then arrived a big fancy truck that looked like a little snow-covered island with a small house and a sculpture of a snowman in it, where the kids dressed in red threw white balls of cotton at each other.

That was followed by a fine display of performances, including singing (solo and chorus), music (band and orchestra), and dancing by large groups of beautiful, colorful, and talented people. Several songs were sung, and tunes played, keeping with the theme of Christmas.

More trucks passed by, amidst cheering from the crowd, one disguised as a giant Christmas tree on wheels, glittering with the embellishments, and another one transformed into large boxes wrapped neatly by shiny glossy papers, giving the impression of a pile of presents. There was one more, an open truck carrying little children dressed as pink lilies and yellow sunflowers, waving joyously at the flock of people.

At last, the most awaited and coveted person arrived. The chief, the mascot of Christmas celebrations. Santa Claus arrived, the vehicle modified to appear as a sleigh led by reindeers, chanting "Merry Christmas" on the microphone in his heavy bass voice.

As Santa neared, the children became ecstatic, squeaking with joy, and I noticed a person standing beside him in the giant ride. It was the man I had seen in my dreams for five nights in a row.

It was Jack.

Chapter Four

Oh my God! That's him! That's Jack, the man I see in my dreams! I thought as my heart started to beat rapidly. *Who else could he be? The same black cloak, the long hat, and the long-pointed nose. So, the man does exist.*

I had wondered before if this man was only the concoction of my dreams, or if he existed in the real world.

Wait, is this the real world? Could it be a dream too? Is it possible what I am witnessing right now is a part of some daydream? Or is it possible what I thought to be a dream before was a reality?

I pinched myself to make sure what I was witnessing was indeed for real.

So, I had been dreaming of an actor, some artist who performed in the Christmas parade! But why? And why was he standing next to Santa in that sleigh? What role was he playing here? Why would anyone be standing beside Santa on that ride, let alone a mysterious-looking man? That did not make any sense.

He was not moving much and looking in only one direction. In fact, he was looking in our direction.

Wait, is he looking at me? Yes, he is definitely staring at me. But why? Oh my God, what is this? My head was exploding with a rush of thoughts that contradicted one another.

Viru, who had been glancing meekly at me now and then since Anu had left perhaps noticed the rapid transitions in my facial expression, from crimson to pink and then to pale, that was inconsistent with his perception of the present circumstance. He asked, "Mandy are you ok?"

The sleigh continued to approach, and so did the smiling Santa looking around everywhere, and poker-faced Jack, staring only at me.

As the sleigh stopped momentarily in front of me, it felt like my dream all over again, where I would freeze at the sight of the mysterious old man.

The sleigh carried on.

The day progressed according to Viru's plan of lunch, followed by shopping, and I tagged along absentmindedly, barely speaking or participating. Even my favorite part of the day, the shopping, failed to arouse any interest in me.

Viru continued his effort to get me to talk to him. He perhaps took my silence as a consequence of seeing Anu, although that was not the only conundrum occupying my mind that day.

In bed, Viru gently put his arms around my waist in a bid to make up with me.

"Mandy, c'mon. Talk to me, please. You have been silent all day. How can I work if you don't trust me?"

On any other occasion, following a chance encounter with Anu, such as today, I would not have spoken to Viru for at least two days. But it was different tonight. In fact, something else was bothering me.

"Did you see that man in the sleigh today?"

"What sleigh?" asked Viru, visibly comforted to see me speak.

"Santa's sleigh, in the parade! Remember a man in a black hat standing next to Santa?"

"Oh. The parade. Yes, I saw Santa, but don't remember any other person with a black hat."

"That's because you hardly pay any attention. The only other person you remember is Anu."

"Mandy, why is your mind hung up on Anu? I have told you many times there is no other person in my life. You are the only one. And there were so many people in the parade in colorful outfits. How would I remember all of them? But what about the man?"

"That was the man I see in my dreams."

"Oh really? Did you see him in the parade? You mean the man you see in your dreams is a performer in the Christmas parade?"

"I don't know, but I saw him there. And he kept staring at me with a stern face."

"Oh. Wait, was he wearing black?"

"Yes, cloak and trousers."

"Hmm…and a black hat?"

"Yes."

"Did you notice a short mustache?"

"Mustache? I don't think he had a mustache. Or maybe he did. Yes, perhaps he did. Why, do you know him?"

"Of course, I know him. Everybody knows him. You know him too. He's an actor."

"An actor? Where? Stage actor? Like in a play or something?"

"No, in movies. The old ones. A man with a stern face."

"Who? Do I know him?"

"Of course you do! Everybody knows him. Finally, now I know who your mystery man is."

"But, who?"

"Charlie Chaplin!"

"What?"

"Yes, black hat, black coat and trousers, and a short mustache. Who else could it be?" Viru burst into laughter, making me angry. I shoved his hand off my waist.

"Always non-serious. Everything is a joke to you. Charlie Chaplin? Really?"

"Or maybe some actor playing Charlie Chaplin."

"No, it's not. Charlie Chaplin is dead. And it makes no sense for an actor playing him to join Santa on the sleigh. There is a difference between a mustache and a toothbrush mustache. Also, wearing a coat and a cloak are not the same thing."

"Ok, ok. I am just joking, Mandy. I am sorry. I understand that you saw a man in the parade today who resembled the man in your dream, or maybe it was the same man. So what? We see so many people every day on the street and do not remember most of them. We also see people in dreams. What's the big deal?"

"Big deal? The big deal is that he was staring at me!"

"Again. Haven't you seen actors performing on stage in a play? Everybody in the audience thinks that they are looking at them when in fact, they are so engrossed in their character that they look through them. This man was an actor looking in one direction, and don't you remember hundreds of people around you? How can you be sure he was only looking at you?"

"You don't understand. Why do I see this man in dreams every day?"

"Mandy, dreams do not mean anything. I remember having a dream once in my childhood where this man came close to my face and said, 'titch button.' That dream scared the hell out of me, and I slept in my mother's room for almost a week. When I grew up, I realized how useless that dream was. Imagine a guy I never saw before scaring me not by yelling or attacking me, just uttering trivial words, 'titch button.' Now tell me, should I spend the rest of my life thinking about that man and the lame dream trying to break it down? Should I start looking for all types of buttons? Shirt buttons, shank buttons, wooden toggle buttons, stud buttons!"

"Leave it. No point talking sense to a senseless man who talks about buttons."

"Look, Mandy. You think a lot, and I know you worry about Ryan. But we are doing what we can. Everything will be ok, just start living in the present. Take it one day at a time. And stop overthinking about the past, the future, or meaningless dreams."

I made no reply, and Viru slipped under the quilt. I wondered if he really didn't care much or if he was just pretending to be cool.

"And go back to sleep now. You won't see Charlie Chaplin anymore since I cracked the code. Next time it will be Laurel and Hardy in your dreams," said Viru as he chuckled under the quilt.

Viru's jokes that would crack me up before marriage did not amuse me anymore. His words that felt so full of wisdom to me before now seemed like mere preaching.

He said I should stop overthinking, as if there was a key to lock your thoughts from popping up in your mind. Sometimes, I think we are tiny insects trapped in an enormous spider web. This web is weaved carefully by infinite fine threads. This limitless web is our mind, and those threads are our random thoughts and worries. We spend our lifetime straining and stretching these threads, but there are times when we get irreversibly tangled in their complex knots and fall prey to the spider. The spider in the middle of the web of mind, weaved by threads of thoughts is depression.

Viru did not want me to quit my job six years ago. He said, "Very few people have a passion for their job, and you are one of those lucky ones. So, don't lose it."

But losing her passion is an easy choice for a mother to make, as opposed to the risk of losing her child. How could I see my child suffering?

Ryan had turned three, but he would not even once call me Mommy, the word that melts every mother's heart when she hears it for the first time. He was this child sinking into oblivion, barely speaking, listening, or following anything of the outside world, but I could see those twinkling eyes pleading for help in a way that only a mother could understand.

I had so many plans, but unfortunately, they did not work out. I believe future planning, or any other planning for that matter, works out only when God's plan coincides with what you envision for yourself.

In my case, God's plan was way out of sync with that of

mine. Only his plans are realized, and we have no choice but to fall in line. This falling in line is what we call the "change of plan" or a new plan. We believe that things work out according to our new plan or change of plan, still innocent of the fact that those are again at his mercy. We, humans, are silly in our delusion of thinking that we control our plans and change of plans. All we do is adapt to His plans, thinking we made them.

I hated to admit that Viru, who was now fast asleep and heavily snoring beside me, was perhaps right in his conclusion that I thought a lot, and I envied him for thinking so little. My train of thought took me to a few more places of suffering before I finally slept.

The next Monday morning, Viru hastily walked Caesar to Mount Mary Hills and later left for New Jersey on his business trip. I, as usual, started my day by spotting the young girl through my window, jogging on the street. The kids got ready, with Reva requiring a little and Ryan a lot of assistance and left for school.

The day progressed. Sebastian accepted food graciously at the Saint Thomas Metro Station and again amused me with his cheerfulness despite his mundane homeless life.

Late in the afternoon, I chatted casually with my neighbor Elena Hayden in the front yard, and she shared her woes of going through the separation with Jim and the pain of being a single mother.

Ryan, sitting on the steps, wrestled with Caesar and pulled his ears, and Caesar, like a docile companion of his master, submitted to him every time. They both looked happiest in the company of each other.

Reva shared the weekend fun with Britney, talking enthusiastically about the parade. When she spoke about Santa and his sleigh, I could not help but overhear.

"Reva, did you tell her about the man with Santa?"

"The man? Who, Mom?"

"That man in a black hat standing still next to Santa on the sleigh, looking in one direction, like a statue, playing some character, I guess." I glanced at Elena for the later part of my sentence.

"Mom, there was no such man in that sleigh. Santa was alone."

"What? No! You don't remember, Revu. There was a man in a black cloak and trousers."

"Mom, I remember everything about the parade. There was no man with Santa."

At that moment, a chill went down my spine. Reva had not seen what I had witnessed, and neither had Viru. The scary possibility presented itself that the mysterious man I saw in my dreams, and who stood next to Santa on that sleigh looking right at me, was perhaps only visible to me.

Chapter Five

It was the day before Christmas eve, and Viru had been away on his business trip for about a week. He called from New Jersey every other day to tell how much he missed the kids and me, and I knew his frequent displays of affection were partly out of guilt over leaving us alone.

When I enquired about Anu, he told me that she had appeared in one of the customer meetings. Then out of habit, he made jokes about it, "Mandy, I kept flashing my wedding ring at the customer meeting so that Anu does not talk to me. I even placed the ring on the table one time, and no woman in that meeting talked to me because they thought I was crazy. One man from the customer's side even asked me if our company sold wedding rings too."

Upon pressing further, he told me that he did not speak to her at all, and that she had left with her boss that same day, which I thought was another lie.

To keep the kids in good spirits and upon Reva's insistence, I invited Elena and Britney over for supper on Christmas Eve. Every year they would visit Jim's parents during Christmas time, but since her separation, Elena was left with only one close companion, and that was me.

Usually, Viru would invite his colleagues from the office for a party, mainly the immigrant families like us, those who had no relatives living around with whom they could celebrate Christmas.

With Reva's help, I installed the Christmas tree that we had bought from Canadian Tire about two years ago, that we assembled every year and embellished with lights and ornaments.

Ryan and Caesar devised a fun game with Caesar plucking the decorations from the tree, especially the ornament balls, and bringing them to Ryan, who would then hang them back on the tree. I wondered how they could do this monotonous back and forth act for hours and enjoy it.

Their silly game made Reva upset, as her meticulous decoration of the tree—the organization skill that she so loved to display—was ruined.

For the past week, I had pondered over several questions. Who was Jack? Why did I see him in the parade? What could an ancient-looking man be doing in a parade, standing beside Santa in the sleigh? Was he really the man I saw in my dreams? How could I see a random man in my dreams? Why didn't Viru and Reva remember seeing him in the sleigh? I understood that Viru was absent-minded, but Reva was always attentive. Was it possible that only I could see him? That did not even make any sense. But then, none of this made any sense.

Perhaps the man I saw in the parade was not the same man I dreamt of, but somebody who resembled him. Perhaps seeing an unknown man in my dreams was as trivial as Viru's childhood nightmare where the man said "titch button." However, I was not sure if that story was true or if Viru had made it up. I mean, what was "titch button"? Was it some silly term invented by Viru to prove that dreams are stupid?

Viru always had a story to justify the worthlessness of every little thing I worried about. When I wondered about Ryan's oversleeping, Viru would pacify me by giving an account of his friend back in college who would often wake up at lunchtime, thereby missing all their morning lectures. He had a friend who once slept on a Friday evening and woke up on Sunday morning. The boys joked that he followed a personal calendar comprising six days in a week and twenty-six days in the month.

When I expressed my disbelief of this exaggerated account, Viru quietly mumbled the real reason. What Viru had conveniently avoided mentioning before about his friend who slept on a Friday evening and woke on a Sunday morning was the fact that he smoked pot and was addicted to drugs.

From morning till noon, I spent the whole time in the kitchen cooking a sumptuous meal for the guests. With my favorite deputy Reva by my side, who always came to my rescue under such time-bound situations, I accomplished the uphill task before the deadline.

Reva helped me with all the washing, peeling, and chopping. The other two members in the house, as usual, did not contribute. The only help expected from them was to leave us alone, that they happily obliged, by continuing to play their favorite unproductive game of plucking and hanging the ornaments on the Christmas tree.

I was well known in the neighborhood for my cooking skills, but then it became a responsibility to uphold the reputation by setting a benchmark, and then topping it the next time.

Being a vegetarian all my life, I specialized in vegetarian Indian cuisine, but after getting recognition in the neighborhood for my cooking talent, I realized the need to expand the scope of my cooking to get more admiration.

When I cooked chicken for the first time, Viru became so ecstatic that he called me "the best chef in North America." As usual, he did not restrict his titles within the neighborhood, city, or country limits, but was generous in his scope to assign a continent, world, or even universe to it.

Reva tasted the salt and spices for me, and according to her, I had managed to keep my status.

I was half-vegan before, consuming dairy products but not eggs. Recently, Viru had managed to convince me with his protein-rich argument, and I started having eggs. That turned me from half-vegan to a wholly vegetarian, or eggetarian, for that matter. Viru continued to allure me into meat-eating in the hope of getting more variety in my cooking at home, but in vain, as I had limited my cooking to chicken only.

I told him that my resolve of not eating meat was like an immovable rock, but he believed that a persistent effort of pressing against the rock could ultimately push it off the cliff.

I tried my best to keep the menu consistent with the Christmas theme, with roasted potatoes, Brussel sprouts, vegetables, apple pie, and fruit pudding. Everything except turkey. I knew turkey would be a great choice and was poultry, the same family as chicken (so I would have gone only a step further in my resolve to cook chicken only). Still, I would rather have stuck to my comfort zone than experiment with something that was not my strength. I cooked roasted chicken and chicken curry instead, that Britney loved very much.

Elena and Britney joined us in the afternoon, and our little Christmas party began. Britney, as always, lit up the atmosphere with her non-stop witty babbling, primarily talking to Reva and making sure to include other household members now and then.

Her mother, Elena, was visibly relaxed—a contrast to her stressed demeanor of late—and updated me with the neighborhood's gossip. She told me about Mrs. Bergenza, who recently purchased her fourth cat, and was now known as "Cat Woman." And that the hot man, who lived alone across the street, was seeing a woman much older than him.

Reva, who had helped me with cooking before, seamlessly switched her role from assistant chef to assistant hostess, making the guests comfortable by offering soft drinks and lending an ear to Britney's childish chatter.

Ryan stayed quiet for the most part and occasionally gazed at Britney. In the gathering of familiar people, Caesar expressed his delight by wagging his tail and pacing here and there, but mostly staying close to Ryan.

Reva and I served our elaborate supper at the table. Before, it was only the tantalizing aroma of my cooking, but now the presentation also garnered favorable reaction from our guests. We were about to start when the doorbell rang.

I opened the door to find Jim.

"Hi, Mandira."

"Hi, Jim...how are you?"

"I'm good. Is Elena here?" he asked after an awkward pause.

Before I could reply, Elena, who had perhaps seen him from the living room, approached. "Jim, what are you doing here?"

"Elena, I came to talk to you."

"About what?"

"About what we discussed this morning."

"But we spoke over the phone about that."

"Yes, but you did not hear me out. I just want to talk for a few minutes."

"Daddy! Wow, you are here!" Britney came running to the door and hugged her Daddy.

"Hi, Britney! How are you, dear?"

"Daddy, did you come to eat with us? Come, look, Mrs. Sharma made chicken curry."

"Britney, I came to speak to your mom. Elena, can we discuss this, please?"

Elena was noticeably vexed by Jim's unannounced dropping at my house but was wise enough not to create a scene with company present.

"Britney, honey, you stay here with Aunt Mandy. I am going home to talk to Daddy. I will be back soon, ok?" Elena said, then turned to me with a face that tacitly expressed both apologies for her leaving and a request for me to keep Britney. I quickly nodded my reassuring assent and they left.

Britney, no more in her former spirit, now spoke less. I tried to cheer her up. "Your mom will be back soon, Britney, and then we will have fun and eat. I made your favorite dessert, and then we will open presents!"

"They are fighting, aren't they?"

"No, there are not, honey. They just want to talk to each other. Moms and Dads do that all the time."

"You don't know, Mrs. Sharma. When Daddy lived with us, mom would say, 'Daddy and I will talk in the other room.' And then they yelled at each other. I stood outside the locked door many times."

"But your Daddy does not live with you anymore. So, no more yelling. Right?"

"Yes, but you know, Mrs. Sharma, I liked it more when Daddy lived with us."

Britney had always amused me with her non-stop blabbering, but this time she bemused me with her sensitive side. I knew the estrangement of parents took a toll on their children, but then watching nonchalant Britney pour water on her doll and ask Elena, 'Mom, Mrs. Stella peed on her skirt, can I take her to the toilet?', I thought that Britney perhaps did not care that much about her parents' separation. I was wrong, and she cared as much as any other child would do.

After twenty minutes, Elena returned without Jim, but only to take clueless (and hungry) Britney back to her house. She came back later, this time without Britney.

With a heavy heart, Elena unfolded the mystery of the unannounced appearance of Jim, and later, the disappearance of Britney. Every year, as a Christmas tradition, they had visited Jim's parents for their evening supper. Jim, post-separation with Elena, wanted to continue the practice without her, but with Britney. They spoke about this on the phone, and Elena refused, stating that she had already promised me that they would eat with us, but Jim would not let go. He came to fetch his daughter.

Elena argued, but then Jim played the best card in his deck by threatening to take Elena to court for Britney's custody, and thus won the argument. Unlike her usual self,

Britney accepted the final decision of her parents with no questions asked and left with Jim.

Could Jim's timing be any better? I had spent almost a week planning and worked all morning to execute my finest recipes, and he had spoiled it all. I was upset, but a woman complaining of her missing hatpin certainly does not make a better case when another one just got robbed of her fine necklace. Clearly, I was less miserable than Elena, as I would still spend the rest of the evening with my kids.

Elena stayed for a while and apologized for the inconvenience caused. Without her daughter, she had no appetite left to eat, let alone enjoy the hospitality. I did not insist on anything as I knew she only stayed for courtesy, and when she expressed her wish to leave, I packed some food, and she took it back to her place.

I glanced at the dinner table. The roasted chicken with the spicy garnish around it looked dry and upset. The chicken curry with soft pieces of chicken immersed in thick creamy gravy was now sad and cold. The roasted potatoes and Brussel sprouts stared at me as if complaining. And the apple pie and fruit pudding felt left out. It was one of those rare moments when there were no happy hands to grab them and devour eagerly.

I thought of Sebastian. Who else could value such exquisite cuisine more than a poor homeless old man? *But he told me last time,* I thought, *that he was putting up at the Victoria Hospital shelter for the evenings until the new year. But it is not late. I can probably find him at the metro station.*

Chapter Six

Leaving Reva in charge of the house in my absence, a responsibility that she would manage efficiently, I headed for Saint Thomas Metro Station, which was about five minutes walking distance, holding my carefully packed food, hoping to see Sebastian.

As I entered the subway and approached the escalator, Sebastian was not present at the other end in his usual place. Arriving at the other end of the escalator, I looked around and then punched my metro card and walked down, hoping to find him around the platform, but no luck.

I turned back, and just when I was ascending the escalator and regretting my instinctive decision of coming down to the metro station and leaving my kids alone at home, I heard someone calling my name.

"Mandira! Hi, Mandira!"

I turned around. It was Sebastian with his smiling face, walking briskly towards me.

"Hi, Seb. Where were you?"

"I was in the metro. I saw you at the platform when I got off and came running to wish you Merry Christmas."

"Merry Christmas, Seb. I thought you had left for Victoria Hospital."

"Yes, I will go in sometime. I went to see my friend Jill. She lives near Metro Pearl."

"Oh, you have a friend! You never told me about her."

"Well, Jill is a fine lady. I met her in the fall, and we became friends."

"Wow, you are blushing. It looks like this Jill person is special."

"Now that you have mentioned it, I must admit that I become animated when I talk about her. Jill is an amazing person. She listens to all my nonsensical speeches. She even laughs at my unfunny jokes. I wonder how a person can make you feel so good about yourself."

"I am happy that you found a companion, Seb."

"Thank you, Mandira, me too. She will be joining me in today's evening feast at the shelter."

"That's great. Here is a little feast from me. Don't forget to share with Jill."

"Ah, lovely," said Seb, as he always did when referring to my food. "No feast is better than your food on a Christmas Eve, my dear lady. But this is only for me. I will not share this with anybody."

"As you wish," I said, smiling to reciprocate his still-animated grin, "have a good evening."

"A very good evening, dear lady. You have a heart of gold. I wish all your dreams come true in the new year."

I came out of the subway station. It was late in the afternoon, the day on the cusp of transition when it was no longer bright and not quite dark enough. The time when the cars' headlights are turned on to compensate for the fading daylight, but that contribute less to the visibility and more to blinding the oncoming drivers. The fresh snow from the morning snowfall, a befitting tribute to Christmas Eve, gave the impression of soft cotton wrapped around an infinite landscape, like a splendid gift of nature.

There is a common saying that translates to: "Every grain of food is labeled with the name of the one who eats it." It had not occurred to me before that it was a well thought of and logical saying. For the past week, I had been planning the Christmas dinner, keeping in mind the likes and preferences of Elena and Britney and thinking how they would like this and enjoy that. I had still planned to give the leftovers to Seb but did not realize that the food was meant for him in its entirety. The grains (that Elena and Britney did not enjoy), all this time, were labeled with the names of Sebastian and Jill. I knew he was going to share it with Jill and had joked about eating it all by himself.

When he wished for my dreams to come true, the image of Ryan flashed in my head. What would a mother dream of other than her child's development defined by the norms of society? I hoped the wish of one of the nicest and selfless souls I knew would get the priority in God's answers.

"Mandira!"

As I walked along the sidewalk just one block away from my house, my train of thought broke as I felt someone call my name.

"Hello, Mandira."

The familiar-sounding voice was now clear.

I turned around to see who it was and suddenly froze, as I did in my dreams.

"Hi, Mandira. Do you remember me?"

I could not believe who I was seeing in front of me. Someone who had clogged my brain with perplexing thoughts for weeks was standing right in front of me, and their presence was even more baffling. For a moment, I felt that I could not speak. Then with great difficulty, I cleared my throat and said with my voice trembling with fear, "Mmm…No. Who are you?"

"I am Jack."

"J–J–Jack? Who?" I returned, fumbling again.

"Jack, the man you saw in the parade," he replied with his deep voice that sounded as confident as it did in my dreams.

"In the parade?

"What parade?"

"The Christmas parade."

"No. I don't think I saw you in the Christmas parade," I replied nervously, in denial about whatever I had seen or heard.

"Yes, you did. You saw me in the sleigh alongside Santa."

"B–b–but who are you? I don't think I know you?"

"Well, I think you know me a little by now. I am the one who you see in your dreams."

I was terrified. I could now hear my heart pounding, like in a band; we sometimes hear the sticks beating the drums so distinctly that the ensemble of other fine instruments sounds feeble.

How does he know that I see him in my dreams? How can he be certain of seeing me in the parade among hundreds of other people when Viru and Reva had no recollection of him? Who is he, and why is he here? Many such questions popped in my head, but I was scared to ask as I had this uncanny feeling that the answers would be overwhelming.

"You must be wondering how I know this about you. Well, Mandira, I know a lot more. But before I tell you, I need you to hear carefully and trust that whatever I say, no matter how extraordinary or impossible it may seem to be, is all true."

Jack's words only helped to catalyze my fear. I now felt palpitations as it seemed that some revelation beyond my comprehension was about to unfold.

"Hold on. I do not know you. Why would you tell me anything? I do not talk to strangers. And why should I hear you out?"

"Mandira, I think you should hear me because it is important. This concerns your son, Ryan."

"Wait, what? Did you say Ryan? My son, Ryan?" I was taken aback by the mention of him.

"Yes, Mandira, your son Ryan is the important reason for me to meet you."

"What about my son? How do you even know him? No! Stop right there. I don't want to hear anything."

"But Mandira—"

"No. Go away! I don't want to hear another word about Ryan. Please, go away!"

Without waiting to see if he acted upon my anxious

supplication, I turned around and hurried away. He called my name, but I did not stop or turn back. The snow flurries that fell lightly before continued to intensify, perhaps catching up with my pace, as I hastened from one block to another and almost sprinted from the sidewalk to the front yard.

I banged the door and Reva opened it. I barged right into the living room and panicked.

"Mom, what is it?"

I rushed to the playroom and then to the kitchen area.

"Are you alright? What are you looking for, Ma?"

"Where is Ryan?"

"He is in his bedroom."

I ran upstairs and Reva followed me. We entered the room and found Ryan in the bed cuddling Caesar. Ryan and Caesar glanced at me momentarily, then carried on with cuddling. I took a deep breath.

"Mom! What's the matter?" asked a worried Reva, standing at the door behind me.

"Nothing. I just…nothing at all!"

"Why are you so tense? Anything wrong?"

"No. Just checking on Ryan. I was thinking of him." I desperately tried to make up something.

"But you're sweating, Ma. Do you need to see a doctor?"

"No, no, dear. It was snowing heavily, so I came running."

"Something's wrong with you, Ma. Do you want me to call Daddy?"

"I am fine, Revu. I just panicked a bit. You know how I sometimes worry about Ryan. It's just that…nothing. You go back to work. I will be in my room, having some rest. Go, go."

Reva did not look convinced by my reasoning but carried on.

I lay in the bed and closed my eyes, thinking about what had happened. My mind went blank for a few seconds, as if incapable of comprehending this unusual occurrence.

Suddenly, I opened my eyes.

Was it a dream? I thought, *It must be. How else can anyone explain this? How can a man appear in my dream and then show up claiming to know about it when I had not disclosed my dream to anybody except for Viru? And he knows Ryan? What does that mean? Is there something wrong with me? Why did I run away from him?*

In my head, I analyzed my reaction to this strange occurrence. I was already stunned by the existence of this man who had mysteriously appeared in my dreams and surprisingly knew about them. Then he mentioned Ryan, my most precious possession. It felt like an indication of impending danger to my son, for whom I would go to any length to protect.

Like a pile of books, my emotions kept stacking up rapidly, ranging from fear when I saw him in front of me, to anxiety as he said about revealing something extraordinary, to anger when he mentioned Ryan. At that moment, it became unbearable, so, I ran away.

When I met Sebastian, I hoped God would prioritize his wish for me. It looks like God did prioritize Sebastian's wish and took him literally for saying, "I wish your dreams come true." And the person I saw in my dreams came to life.

Jack had something to tell me about Ryan, I thought, *something that he felt was important. What could be so important?*

Wait, what if it was *important? Oh my God. Why did I run away? I should have waited to hear what he had to say about Ryan! God, what have I done?'*

Rohit Dharupta

"Cherry blossoms blooming in the bosom.
The gardens in the spring, spring to life."

Chapter One

Ever wondered what the greatest vehicle known to mankind is? The transport vehicle that weathers every storm and braves every adversity on its way without wearing out even a tiny bit.

This unstoppable vehicle requires no fuel to propel, no repairs, nor does it need servicing. This magnificent vehicle is a *cycle*. No, not a manmade bicycle or motorcycle, for man can only be a tiny part of this cycle. This is the cycle of time.

And what does this grand vehicle, the cycle of time, transport? Well, it transports life through the transition from mornings to evenings. This cycle of time identifies itself through this perpetual transition of days into nights and back to days again.

In the absence of transition, the cycle of time would perhaps not find significance, like a treadmill enabling continuous motion without moving anywhere.

Day and night attribute a meaningful state to time, and this cycle of time repeating itself over and over leads to the milestones of weeks and months.

At 6 a.m., I had been up for about half an hour, and was gazing at the first ray of daylight penetrating through the glass windows, absorbed in the anatomy of days and nights for no apparent reason. But then, the train of thought does not follow the track of structure.

The morning light in springtime appears earlier than in

winter (though not early enough compared to summer).

I now vaguely understood the concept of short days and long nights in winter and long days and short nights in summer, thanks to Viru's colleague Sylvain, who had once passed on this wisdom of the solar system during one of our potluck parties.

When a layman like me complained about winter, he had explained how the rotation of the earth's axis is tilted at an angle of 23.5 degrees away from vertical. Since the earth also rotates around the sun, this means the earth's northern hemisphere is more exposed to the sun in June (long days) than in December (short days). I learnt, to my amazement, that the tilt is responsible for the seasons.

Sylvain also talked about other imaginary scenarios of possible angles for the earth that would mean a whole lot of lousy seasons. I wondered why he would imagine tilting the earth at different angles, only to analyze how miserable our lives could be.

Viru's friend Sylvain had something to say on every topic. Viru often joked that if we broached a subject in Hindi, the foreign language he did not speak, this human encyclopedia would still have some story to tell.

Viru went far with his self-proclaimed creative talent by proudly coining the term "mencyclopedia" for such people. When I made fun of his creativity, Viru expanded his imagination further by comparing "mencyclopedia" with "womencyclopedia," and his favorite girl Reva laughed heartily.

I remembered one story by Sylvain vividly. The time he visited the chalet that he owned up north in the summertime and had an unexpected encounter with a wild animal called a skunk. I had no knowledge of this animal before who, as per Sylvain, attacked him in his living room.

When I inquired if he was injured, the master storyteller Sylvain then revealed the mode of attack of the skunk, and that, according to him, was peeing right at him.

That made us laugh, though it was not the best part of

the story. He then decided to recreate the horror story in my living room by demonstrating how the skunk peed (by enacting as a man peeing) and how he narrowly escaped the piss by collapsing on my couch.

The fun of action replays soon vanished when he mentioned that he had to throw away most of the furniture, including the couch, and disinfect and purify the house for several days.

I was so disturbed that I later googled it for more information. This animal, with black and white fur, sprays liquid as a defense mechanism that is unbearably pungent and utterly repelling.

I heard the main door creaking open, bringing my abstract train of thought (ranging from earth's tilt to skunk's piss) to an abrupt halt. Viru, who had returned from walking Caesar, was muttering something in the living room. He soon came upstairs.

"Mandy, when did you wake up?"

"A little while ago. What happened?"

"What happened? I brought this stupid dog three years ago and since then I have walked him every morning. That happened."

"Calm down and tell me."

"Today, he started barking for no reason."

"What do you mean?"

"As we walked back from Mount Mary, he suddenly started barking!"

"Do you mean he started barking at somebody?"

"No, Mandy! That's how foolish he is. He pretended to bark at somebody. He pulled so hard that I dropped the leash."

"Then?"

"Then he chased the air, barking furiously, and sprinted back. There were people around panicking at his behavior, I was so embarrassed."

"That's strange. Why would he do that?"

"He just wants to piss me off. That's why!"

Viru's "piss me off" comment reminded me of the skunk that I had been thinking of for no apparent reason.

"Could he be sensing something? People say dogs have a sixth sense," I wondered aloud.

"Why, which people say that? The people in your dreams? For God's sake, Mandy, stop overthinking! I tell you, this stupid dog keeps playing pranks on me," Viru returned irksomely.

Viru went downstairs, mumbling something followed by his favorite catchphrase, "I tell you," and I pondered over the behavior of Caesar. I knew he often played mischief, especially with Viru, but this seemed unusual.

It somehow reminded me of Jack, though there seemed to be no connection. I hadn't seen him again after that Christmas Eve, so I didn't know why I associated every peculiar occurrence to his existence.

Over the last three months, I had often felt as if somebody was watching me on the street or following me on the metro. However, linking this feeling to mere instinct or conjecture could not be ruled out. Sometimes I wondered if I had actually met Jack or if it was just a part of some elaborate dream.

I did not tell Viru about my unexpected encounter with Jack on Christmas Eve, because I knew he would either attribute it to my fantasy or obsession with dreams and make fun of me or think that I was losing my mind.

Knowing that that evil witch Anu had laid eagle eyes on my husband and followed him everywhere, the last thing I wanted was Viru to suspect that I was mentally unstable.

I rose from my bed, approached the window, and, as usual, saw the young girl on the street heading for Mount Mary Hills. This girl, who would amuse me before for her infatuation with running, now left me inspired by her perseverance.

Viru, still not able to let it go at the breakfast table, recounted all the other mischiefs of Caesar dating back to winter and later left for the office.

Ryan and Reva were upbeat after our trip to Chadwick Falls, another of Viru's initiatives, or rather an excuse to make up for his frequent absence due to business trips. They boarded the bus for their first day back at school after spring break, and Caesar, as expected, ran after the bus for about two blocks.

A little more relaxed after finishing my morning chores, I casually strolled into the living room. I noticed Britney in her backyard through my sliding glass door and went outside to talk to her.

"Britney, how are you?"

"Hi, Mrs. Sharma. When did you come back?"

"Last night. Why are you still at home? No school today?"

"Do you know, Mrs. Sharma, that Daddy is dead?"

"Daddy what?"

"He died."

"Why? When? I mean, what are you saying?"

"Last week. Today is the funeral."

"Is your mom at home?" I asked in a state of shock and ran into her house without waiting for her to reply.

I found Elena sitting at the breakfast table, listless, gazing at the bowl of cereal that she had not eaten. When her sad eyes met mine, the fragile bridge of restraint could no longer hold the flood of emotions, and tears rolled down her cheeks. I lent her my shoulder, and she sobbed like a child.

It had been about one year since Elena had separated from Jim, and she often grumbled about him, but never ceased to love him. Deep down, she was perhaps waiting for him to return to her.

Things did not always stay the same. Jim and Elena had been an enviable couple when we had moved to this neighborhood seven years ago. They would throw these lavish barbecue parties in their backyard over the weekends and invite all the neighbors. Everybody loved their warmth and hospitality. Then, Jim fell for a woman at his work, and Elena's dreamworld fell apart.

When Elena collected herself, she told me how Jim had gone to sleep that night, four days ago, and never woken up. His girlfriend was out of town and everybody became curious when he did not show up at work for two days. Doctors could not find a reason for his death.

It reminded me of the news on TV I had seen a week ago, about a family in Long Island dying in similar circumstances while sleeping, and nothing could be concluded in the post-mortem.

Elena also mentioned, and it scared the hell out of me, that days before his death, Jim had confided to one of his friends about seeing his dead ancestors in dreams.

I called Viru, and we attended Jim's funeral. I looked at Britney, who was holding her mother's arm and gazing at everyone at the funeral. Her sparkling green eyes offered a glimpse of a lonely new world where her loving Daddy would not see her anymore over the weekends.

Her little mind could not fathom why her happiness had eroded, from the days when Daddy was always around, to the times when he visited once a week, and now, he had disappeared entirely out of her life.

Chapter Two

"Where does a baby come from?"

"A baby comes from Mommy's tummy."

"Mommy's tummy! But who puts a baby in Mommy's tummy?"

"Nobody puts them there, babies are born in the tummy, like a seed...tiny at first, and then they grow slowly."

"Was I also in your tummy?"

"Yes, of course, when you were tiny."

"And what about sis?"

"She too was in my tummy."

"But I am a boy. Boys should be in Daddy's tummy. Mommy, why didn't Daddy make me in his tummy?"

"Ha ha. Your Daddy's tummy can only make gas. Only a woman can make babies, a boy or a girl; it doesn't matter."

"But Aunt Disha is a woman too. Why is she not making a baby?

"Aunt Disha is single. You need both Mommy and Daddy to make a baby."

"But you said Daddy's tummy can only make gas. What does Daddy do to make a baby?"

"Umm. You should ask Daddy this question."

"Ok. But why are babies born?"

"I don't know. God creates babies. God wants beautiful babies to be born and grow up and become big."

"Ok. So, God creates babies. But you said that Mommy

and Daddy make babies. Then what does God do?"

"I don't know. Ask your Daddy."

"Where is God?"

"Ryan, I am busy right now. I told you to ask Daddy in the evening."

"Ok, Mommy. But how did I come out of your tummy?"

"Go away."

I often had these imaginary conversations with Ryan in my head, where he surprised me with his questions, and I would struggle to satisfy his curiosity, trying to get away by ascribing his "whys" to God's will. But when he bewildered me by asking about the existence of God himself, or more awkward questions, I, pretending to be busy in my chores, would refer him to Viru.

Viru, who loved bragging about his knowledge and articulation, would seem to be smarter in my head and answer Ryan's questions with appropriate reasoning.

But only my imagination blessed me with such pleasures of motherhood. The reality, on the other hand, would laugh at my daydreaming as if making a cruel joke.

Ryan did not express curiosity about anything, nor did he ask questions. The words "what" and "why" were so insignificant in his limited vocabulary that he barely felt the need to use them. He cut every conversation short by making replies either reluctantly or in haste.

He played alone as if he needed nobody to join. He examined his toys for the finer details like never was done before. He gazed at objects for hours as if they were not visible to him any longer.

He lined up all his toy cars in a strange fashion every day, with the red roofless car always ahead, as if leading the rest of the fleet.

His peculiar play games involved sitting on this red roofless car, looking like a giant passenger in the world of tiny hot wheels cars, who could not fit in the entire space in the car, even if it was a hundred times bigger, let alone in the passenger seat. He pretended to ride by sliding on it, pushing himself forward with his hands and feet, and I would try to stop him lest he should break the car.

The only time he laughed was when playing with Caesar. Sometimes, sitting alone on a chair, he shed tears for no apparent reason.

On a sunny Saturday morning, we went for a picnic. Since Viru was away on yet another business trip, I hit the road with Elena Hayden and the kids. Elena had been mainly staying indoors since Jim's death, and I missed our evening chitchats in the yard. So, I planned the outing to cheer her up.

As I drove up north at a temperature of twelve degrees Celsius, the gentle breeze, intensified by our speeding vehicle on the quiet and lonely roads, blew the outside vegetation into my nose, with fragrance stimulating my olfactory receptors and the fresh air giving new life to my lazy, bored lungs. About two hours later, we arrived at the tulip gardens.

Now, I had not seen paradise, well nobody had, but I thought this place perhaps bared the closest resemblance. There was a vast bed of tulips aligned in the form of well-designed stripes of colors ranging from red, yellow, purple, pink, and white. This heavenly mat of colorful tulip bulbs was adorned in the middle by the dreamy pink cherry blossom trees bordering the sleepy walkway that stretched up to the serene blue lake at the other end.

We walked lightly on the pathway that appeared to be pink under the reflection of the cherry blossoms on either side.

The children seemed to be equally mesmerized by the scenery. Reva and Britney, visibly beaming, admired the sea of bright bulbs of tulips and the general surroundings.

A mild glow appeared on Elena's face that I had not seen in a while, as she appreciated the blissful feeling of being present in the bed of flowers under the quilt of fragrance.

And Ryan, well, oblivious to the wonders of nature, he continued to play with Caesar, who also seemed to be interested only in flattering his master through his antics and nothing else.

We found a fine spot under a tree by the lake, and like many people around us on the sprawling grassland, we spread our mats.

I had noticed a change in Britney in the sense that she was not as chatty as before. She did not bombard me or anyone else with the shells of her curious questions.

I spoke to Elena softly about my observation, and she confirmed that Britney had talked less since Jim's demise. Elena told me that before, she would ask about her Daddy all the time and want to call him, but since his demise, she had barely mentioned him in any of her little conversations.

It pained me to think about what would be going through the mind of this innocent child who saw her Dad separating, first from her mother and later from this world.

The most striking thing was that she did not exhibit her well-known fondness for Ryan anymore. She did not go up to him or sit beside him, nor did she ask questions as she had before, despite knowing that Ryan would not respond.

She would say, like before, "Look, Mrs. Sharma, Ryan put his hand in Caesar's mouth," or "Mrs. Sharma, Ryan is pulling Caesar's tail."

I tried to engage her. "Britney, dear, did you notice Ryan has combed Caesar's hair today?"

"I know, Mrs. Sharma; he always does that."

"And this morning, he picked him up by his legs."

"Yeah, I have seen that."

It turned out Britney was already as familiar with Ryan's antics as if Ryan performed them only for her, and hence showed little interest.

Seeing me try, Elena pressed my hand softly, "Don't worry. She will take some time."

Britney did not ignore Ryan on purpose, for she was far too innocent to play games like adults. Something lately (perhaps her Daddy's death) had made her realize the worthlessness of expectations and she had inadvertently stopped trying altogether.

Anyone else would think that Ryan did not care about people around him and notice no difference, but I, his mother, saw clearly that this lack of attention from Britney bothered him.

Though Ryan played with Caesar as usual, I could tell that he was distracted. Every time Ryan wrestled with Caesar, held him on his lap or his back and pulled his ear or tail, he would momentarily glance at Britney, perhaps hoping that she would go back to her previous self and take notice. But that did not happen.

In my imagination—or daydreaming, if you will, where things happened according to my wishes—Ryan would initiate a conversation with her and inquire about her coldness. But then my wishes were only fulfilled in my imagination. The reality, on the contrary, only added them to my wishlist.

There was nothing special with the food that we had packed from home, but everything we ate tasted better than ever, thanks to the joy of eating in a picturesque location.

It turned out it was not perfect cooking, pleasant aromas, and good presentation that always made food great. Sometimes the empty belly and elevated experience of eating alone could do the trick. Why else would sandwiches stuffed with potato and eggs feel like an exquisite delicacy, and sliced cucumbers and tomatoes taste like an exotic salad?

I did not know about others, but this dose of nature helped invigorate my spirit and rejuvenate my energy for a few hours.

Late in the afternoon, we headed back to Abbynton. As I entered a secluded narrow stretch after driving for about an hour, I slowed down after noticing an animal on the road.

It was a bear who turned as our vehicle approached. The big black bear looked at our car through his fuming red eyes, and our vehicle and my senses both came to a halt.

In the backseat, Caesar was barking furiously, and Reva and Britney started panicking.

I was frozen by the angry, illusionary eyes of the bear, like a deer caught in the headlights, when Elena, sitting next to me, shouted, "Shut the windows, shut the windows, Mandy!"

Elena's shriek helped restore my senses with a shudder, and I slid up all the partially open windows and applied central locking to the doors and windows.

Seeing some action in the vehicle, the bear roared vehemently by opening his big jaws, displaying sharp, protruding teeth, and our jaws dropped in fear. All this time, Caesar continued to bark profusely.

Suddenly, the bear turned around and started, first walking briskly ahead of our vehicle, then running straight in the middle of the road, and after that, running in a zig-zag manner. Since it was a narrow, straight road, we could spot the bear for about two hundred meters, still roaming on the road.

A few vehicles had closed in behind us by this time, so I started the engine and drove slowly. To our relief, the bear disappeared into the bushes after some time, and I drove on.

Within minutes, I noticed another figure at the shoulder of the road, some distance away. It was a man clad in a black hat and cloak, attire that seemed familiar to me.

Oh my God, who is that? I thought as I approached. *Is it, Jack?*

The man was looking into our vehicle, perhaps at me, but I could not yet make out from the distance if it was really Jack. Caesar was again barking from the backseat like a mad dog.

Then something strange happened. The man suddenly appeared in the middle of the narrow road.

Petrified, I forcefully applied the brakes, and the vehicle came to a sudden halt, jerking everyone to the front.

The man was not Jack, for I could recognize him among a hundred men, thanks to his conspicuous long nose, but someone younger dressed like him, standing right in front of the car, staring at me with red eyes, with no fear of getting crushed under the wheels.

"What is the matter with you, Mandy? Why did you apply

the brakes?" asked Elena, perplexed.

"What? What do you mean?" I returned as I tried to make sense of Elena's question.

"We are lucky there was no car behind us, or else we would have banged our heads on the windshield."

"What, Elena? Don't you see the man that came into the middle of the road?"

"Man? What man?"

I turned my head momentarily towards Elena. "That man. Don't you see?"

I looked to the front, and there was no man.

"Where did he go? How is that possible? Didn't you notice a man who came in front of the car?" I asked aloud.

"There was no man, Mandy."

"I swear, Elena! I just saw a man."

"Reva, Britney, did you see any man on the road?"

"No, we did not." both replied together.

"What? That is ridiculous. How come Caesar was barking then?"

"I don't know. Maybe still thinking about that mad bear. Are you ok, Mandy? Do you want me to drive?"

Despite being paralyzed by a frightening experience in one moment and the startling revelation in the next that I was the only one to see the man, I tried my best to collect myself.

"No...Um, I'm fine. Yes, you are right. Perhaps I was distracted since we saw that crazy bear." I said and carefully drove on.

Chapter Three

I had established three things by now. One, I'd had encounters with two strange-looking men wearing a black hat and a cloak. Two, I'd had several meetings in my dreams and a brief but baffling interaction in person with one of them named Jack. Third—and the worst—the above two things were only known to me. Usually, if you see something, there is no reason why you should not believe it, but what to make of the existence of something that only you had seen, and nobody else?

As soon as I walked out of my house, I was in a state of constant fear of being watched or followed by some mysterious humans, who I could see but the world could not.

I dreaded an encounter with these weird men, so much so that even hats or cloaks lying on display in showrooms were enough to send shivers down my spine, let alone people wearing them.

The worst part? I was bearing this torture all alone. I missed my former life when I regarded Viru as the only weird man in my life.

I could not take it anymore. I was not one of those people who could keep information to themselves, and certainly not information of enormity, such as this. I could not tell Elena as she had been in low spirits since Jim's death and needed cheering up, rather than scaring. Moreover, I did not want her to think that I was going crazy.

I must tell Viru, I thought. *He will make fun of me as he always thinks I make up stories in my head. He will make lame jokes like, "Oh, you finally met the man you saw in your dreams? What did he say? 'Remember me? I am the one you see in your dreams?'"*

When I tell him that he indeed made comments precisely to that effect, Viru will start rolling on the floor laughing. He will continue, something like, "And now there's another one, who, instead of dropping by in your dreams, drops right in front of your car? To kill himself?" He will then make follow up jokes for a few days on this topic that only he finds funny, something like, "So, now there are two Charlie Chaplins!" or "One is Charlie and the second is Chaplin!"

This unbelievable experience would be an uphill task for me even to explain to any caring and understanding person, let alone to insensitive and nonchalant Viru.

So what? I resolved in my head, *I will still tell him when he returns next week from his trip. I must get this plague out of my system, it is killing me. I will open up to him even if that means dealing with his piercing sarcasm or suspicion about my mental state.*

My train of thought ended abruptly at 5:30 a.m. in the morning when Caesar, who I was walking to Mount Mary Hills, stopped abruptly at the entrance gate of the cemetery and gave a loud, angry growl.

The wide gravel road, a popular walkway for morning walkers, where Viru (or I, in his absence) walked Caesar in the morning, bordered a large cemetery that stretched deep into the forest and all the way up to Mount Mary Hills. This cemetery boasted of lush green lawns embellished by a dense covering of dandelions. A web of narrow roads comprised hundreds of rows where thousands of tombstones were aligned neatly, many of them adorned by multicolored bouquets of fresh and stale flowers.

Favreau, Desrosiers, Turcot, Teolis, Dumas, Perron, Forlini, Gualano, Dinarzo, and many others whose names I could not read when walking on the gravel road, laid peacefully beneath their intricately carved tombstones.

As happens with the large and ancient ones, this cemetery

was no stranger to scary ghost stories. Elena Hayden, who had shown keen interest in such stories, often told me about incidents like ghosts of dead men spotted walking in the middle of the night, or passersby hearing loud cries at night and I, out of fear, would not let her finish.

I looked in the direction of Caesar, expecting to spot a dog or a beaver or some person nearby, but could not find one. I pulled the leash gently, but he did not budge. Caesar continued his attacking stance and angry, wild growl as if guarding against a threat not from someone or something in particular, but the entire cemetery in general.

At seeing the otherwise charming and docile Caesar so angry and rigid, anxiety engulfed me, and I, yelling at him, pulled the leash forcefully. The next moment, he responded to my temper and the tension (in the leash) by relaxing both his mood and muscles.

Pondering over Caesar's abnormal behavior, I remembered Viru telling me one morning about Caesar barking haphazardly with nobody around, the incident that I had casually passed over, ascribing it to Viru's usual morning grumble.

I wondered if Caesar was losing it. What else could explain this unpredictable and aggressive behavior? I had heard that dogs have a sixth sense in addition to the regular five senses (smell, sight, touch, hear, and taste). They can sense something unusual or perhaps see an impending danger.

I wondered if Caesar's attention towards the entrance of the cemetery was indicative of something supernatural. Could there be any merit to Elena's gossip regarding ghosts walking in the cemetery?

Can Caesar see dead people? The eerie thought crossed my mind.

A few days earlier, when the mysterious man had jumped in front of my car and everyone else thought I was crazy to pull over abruptly on an empty road, Caesar had barked furiously, indicating he saw him too.

Can Caesar see what I see and others do not? Are these people ghosts of dead men? Is Jack a ghost?

That thought felt like a needle sticking in my heart, injecting a fresh dose of anxiety into my brain. The only glimmer of hope was the feeling that I was not crazy or alone. Caesar, perhaps, was witness to this, or even more.

"Hello!"

A faint female voice sounded in my head that felt distinct from the voices of ambiguity and transported me abruptly from my train of thought to the station of reality. It was the young girl who jogged every morning that I could see from my window.

"Hi! I am sorry...did you say something?"

"I was asking about him," she said, pointing at Caesar. "What's his name?"

"Oh, he is Caesar."

"Caesar! Lovely name. How old is he?"

"Five years old."

"I see. I meet him sometimes in the morning with the gentleman, um..."

"Yes, that's my husband."

"Ah, ok. Can I?"

"Yes, sure."

Bending forward, she reached out to Caesar's forehead, gently caressing down his back. Caesar reciprocated with equal warmth by wagging tail and leaning over her lap.

"Oh, he is so adorable. Such a happy dog. You have a great day." She parted with a broad smile and carried on her usual trot.

Meeting her served as an assurance. I also perceived Caesar as adorable and naughty, with unconditional devotion to Ryan, as opposed to Viru, who believed he was a mad dog.

The day progressed with the usual pace, not coinciding with mine thanks to my mind and action being entirely out of sync, something that had happened to me more frequently of late. I was so lost in the shower that I mixed up my shampoo and facewash, leaving behind a thick, frothy face and a wet, slimy head. My absentmindedness was such that I would start from the living room with an object in mind but forget the objective by the time I reached the kitchen.

The better part of the day came through my appointment with Ryan's therapist Estelle Silver. For the past three months, I had been regularly taking Ryan to Estelle's clinic twice a week by skipping his school after lunch to work on the new interactive program that she had introduced. Estelle shared some positive feedback that Ryan was making progress in social interaction and communication.

Another light moment on my way back was my conversation with Sebastian at the Saint Thomas Metro Station.

"You look tired today. Is everything good, Mandira?"

"Yes, Seb, life is full of problems. What can you do?"

"Ah, problems? Well, you can surely do one thing about them."

"Like what?"

"Solve them."

"Ha! I wish it was as simple as you say."

"You know, Mandira, every problem seems complicated until it is solved. Now, I do not know what is bothering you, but in a few years, when we look back, all our problems seem simple in hindsight. And perhaps that's the way to deal with them."

"You may be right. Our problems might sound simple in hindsight but certainly not in the present when we must deal with them. I don't know, perhaps I think too much."

"Thinking is good, it is the first step towards solving any problem."

"Funny that you say that, my husband says thinking is my only problem."

"Ha ha, that is funny."

"So, according to you, thinking is the first step to solving the problem. What is the second step?"

"The second step is understanding it. And before you

ask, acting on it is the third one."

"Nice. Think, understand, and act. I'm amazed by your outlook on life. There is a lot I can learn from you."

"We all learn from each other, Mandira. I learn from you every day."

*

Estelle's feedback, followed by my chat with Seb, helped change my state of mind. However, my positive outlook, like all good things in my life, was short-lived.

That afternoon, Caesar seemed anxious rather than excited while waiting for Ryan and Reva to return from the school. He ran down the street, many more times than usual, looking for the school bus, and returned to me every time, tapping with his paws, complaining, and imploring me to look out with him. As there was some time left for the bus to return, I comforted Caesar, only for him to run down the street again.

The bus arrived at the stop on time, Reva and Ryan disembarked, and I received them along with visibly agitated Caesar. Caesar sniffed and licked his master as a display of affection and concern that, as opposed to other days, did not excite Ryan, for he continued to be his subdued and indifferent self.

Reva told me that Ryan wept on the bus, and when she enquired, his classmates expressed no knowledge of any unusual occurrence during the day that would have upset him.

"Ryan. Look at me, dear. Did something happen at school? Did anybody hurt you?" I asked.

"No, Mommy."

"Are you sure?"

"Yes," he nodded, shyly pressing his hand on his neck as if hiding it under the collar of his shirt.

"Wait, what is that?" I checked his collar, removed the sweater, and unbuttoned a blood-stained shirt to find two wide scratches from the lower part of his neck down to his chest. "Oh my God! Who did this? Did anyone hit you in class? Please tell me, what happened? Don't be scared, Mommy will fix everything."

As I spoke, tears filled those limitless brown eyes to the brink of his thick eyelashes, and like gushing waves of floodwater overflowing from a dam, they rolled down his gloomy crimson cheeks.

My motherly concern and a barrage of questions did not comfort him, and rather aggravated his misery, as Ryan would not utter another word from the helpless mouth that twitched repeatedly.

Silence is golden, but not for a child who bears pain. Patience is a virtue, but not for a mother who witnesses her child's misery. Silence and patience may appear complementary to each other, but there is a dichotomy between the two. When the effect of the former is high, the latter's influence is suppressed.

When Ryan's silence became unbearable, I ran out of patience and called his class teacher, Miss Stella. She also expressed ignorance about the matter. She tried her best to placate me by promising to check with the support staff and Ryan's classmates first thing in the morning.

My restless state that evening was followed by a sleepless night with Ryan cuddled close to my chest. He shuddered sporadically out of fear of the memory of some incident, perhaps dreadful, that was unknown to me.

All the other worries that had bothered me before had vanished in light of my son's troubles, which now occupied all the space in my mind.

Chapter Four

Miss Stella's investigation the next day did not pay off, and the injury marks on Ryan's chest remained a mystery. Sister's protective instinct in the school was activated for her little brother, more than it had previously, for Reva almost assumed my role, and made it a point to keep a check on Ryan by frequently stepping out of her class on the pretext of water or toilet breaks.

Upon their return in the afternoon, my beautiful and dutiful daughter would give me a detailed account of her action and observations at the school. It seemed to me that she had resolved to get to the bottom of the incident.

Ryan, now timid and lost, went back into his shell, the shell that became much harder to intercept than before. His buddy Caesar tried all the antics of the dog book to bring a smile to Ryan's face and often succeeded briefly, but his magic did not work like a charm as before.

Reva's determination yielded results two days later, and I sensed it even before she spoke from her enthusiastic waving gesture as she stepped off the bus with Ryan.

"Mom, I found them. I found the culprit!" shouted Reva from the street, letting go of Ryan's hand, handing him over to his other guardian, Caesar.

"What happened?" I returned curiously, standing at the entrance to our yard.

"I knew it was him. I caught him red-handed."

"Who?"

"Who else? That boy Ben."

"Ben? Who is Ben? Tell me what happened?"

"Ben is in Ryan's class. A tall and fat boy, always mocking him. Today I stepped out of my class to see Ryan about a minute before the recess started. By the time I reached his block, the bell had rung, and I saw the boys and girls coming out of their classes. And you know, Mom, he pushed him down the stairs."

"What? Which stairs?"

"The main stairs, going down to the first floor."

"Oh my God! That's a lot of steps."

"Yes, Ryan came rolling down."

"Did he get hurt? Ryan, come here, honey."

"He's fine, Mom. I checked him. Luckily, he escaped injury."

Despite Reva's confirmation, I checked Ryan thoroughly for my satisfaction.

"Why would this boy Ben do that?"

"No reason, that boy is just a bully. He was probably irritated at Ryan walking slowly ahead of him."

"Then what happened?"

"Then I rushed to pick up Ryan. Ben was not expecting me. Before he could run away, I grabbed his arm and he got scared. I took him to Principal Elizabeth. She was very angry and called Ms. Stella, and they both scolded him and made him apologize to Ryan. Principal Elizabeth is also going to talk to his parents."

"Did he also admit to the scratching?"

"No. But he also didn't admit to pushing him today, even when I caught him! That boy is a liar, Mom, I am sure he is the one who scratched Ryan."

The matter of scratch marks could not be concluded due to Ben's blatant denial and lack of any eyewitnesses. Since that day of the incident, I had noticed a change in Ryan. Now, I would not expect a change for the better in any child who had gone through such trauma, let alone in the case of

Ryan. Still, considering how detached, disengaged, and disinterested he had always been, it was rare that the external environment affected him at all.

But the change I had noticed was undoubtedly for the worse, as he looked nervous all the time. He would starve himself at the school by not eating his lunch or drinking water. I fed him well upon returning, and he devoured all the food in just a few quick bites. But he would not tell me why he brought his lunch box and water bottle back in the same condition as in the morning.

I was worried about Ryan's health and nutrition. Since he had stopped eating at the school and would be hungry by the afternoon, I decided to cook fresh food and not feed him the lunch I packed in the morning upon his return.

Usually, I did not cook lunch on the weekdays as I lacked the motivation to cook only for myself, and thus ate the leftover food from the morning or the previous night. But a mother cannot remain lazy when it comes to her children. She needs to adjust her routine and always stay on top of her game.

So, I set off to buy some fine spices to add flavor and variety to my cuisine. I visited one of my favorite stores for my condiments in Summerhill, a town relatively far away from Abbynton, but worth it.

Over the years, I had done extensive research on grocery stores in the city and gathered much insight into the right stores for specific products.

I would never let Viru shop for the groceries as there was only one grocery store near our house that he knew of. According to his logic, it was within walking distance, and that meant it was the best option. "Since they all look the same, the food will taste the same," was his philosophy. But when I confronted him about the quality, he defended it with the logic of accessibility. He would go far in his silly logic and invent bizarre mathematical reasoning according to which the quality of the product was inversely proportional to the distance required to travel from the house, meaning high quality ~ low distance, and vice versa.

I came out of the store holding bags of groceries, satisfied with my shopping in Summerhill, and took to the sidewalk of the narrow path, a shortcut connecting the main road where the car was parked. Since Viru was out on his trip, I had the car at my disposal to make my life and the commute easier.

"Hi, Miss Sharma."

I turned around to take a look at the owner of that friendly voice. It was a tall and handsome gentleman, clad in a white shirt folded stylishly at the cuffs and a pair of black trousers. He must have been in his late thirties, but with that athletic body evident through his slim-fit shirt, this Brad Pitt look-alike could very well have given twenty-five-year-olds a run for their money.

"Hello, I am sorry, have we met before?" I asked.

"We have not, but I have seen you quite a few times at Saint Augustine School."

"Oh really?" I returned, wondering how I never noticed a man like him, who could be easily noticeable even among a crowd of hundred men.

"Yes, you are Ryan's Mom. I'm Bob, by the way."

"Hi, Bob, how do you know Ryan and me?"

"I'm Ben's Dad," Bob uttered hesitatingly.

"Oh."

"Miss Sharma, I am deeply sorry about Ben's actions," he added quickly, seeing me change color at the mention of Ben. "The principal summoned me to school the other day and informed what Ben did to Ryan. I am ashamed of my son and have grounded him. I assure you he will never harm your son in the future."

"That's all right. He's a child; children make mistakes."

"Thank you, Miss Sharma, you are very kind. How is Ryan doing?"

"Not taking it very well, but he will be fine."

"My apologies, Miss Sharma. Ben was not always like this. His mother died in an unfortunate accident a year ago, and since then he has become a rebel."

"I am sorry to hear that."

"No matter how much you do, one cannot replace a mother's love and care. It's my fault too as I keep busy at work and the poor child feels neglected."

"I understand. I hope everything will be ok."

"I wanted to apologize to you but did not know how to contact you, and then I saw you here and couldn't help coming over. I will do my best but do not hesitate to call me if Ben causes any trouble to your son in the future. Here's my card."

"Robert Sutherland...you are a psychiatrist!" I said, glancing at Bob's business card.

"I am."

"Do you practice here in Summerhill?"

"Yes, my clinic is two blocks away. It's expensive to afford a modest clinic in the city of Abbynton, you know, so I opened one here."

"Very well, Mr. Bob, thank you. Nice talking to you."

"Thank you for talking to me, Miss Sharma. I feel relieved now. Do you need help with those bags?"

"No, thanks, my car is right there. Goodbye."

*

My unexpected meeting with Bob turned my resentment into empathy for the dad and sympathy for his son. I regretted the prejudiced perception that I had developed in my mind towards poor, motherless Ben without even knowing him properly. It is not a child that is bad, but his circumstances, I reminded myself. I could not imagine Ryan's life without me and wished no child was deprived of a mother's love.

Viru returned from his two-week long business trip to New Jersey in low spirits, a trait uncommon in him. He did not greet the kids warmly and Caesar poorly like he always did. He talked less and did not tell stories of his trip. Moreover, his unfunny jokes—of which only Reva would care to laugh at—were missing at the dinner table.

In bed, I asked him about the reason for the gloominess, and he opened up after initial reluctance. Viru told me that his company was considering downsizing to optimize the manpower operational cost structure. When I got lost in the heavy business terms, he clarified that a friend of his in the human resources department, who also accompanied him on the trip, had hinted at the possibility of Viru losing his job.

"What? How can they do that? You work so hard! You received an award for the best employee last year!"

"Performance does not matter, Mandy, when it comes to cutting costs. That's how the corporate world operates."

"But that's wrong. It's an unethical practice."

"Yes, from our perspective. But the decision-makers at the top have to put business first, even before people."

"To hell with the business. I cannot believe you are still taking their side. How can these people sleep at night knowing they robbed someone's livelihood? If the business is so important, how come those so-called decision-makers don't get laid off?"

Viru tried to explain how complex business decisions were made, which was beyond my simple mind's comprehension. To me, a person who gave everything for his company should have every right to keep his job with dignity. My simple logic did not fit in with the complex business decisions. Viru pacified me by saying that the formal announcement had not been made yet, and that the final decision could change, but I was angry and scared.

I would often complain at Viru for not helping much with the household chores or kids' homework, and for taking everything for granted in general, but one thing I was proud of was his job.

Viru put his work before everything. He always started at the office early and finished late. He avoided taking vacations but would not skip business travel which kept him away from family and the comfort of home for several days and weeks. He won awards for his work, and it occurred to me that he was indispensable to his company.

I disliked his obsession with work as much as his jokes and often wondered if the business trips meant work or some excuse for having fun. But with Viru, there was always a sense of security. I did not worry about our finances, despite Ryan's expensive therapy.

I had left my job a few years ago to focus on the kids as I was confident about Viru's capability to ensure food on the table. And believe me, a few bad jokes did not hurt when you had sumptuous food on the table.

If ever there was a limit to the sufferings from that point onwards, I wished I were at the brink of such a threshold.

Chapter Five

Since Viru was dealing with the setback on the subject most dear to him—his job—I dropped the idea of telling him about the sufferings of the past two weeks while he had been away.

Viru now talked less and joked no more, walked Caesar in the morning without complaining, and left for work reluctantly. He still spent long hours in the office but lacked enthusiasm. I dreaded the possibility of Viru sitting at home jobless, as he derived all his energy from work. I felt terrible seeing him engrossed in his thoughts all the time and did not wish to have another overthinking person in the family, a habit that he would exclusively attribute to me.

Meanwhile, Ryan continued to starve himself at the school and would only break his fast at home in the afternoon, relishing my freshly cooked delicacies that sometimes Reva would also find irresistible, even after having lunch at school.

In addition to Ryan's problems and Viru's latest situation, one thing that bothered me constantly was my strange experiences over the past few months. It was becoming increasingly difficult for me to hold this information any longer, and I felt a desperate need to talk to someone and let it out.

I had earlier thought of telling Viru, who would have made a few jokes about it and declared everything fine without judging me. Honestly, his reassurance was always a relief, something I liked to hear, even though his casual approach would hurt me.

But I figured, given his present circumstance, he was himself skeptical about things being fine—the reassurance that he would conveniently give me—and the last thing he needed at this time was to be introduced to my troubles.

An idea came to my mind that at first felt silly but started to make sense when I contemplated it for a while. *I know I don't have any mental illness, well I don't think I do,* I thought, *but people seek professional help for various conditions such as stress, depression, or just to clear their mind, like in my case. And I recently met a person who is a psychiatrist by profession and who made an amiable impression on me.*

I decided to consult Bob, who had left his card with me that day outside the grocery store in Summerhill.

I called Bob for an appointment, and he sounded a bit relieved upon realizing that it was about me and not in reference to his son Ben. He generously accommodated me for a slot on the following day, despite his seemingly busy schedule.

Since the car was not at my disposal anymore as Viru used it to commute to work, I took the metro and traveled all the way to Summerhill, the last stop on the green line. From there, I walked three blocks further, to the end of the street, and finally arrived at the clinic, which was in the basement of a three-story building.

An elderly lady at the reception showed me to the clinic entrance, where Bob greeted me warmly before I settled down on a comfortable couch, and he sat on his easy chair. It was a cozy room with a wooden table and a few easy chairs on the left. A large bookshelf filled with neatly arranged books occupied about half of the wall on the right. There was a door next to the bookshelf that I guessed opened to a retiring room.

I was anxious at the beginning of the session, still wondering if I had made the right decision to visit him, but

Bob made me comfortable by initiating a casual conversation rather than asking direct questions, something I would not expect from a regular psychiatrist.

I don't know if it was the magic of his smooth-talking or my desperate desire to share the misery of the past several months with another human, but I gradually started to uncover my unprecedented encounters hitherto guarded carefully, like an onion peeled layer by layer.

While Bob listened patiently, I opened up about my son's struggles, and my dream encounters with a stranger followed by an unexpected meeting with him, that according to my husband (who only knew about the dreams and not about the meeting), was an effect of my obsessive worrying about Ryan.

Bob took a keen interest in my account, particularly the part where I mentioned meeting with the unknown man and asked me to elaborate on the minute details.

I told him how I saw a man in a hat and cloak, who identified himself as Jack, in my dreams for several days, before finally seeing him at the Christmas parade for the first time, and how I cut him short and fled to my house when he showed up another time. I also told him about the outing with my neighbors, the Haydens, when I had a momentary illusion of another man dressed in similar attire to Jack bumping into my car.

Bob interjected for the first time by asking if my family members or the neighbor Elena confirmed witnessing the encounters with those men.

I explained how absentminded Viru was, in general, to noticing people, especially in a crowded place like the Christmas parade, and that when Jack met me in person, I was alone on the sidewalk. As for the incident in the car, I told him that it was a brief observation, perhaps a daydream or my overthinking, as often suggested by my husband.

"So, nobody else other than you have seen these men," he remarked.

Bob's inference evoked such a sensation as if a bucket of

ice-cold water were tumbled over my warm, bare body. I had thought about those men and the finer details of the encounters with them on numerous occasions, and somewhere deep down knew this all along, but hearing from another person that nobody else witnessed what I did felt like a fresh, eye-opening revelation.

The justifications, like Viru's absentmindedness, Reva's oversight, or my fantasy suddenly seemed to me like mere excuses. It was clear now that only I could see those men. What was not clear was why, and who were those men?

Bob then asked if I suffered from anxiety, irritability, sleeplessness, or whether I heard voices in my head, felt like someone was plotting against me, or had suicidal thoughts. He also asked if I had any history of trauma or drug abuse.

The series of questions made me realize for the first time that I was not casually chatting with a caring acquaintance but consulting a professional, and my response to most of his questions was an emphatic no. I had none of those symptoms, except for the stress of family problems like Ryan's regression, Viru's frequent business trips, his likelihood of losing his job, and his evil colleague Anu's plot to steal him from me, which gave me a few sleepless nights.

Finally, Doctor Robert Sutherland began to share his observation. "Miss Mandira, I have now collected most of the details about your situation. I require a few tests and screenings to rule out certain things and come to my final conclusion."

"I see. So, you will help me with my stress? Give me some exercises, I guess?"

"Well, I am afraid it is more than stress."

"Oh, that means you already know what it is. Will you tell me? Is it depression?"

"Generally, I prefer to finish my screening first, but, in this case, I have a fair idea of what it is. Now, before I tell you, I need you to keep in mind that I can treat your condition very well."

"My condition? What condition? Tell me, Bob, you are

making me nervous."

"I am suspecting signs of schizophrenia."

"What? Schizophrenia?" I said, pausing to make sure I had heard him right. "That cannot be true! How? But how can it be?"

"There is no specific reason. This condition can happen to anyone."

"I don't believe you. Do you mean to say I am mentally ill?" I flushed crimson with disbelief.

"Well, I would not put it that way."

"I am completely normal. With all due respect, Bob, I think you are mistaken here." I shuddered, and my hands trembled nervously.

"Well, I will be happy if I am proven wrong after finishing the tests. Calm down, please," Returned Bob at seeing me becoming impatient.

"Calm down? How? Ok, prove it to me, Bob. What led you to think that I am schizophrenic?"

"Ok, how about seeing people who do not exist?"

"Which people? Do you mean Jack? When did I say he doesn't exist?"

"You didn't say it but isn't it obvious when you see a person, but your family members and neighbors don't see anything?"

"But…but I told you there was nobody around when Jack met me near my house."

"Ok. And what about that time in the parade and the other time when this man bumped into your car?"

"Well…" I fell short of words.

"Mandira, you might have heard of something called hallucinations. It means you see things or people that are not there or hear voices that do not exist."

"So, are you saying the man named Jack, who I have seen in my dreams many times and also met in person, is my hallucination?"

"Yes, and what you believe is a dream is also a form of visual hallucination called hypnogogic hallucination that occurs in the conscious state between waking and sleeping. Look, to explain in simple terms, these hallucinations at play have produced an illusion of an unknown man coming to life and even talking to you, when there is no such man or men. I still need to complete the screening, but based on our discussion, I am quite sure that the underlying condition is schizophrenia. The good news is that I can treat you through psychosocial therapies. Also, I will prescribe medication."

"I don't know what to say. This is…"

"Miss Mandira, I know this is a lot of information. Believe me. I have treated many such patients who were able to get on with their life. I need you to go home and think it over. We can fix this. And yes, one important piece of advice: If you see Jack again, do not give him any attention. Also, ignore any strangers or any occurrences that you perceive to be strange or bizarre."

Back home, everything that Bob said in the clinic that then had seemed impossible to me started to make sense. Knowing the truth was certainly not comforting. I wished I could go back in time and continue living in my world of fantasy and confusion without knowing that they were, in fact, hallucinations, and know that Viru would blame my weird sightings on my obsessive worrying. I knew that living in denial would not solve any of my issues, as acceptance, no matter how painful, was the first step towards a solution.

I felt weak and helpless but decided to keep it from Viru until his job situation could get sorted. He was barely noticing anyone in the family lately anyway.

Chapter Six

In other news, an uncanny fear was gripping the world. The scientists and researchers of the medical and healthcare world were baffled by yet another challenge that they secretly believed could very well turn out to be a global phenomenon.

This disease or disorder was associated with sleep. What were the symptoms? It was observed that the person, who otherwise had no history of insomnia or difficulty in sleeping, would suddenly start to experience sleeplessness. The person would complain of being awake most of the time through the night with a slight recollection of dozing off. They would not report stress or anxiety or any other symptoms that could lead to sleeplessness, and sleeping pills only worked to the extent of inducing mild sleep for short spans.

The sleeplessness would be followed by extreme weakness and fatigue. Soon, the lack of sleep and burnout took a toll on the patient, who would start to blabber irregularly as if stoned.

The symptoms, that lasted about fifteen to twenty days, would eventually lead to death during one of those rare occasions of mild sleep.

Some smart people were quick to term it "fatal insomnia," a rare type of disease, but failed to explain its properties and why it caused death in just a few days.

While some scientists believed unknown anxiety was responsible for this condition, others blamed underlying health conditions which caused increased levels of weariness.

Then there was another type of disorder observed that was contrary to sleep deprivation. Here, people did not show the symptoms of sleeplessness. Instead, they would sleep well and not wake up. Ever.

Initially, their heart would beat normally, but the pulse slowed down over a few days and eventually stopped completely, and so did life. The defibrillators used to resuscitate would prove to be futile in restoring the heartbeat.

During their abnormal and prolonged sleep, they went into a state that doctors believed to be a type of coma that would, in a matter of days, bring a full stop to the patient's life. Sadly, life for the patients of sleep coma became analogous to the length of a short sentence paused by a comma and ended by a full stop.

Elena's ex-husband Jim's untimely death in sleep was attributed to this condition.

These two conditions of sleeplessness and wakelessness were named "wake syndrome" and "sleep coma," respectively. Such was the dichotomy of these two types of symptoms believed to be originated from a common condition that people dreaded both sleeping and being awake for prolonged durations.

Researchers came up with scientific explanations that fell short of convincing reasoning. Religious gurus declared it to be an act of God, angry at the sins of humans. Environmentalists blamed it on global warming and nature's balancing act against the exploitation by humans.

While the experts of modern medicine bragged about the drugs or vaccines that could cure these conditions, the learned people of homeopathy and Ayurveda made tall claims of treatment by triggering the body's natural defense, exercises, and consuming natural herbs. One thing was common among all the people suggesting remedies: nobody knew of a clear diagnosis yet.

The World Health Organization had downplayed the threat as there was no clear, conclusive research available, and it did not fit the benchmarks of the definitions of endemic, epidemic, or pandemic.

An endemic is a disease or condition that occurs in a certain region at a regular and predictable rate. When an endemic leads to an outbreak with an unexpected rate of increase, it turns into an epidemic. When the epidemic spreads to multiple countries, it becomes a pandemic.

Firstly, the origin of this disease or disorder—whatever you might call it, for it was not clear—was not known. Secondly, the number of cases observed was small, with no news of an outbreak yet, but still alarming enough. Thirdly, there was no evidence of a contagious disease, but it was prevalent over multiple continents, and the rate gradually increased over time.

Governments around the world tried to keep it as a low-key affair. They acknowledged it as a disease but not a global threat, lest they spread panic, but spent hefty amounts on research, as they were careful not to underestimate the risk, thanks to lessons learned from the pandemic of 2019.

Summer

"Early sunrise and late sunset.
Watermelons. Mangoes.
My daughter's infectious giggles."

Chapter One

Long, warm days and short, warm nights. Tiny ripples caused by the light breeze in the calm lake reflected the sunlight into millions of glittering white pearls by day, and the clear, dark sky held billions of twinkling stars in the bosom by night. Melodious singing of nightingales by morning and high-pitched chirping of crickets by night. Cold frosty ice creams in the living rooms by afternoon and hot smoking barbecues in the backyards by evening. Light, colorful, and unlayered clothing. Fans and Air conditioners. Holiday spirit.

Despite the grand arrival of summer, there was no respite to my misery. The bar was only raised, as Viru would say.

When Ryan was born, he would cry all the time. He would wake up in the middle of the night and keep me up. My darling daughter Reva was always easygoing, but she was little at that time. During the first fifteen to twenty days, Viru and I felt extreme exhaustion at taking care of a very demanding newborn and a little girl. Then, it occurred to me that Ryan was perhaps crying less and sleeping more, and there was some relief to my afflictions.

Viru told me that it was not Ryan who had changed within twenty days of his birth, but my capacity to endure that had set a new bar for me. Higher and tougher.

I remember one time when Viru had turned

philosophical while reacting to my usual cribbing and said, "The good times and bad times are just the temporary phases of heightened emotions. Life is about everything in between. It is about the enduring times in which good things cease to stir, and bad things fail to deter."

Since his job loss, Viru had rarely shared the words of wisdom that he would have otherwise considered priceless. He was either engrossed in his thoughts or glued to his laptop. He spent most of the time applying for jobs or going for interviews.

It was a strange feeling, but I missed the old carefree and careless Viru and his habits that used to annoy me. He would not admit it, but I knew that he always took pride in his role as the provider of the house. The idea of living with uncertainty and exhausting the limited savings for daily household expenses was unbearable to him. He was desperate for a job, and I knew only that could bring back his lost pride and annoying habits.

Ryan had not recovered much from the shock of the incident at his school that left deep marks on his chest and perhaps his mind too. He continued to stay away from food and water at school. After getting off the bus, Ryan would first rush to the toilet to empty his bladder and then help himself with the food served at the table by scoffing it down in no time.

Estelle, who'd had a few good things to share last time about Ryan communicating better and making friends with other kids at the therapy sessions, had nothing positive to say in her latest feedback. On the contrary, she yet again noticed what she referred to as "regression," the term that I hated to hear.

My therapy with Bob, on the other hand, had worked well for me. He taught me how to deal with my thoughts and how to tell the difference between what was real and what was not.

I refrained from talking to strangers as per Bob's strict advice. I hallucinated a few times about Jack trying to talk to me on the sidewalk near my house and wondered how it felt so real. But I ignored the illusion of Jack, as Bob had warned me against any such interaction.

Sometimes the guilt of not revealing my condition to Viru bothered me, but I found many reasons not to tell him every time I considered the idea. First, it would be a big distraction for Viru, who was already struggling with the job search. Second, when I discussed this dilemma with Bob, he was confident that I could lead a normal life by taking care of a few things.

Also, I feared the social stigma attached to the disease so much so that I had little courage to tell Viru. The thought of my precious little family falling apart due to my hallucinations was a significant deterrent against disclosing it even to Viru, let alone anyone else. I knew I would run out of excuses for not telling Viru one day and hoped that day was not just around the corner.

The fresh breath of air among the stale course of melancholic events was Sylvain, the ex-colleague whom Viru called "mancyclopedia." He had paid frequent visits to our home since Viru's job loss to keep his friend and his family in good humor.

He cracked the best jokes, though Viru would not admit this to me when I teased him that Sylvain's jokes were funnier than his. Viru stated that there was a difference between living with a comedian and watching his one-hour performance. To prove his point that Sylvain's sense of humor in his wife Molly's opinion was also senseless humor, just like it was for me in our case, he would remind me of the potluck parties where Molly would barely smile at her husband's jokes, let alone laugh.

According to Viru, if wives were to judge the comic sense of their husbands, all the greatest comedians of the world would long fade into oblivion.

Speaking of Sylvain, his travel experiences, which he narrated with enthusiasm, were so much fun. In his most recent visit, he had shared his encounter with a moose while he and Molly were driving to their vacation house located up north during wintertime.

While narrating and enacting his account, Sylvain, sitting on the couch, acted out driving the pickup truck with his hands on the imaginary steering wheel and foot hitting the accelerator, and Reva, here playing Aunt Molly and always eager to put on a good show with Uncle Sylvain, took her place next to him.

The light snow from that morning had been neatly scraped off the road by the snow removal services, but an unexpected freezing rain occurred, forcing him to drive carefully.

Now, freezing rain is no ordinary rain, as the raindrops, while falling through the air under sub-freezing temperatures, get supercooled and freeze as soon as they come in contact with any surfaces, thereby making roads icy and dangerous for driving. Sylvain now pressed the accelerator, gently applying the brakes from time to time, and Reva also shuddered lightly in the passenger seat, knowing that the imaginary truck now moved slowly.

They had hardly driven a few miles on the icy road when they saw a seven-feet-tall moose with deadly, sharp antlers standing right in the middle of the road. Sylvain applied the brakes suddenly, bringing the truck to a complete halt after skidding for a few meters.

The skidding of the truck made the beast angry as mancyclopedia Sylvain, who knew the signs of aggression very well, could tell by the raised hair on the neck, pinned ears, licking, and head shaking.

Panic-stricken, Sylvain backed up, and as anticipated, the moose charged at them.

Now, here is the turning point of his hair-raising story (and by hair raising, I don't mean the raised hair of charging moose), which made it funny, like his previous stories.

The gigantic snorting moose galloping furiously towards the backing up truck had no concept of the freezing rain. It turned out that the moose suddenly skidded and collapsed and began to slide helplessly along the icy road. The moose made a desperate effort to recover from falling, but in vain, as it kept skidding more each time it tried, ending up sliding closer to the truck.

Here was an example of the fastest change of human priority, from self to possession. Before, Sylvain had hit the reverse gear to save their lives from an angry moose of 600 kilograms charging at them. Now, he was backing up to avoid damage to the truck from bumping against the same animal, who was now desperate and sliding.

At last, the moose managed to get back on its feet and darted into the woods after learning the hard way about the futility of its aggression in such dangerous conditions.

The highlight of the act was Sylvain imitating the moose by gliding and sliding on my carpet, leaving Reva in the driver's seat of the imaginary truck, and the curious Caesar, unable to follow all the fuss, trying to drag him along the carpet. While Reva and I laughed uncontrollably at the multiple takes of over-the-top performance—also done in slow motion—Viru giggled for the first time in a while, and Ryan sported a brief smile in a rare display of emotion.

While I prepared tea in the kitchen for the guest to be served with my homemade cookies and samosa, which he would call an irresistible combination, Sylvain talked to Viru in the living room, perhaps about his job and mention of a mistake, something that I could not help overhearing. When I asked about it while serving the irresistible combination, Sylvain and Viru casually laughed it off.

Later in the evening, when I enquired, Viru again pretended to be ignorant of any such conversation, but I had resolved to find out.

"Don't you try to change the subject, Viru, I heard you two talk about your job and Sylvain saying that you made a mistake. Why don't you tell me?"

"Because it's not a big deal, Mandy. I don't work for that company anymore."

"If it is not a big deal, why can't you tell me? Did they

fire you because you made some kind of mistake?"

"What? No! I was the best employee in my department, remember? I don't make mistakes. I correct the mistakes of others," returned Viru, taking offense to my remark that he perhaps felt was alluding to incompetence.

"Then what is it?"

"Ok, you want to hear it? Well, here it is. A week before I received notice of my layoff, I was offered a role in the sales division."

"And?"

"And I did not accept it."

"Wait a second. You knew they were going to fire you but still did not accept the role, correct?"

"Yes."

"Why? Are you out of your mind, Viru? Did you forget that you were the only breadwinner in our house?"

"I am aware of that, Mandy. I was going to accept it, but then I found out that Anu had secured that role for me."

"Anu?"

"Yes. Anu found out through a mutual friend in human resources that the company was offshoring most of the roles in my department. She approached her boss to consider me for a vacant position in her section, and he agreed. Now how could I possibly accept that offer knowing that you hate Anu so much?"

I was speechless, and Viru continued after a pause, "Look, Mandy, though Anu was trying to help as a colleague, I know that taking a favor from her would hurt you dearly. And working in the same section as her would only disturb your peace of mind. You have sacrificed so much for kids, especially for Ryan, managing him singlehandedly, and sometimes I feel bad for not being there and helping enough. So, even if it is uncalled for, I cannot give you another reason to worry. Plus, I want a job based on my competence, not as a favor."

"But why didn't you tell me, Viru?"

We had been married for thirteen years, but Viru had not

ceased to amaze me. Whenever I thought of him as a person who was insensitive and incapable of caring, Viru did something out of the blue that made me reconsider.

Instead of teasing me and making jokes, why couldn't he sometimes tell me that he cared for me? I needed assurance from time to time. This change in the mode of caring occurs organically in a relationship. Initially, the display of affection is more in words and less in deeds, but a few years into the marriage, there are only deeds done with unspoken words left for each other to figure out.

My heart melted for Viru for giving up an opportunity in trying times for my sake, and I felt small for suspecting him all this time.

The guilt of keeping a secret from him about my condition suddenly became unbearable. Without caring for excuses anymore, I opened up about my hallucinations. I told him everything that I had experienced over the past few weeks, and Viru listened patiently with a grim expression.

When I finished, I looked nervously into his eyes while he remained silent for a few seconds. It was now his turn to be speechless. Finally, he spoke. "I don't get it. So, you are telling me that the man you saw in your dreams now shows up and talks to you?"

"Yes, kind of."

"And that psychiatrist, what's his name?"

"Bob."

"Bob says that it is schizophrenia, and these are hallucinations?"

I nodded.

"Can you see that man Jack right now?" whispered Viru as he looked around, rolling his eyes to the left and right.

"Not like that. I cannot see him all the time. I have only seen him a few times," I returned, bringing his low voice back to normal.

"Then how can anyone tell that it is a hallucination?"

"Well, nobody else can see him, that's how."

"But, as per your description, most of the time, you have

met him on the street when nobody else was around."

"Yes, but what about the Christmas parade? You and Reva did not see him, but I did. And then during the visit to the tulip gardens, I almost bumped the car into a man, but Elena, Reva, and Britney did not see him. How do you explain that?"

"I don't know, it could be anything. How can you believe that what you see is not real? It could be an oversight on everyone else's part, considering a crowded place like a parade and a long drive. You could be right, and we could be wrong. Maybe all of us did not notice. It seems strange, but hallucinations are certainly not an explanation. I will only believe you are hallucinating if I find you talking to someone that I cannot see."

"Viru, the man I am consulting is a qualified psychiatrist who has come to this conclusion after detailed counseling and performing tests," I said, trying to reason with him.

"Yes, but that man has not lived with you for twelve years. I have."

"Thirteen!" I returned, correcting him.

"Sorry, thirteen years. I know you better than anyone. I don't need a degree in psychiatry."

Viru was very headstrong and hard to convince when he made up his mind. So, I gave up and agreed to take him to my next session with Bob to get his doubts cleared. I was relieved to see him unfazed by my diagnosis, to the extent of rejecting the hypothesis altogether.

"Mandy, why didn't you tell me all this before?"

"I was scared, Viru. I thought you would think I'm mentally unstable and leave me."

"What nonsense! Why would I think that? I lost my job. Did you leave me for that? We do not leave each other for problems. We face them and find a way to deal with them," returned Viru. He planted a warm kiss on my forehead and held me close to his chest.

I had not felt strong and safe before in Viru's arms. I wondered if he had always been like this, or if the testing times had changed him. In the unusually quiet night, as we laid close, the distance from Viru that I had felt for the past few weeks began to close in.

Now all things were sorted out and doubts were cleared, except for one, and I asked, "Why would Anu try to get you that job? What is that woman up to?"

"See! That's why. That is the precise reason why I did not tell you and asked Sylvain not to speak of it in front of you. I knew you would still find a reason not to believe me."

"No, I trust you. I am just thinking about the intentions of that woman. Why was she trying to get you in her section?"

"Because the vacancy was available in her section. All the people I know, including Sylvain, were trying to save the people in my department. She tried for me, and I refused, and then for another colleague who accepted. Will you ever stop suspecting?"

"I am not suspecting you, Viru. I suspect her intentions. That woman is evil. I have seen her eyes."

"When did you see her eyes? I don't remember you meeting her lately."

"At the Christmas parade. Remember when we saw her there?"

"I don't. She never met us at the parade."

"What do you mean? She talked to you."

"At the Christmas parade in Downtown? I swear, Mandy, I did not see her."

"C'mon, Viru! Don't lie to me."

"I am not lying, Mandy. I don't remember meeting or talking to her. Wait. Now I kind of believe it. Oh my God, I think that was your hallucination."

"What? What rubbish!" I returned irritably, but then seeing the terrified expression on his face, I paused and became slightly anxious, "Really?"

"No, just joking," and Viru burst into laughter, annoying me even more, and proving yet again that nothing could change him.

Chapter Two

The night of sharing and caring brought us closer. After a long spell of agreeable conversation, Viru's voice became softer and dizzier until he was fast asleep sometime by midnight.

However, there was no trace of sleep in my eyes. Though I was relieved that Viru appeared quite relaxed about my situation, or perhaps was pretending to be nonchalant, for he was good at absorbing shocks, I kept wondering if I would ever come out of this whirlpool of sorrows that was sweeping me swiftly towards the center of despair.

My mother would often say, "When you have trouble sleeping, you should put some happy memories in your mind." So, when was I happy? Had I ever been? Of course. My childhood was the best.

When I was a little girl, I did not have to worry about my hallucinations of strange men, my husband's struggle with jobs, my son's regression, and my guilt of not giving equal attention to my darling daughter.

Back then, I would worry about my two elder brothers messing around with my dollhouse or eating the bigger or creamier share of mother's homemade cake, my beautiful birthday dress getting soiled, and my best friend not sharing her scented pencil with me at school. These matters that now seemed trivial would have been of great concern to me at the time but did not last long thanks to mother, who resolved them swiftly like magic.

The best memories of my childhood were the days I spent at my Grandma's. Her house was like a big dollhouse, and I was her doll. Grandma loved me so much, and I was equally fond of her. I would walk with her all day to wherever she went, holding the waistcoat belt that she wore.

She would say, "This little girl is just like me, simple and innocent, and those mischievous boys are like their Grandpa."

I do not remember much about Grandpa, as he died when I was little. My mother said that he was very handsome and was smitten by Grandma's beauty and married her against the will of his parents, who disapproved of the match.

Grandpa turned down the wealth of his rich parents for my Grandma, who came from a humble background, and he moved out to live in a small house with her, a classic love story, rare in those times, that was the talk of the town, or should I say, talk of the villages.

As happened in every loving household, the anger of Grandpa's parents withered when Grandma gave birth to her first child, my maternal uncle, and the desire to see the newborn grow in the yard, in front of their eyes, made them welcome Grandpa and his poor wife back to the family.

So, my handsome and resolute Grandpa had his way with both choosing the love of his life and inheriting the ancestral wealth. I loved to hear this account from my mother over and over before going to bed and then sleeping like an angel, as if stoned by the smoking hot love story of my legendry Grandparents.

Speaking of Grandma, she would take me to her room, untie the complicated knot of her worn-out cloth bag and take out her best candies and cookies for me. She would say, "This is only for my little doll. Don't share it with your brothers. Those monkeys munch all day, like the little calves of our cow Nandini."

Like mother, she would also tell great bedtime stories,

and I had no trouble sleeping, cuddling up in her cozy warm lap.

I regretted not being with Grandma when she parted with us forever, as I was in labor. I wished I could go back in time and see her one last time. I liked to believe that Reva was a reincarnation of Grandma, as she came into the world a minute after Grandma died.

A bang at the door being thrown wide open broke my sleep, or rather my train of thought, for I was not sure if I had slept at all. It was Caesar who entered the bedroom and was sprawled on the floor near the bedside, moaning gently.

I looked at the clock on the side table and noticed Viru fast asleep next to me, and immediately figured out why Caesar had expressed his displeasure in the manner known well to me. It was well past six, and Caesar was still waiting eagerly for his master to take him for his daily morning walk.

I made a slight effort to wake Viru, who was generally punctual with his duties, but seeing him sleeping peacefully, perhaps due to our late-night bonhomie, I decided to take Caesar for a walk.

Getting up reluctantly, I stretched my arms to relax my aching body—thanks to the sleepless night—and shortly hit the road with anxious Caesar, hoping to draw fresh energy from the morning sun.

There was something off about the morning, and I did not catch that right away. The sun was mild and getting eclipsed now and then by rapidly spreading black clouds, scattered as if anxious to cover the limits of the sky. There were abrupt gushes of wind swaying the branches of the trees sporadically but firmly. It seemed like a big storm was about to come.

But wait, that was not all. I noticed that no vehicles were running on the street and that there was no trace of morning walkers on the sidewalks. This was utterly absurd. Even the young girl who had, to my knowledge, never missed a day of jogging was nowhere to be seen.

So, it was low-spirited Caesar and me, only the two of us

walking up to the lonely Mount Mary Hills. *Where are all the people?* I thought, *How is it that Mount Mary Hills, the joggers' paradise known for the hustle and bustle of enthusiastic morning persons, especially during the summer, is deserted today at 6:30 in the morning?* For a moment, I wondered if I was hallucinating about an unreal world. *Is it possible that I am still in my bed and dreaming about this?*

I pinched my arm and cuddled Caesar to make sure that I was not dreaming. I was somewhat positive that it was not a hallucination either, for a hallucination meant seeing people who did not exist, not the other way around. Not finding people who existed would be extinction, or at least not a type of hallucination I knew.

When we reached the top of the hill, there were no white or brown ducks quacking in the lake, no swarm of orange fishes swimming close to the shore expecting crumbled pieces of bread or grains, no colorful birds that chirruped in the surrounding trees and no squirrels that sprinted animatedly from one branch to another.

Even the usual highlight of the morning, the six little brown ducklings following mother duck everywhere it swam, that filled my heart with motherly affection, was missing.

Caesar, who loved the everyday attention and admiration of familiar faces around, was perhaps expecting a better show after the morning deferral by his spoilsport master, for he looked gloomy and disappointed.

I returned home with gloomy Caesar to share my ordeal of the morning walk with Viru, who strangely was still sleeping sideways, in the same position as when I had left him, and so were Reva and Ryan. Leaning forward, I moved my fingers gently in his hair and called out softly, pressing his shoulder, but Viru did not move.

"Wake up, Viru! What is wrong with you? Open your eyes. It is late, and you're still sleeping," I said irritably, now shaking him forcefully.

Fear started gripping me as I saw that Viru was numb and motionless. My constant yelling and pushing and

Caesar's tapping had no effect on him. I could tell that he was alive as his nostrils exhaled air, and I felt his heart beating when I lay my head close to his chest. My mind went blank for a few seconds, not returning any results to my anxious queries.

When my mind became slightly more responsive, I thought of the kids and rushed to Reva's room. I again yelled, jerked, and begged, but in vain. My girl, who would usually wake up at the sound of water dripping from the kitchen tap, hardly audible to me in the other room, was now lying unconscious and unresponsive to my loud voice and excessive jolting. I also found Ryan in the adjoining room lying motionless.

Could this be that dreaded disease sleep coma that they frequently mention on TV, in which people sleep and never wake up? The horrifying thought that flashed in my disoriented mind shook me to the core.

No, this can't be that hideous disease. Many scientists are not even sure if any such thing exists. And I saw on TV that some guy mentioned that it is only people with some rare genetic disorder who have these sleep diseases. Viru, Reva, and Ryan are fit and healthy. They have never complained of any problems. This could be a temporary unconsciousness of some kind. Maybe some sort of intoxication from food or water. Or maybe all of this is an illusion. Perhaps I am hallucinating, and nothing I am seeing right now is real.

I filled my mind with reassuring thoughts, pacifying that my family could not meet a tragic end like those people with sleep coma did, defying the slightest possibility of any logic that suggested otherwise.

I could not afford to lose time in figuring out what it was, as the paramount question that presented itself was to figure out what to do.

Panic-stricken, I grabbed the phone and dialed the emergency number once, twice, and thrice, but there was no answer.

Elena must be up by now, I thought as I dialed her number with my trembling fingers. When she did not answer, I rushed to her house and haphazardly banged the locked entrance door. My heart was beating faster with every passing second.

Since Elena was not answering the door, I hurried back to the house to get the copy of the keys that she had given me a long time ago to look after Britney in case she was stuck at work, for nobody could have predicted a bizarre emergency such as this.

Opening the first and second drawers in the storage box in the hall, my dizzy eyes finally got hold of the keys in the third drawer among the topsy-turvy of pens, erasers, watches, purses, cards, belts, and other household articles.

I ran back across the yard, opened the door, and barged into Elena's bedroom. My worst nightmare was unfolding in front of my eyes in this ominous morning, as Elena and Britney laid in their bedrooms like motionless vegetables, just like Viru, Reva and Ryan were.

Aware of the futility of my effort, I halfheartedly jolted Elena and Britney, which, as expected, produced no results.

After instructing Caesar to stay inside, I ran out of the house and down the empty street, wandering around like a nomad fearing that her world had come to a standstill, and this is not even speaking metaphorically.

My footsteps matched my heartbeat, both competing to outdo one another as I marched spontaneously towards the metro station for no apparent reason. Perhaps, subconsciously, I was hoping to find somebody who could help; a familiar face like Sebastian or the ticket attendant or the guy who ran the small candy shop.

When I entered the Saint Thomas Subway Station, I did not see the sagely wrinkled face of Sebastian on the other side of the escalator. He would always welcome me graciously and add the color of wisdom to my otherwise black and white life.

I found the candy shop on the corner open, but the owner, that friendly middle-aged man, was nowhere to be seen.

No passengers were queued up at the booth or the ticket vending machine. Nobody waited at the stop for the metro, and no metro arrived.

I wondered if I was the only person (except for Caesar) awake and conscious in the entire city. (At least, I liked to think I was conscious, though I was not sure.) I was like a lone fish, desperate and directionless, lost in the water, hoping to catch up with my large clan that had suddenly vanished from the lake.

I came out of the subway with a heavy heart and a blank head. I did not know where to go and what to do now. Even my subconscious did not guide my footsteps anymore, which now lagged miles behind my beating heart.

I took a temporary refuge on the old bench in the little park across the street. Tears rolled from my eyes, joining the tiny droplets of sweat on my face, marking a union of melancholy.

"Oh, God! Oh, the creator of this Universe! Help me, please! Help my family! I do not know what is happening. What wrong have I done to deserve this pain? I cannot take it anymore. Forgive my family and me for any sins and restore my world to how it was. I can endure all the sorrows of my life with my little family by my side but cannot do without them…"

Just when I was trying to establish a one-sided connection with the Almighty through my desperate plea for mercy, I heard a voice.

"Hello, Miss Mandira, how are you doing today?"

Bewildered, I turned around, wondering if I had succeeded in establishing a two-way connection for the first time in my life.

It was Jack, the man from my hallucinations, standing on the freshly mowed grass of the small lawn and smiling under his long nose.

The presence of Jack in his usual black hat and cloak led me to think that this unreal experience was perhaps a hallucination, and the idea of a hallucination, for the first time in my life, was comforting rather than terrifying.

"Are you ok, Miss Mandira?"

Ever since Dr. Bob had advised me to, I had stayed away from anyone or anything that remotely alluded to an illusion, including Jack, but today I was curious. I thought it better to talk to a person in my perceived illusion than to myself, for there was nobody else.

In either case, I would be talking to myself, so what difference does it make? I thought, trying to justify my desire to engage in conversation with Jack.

"If you talk to me, I can help you," said Jack.

His confidence in this chaos seemed to confirm my fears of hallucination.

"You can help me?"

"I certainly can."

"I am pretty sure you cannot help and that nothing good can come out of this conversation. But, since you insist, may I ask a few questions?" I asked, wiping tears off my face.

"Of course."

"What is happening?"

"What do you mean?"

"My husband and kids are not waking up, or my neighbors. The streets are deserted. The whole neighborhood looks like a desert. Is it some sort of illusion?"

"Absolutely not. This is all Real," returned Jack.

"Oh really? Are you saying that only this part of me talking to you is a hallucination, and everything else I have experienced this morning is real?"

"Hallucination? What hallucination? Every part, including this one, is real."

"Hmm, as expected. This conversation is worthless. What was I thinking?"

"Wait. Do you think seeing and talking to me is a hallucination? You think you're hallucinating right now?" Jack asked.

"I don't think it, I know it. The condition is called schizophrenia, and it feels awkward to explain hallucinations to a person in my hallucination."

"But that's not true, Mandira. This is not a hallucination."

"Oh really? Then why is it that only I can see you? Can you explain this to me?"

"Well, technically, there are two more people that can see me. But you are right to say that others cannot see me."

"Ok, I do not have time for this. I need to wake Viru and the kids. I must do something. And please do not follow me," I returned as I rose from the bench to leave.

"I can help you with that."

"How?" I asked, turning around hastily.

"Well, to start with, go home and wake Ryan. He is fine. Take your time. You know where to find me."

Chapter Three

I had no reason to believe Jack, but in inexplicable circumstances such as this, hope, rather than reasoning, guides action. So, as soon as I arrived home, I did exactly what he said. I went straight to Ryan's bed, pressed his forehead gently, ran my fingers through his shiny black hair, and uttered the exact words I always did to wake him up.

To my pleasant surprise, Ryan opened his eyes, and like every morning, took my hand into his arms and closed his eyes again. Seeing Ryan open his eyes and witnessing his idiosyncrasy, which would have been a mundane affair on any other day, was a precious and overwhelming moment for me that morning, so much so that I broke down in tears.

Sitting up with lazy, half-closed eyes, Ryan wiped off my tears with his little hands and opened his mouth, something he did mostly for eating and rarely for speaking.

"Mommy, don't cry," said my little man of few words.

Our affectionate embrace lasted for about a minute until Caesar, feeling left out, jumped right in the middle, and shared in the bonding.

While Ryan got busy playing a chasing game with Caesar, oblivious of the fact that his Daddy and sister had still not left their bed, I made another attempt to wake them up, but in vain.

As the clouds in the sky became dense, I turned on the TV, hoping to catch some news about Abbynton city that might disperse the clouds of confusion. As I switched from one channel to another, most of the local channels being either blank or displaying merely their logo, I finally stumbled upon BBC News, where a tired-looking anchor announced the unprecedented situation.

"The world has hit upon a disaster situation. The sleep condition that was, until yesterday, believed to have been dormant and non-contagious caused havoc last night. As per reports, around sixty percent of the population of the UK, France, Germany, and other parts of Europe did not wake up this morning. Hospitals with inadequate and unprepared staff have been flooded with cases of sleep coma. The entire nation is devasted by this unexpected catastrophe.

"Declaring the worst international emergency that has ever been known to mankind, the Prime Minister of the UK has urged citizens to remain calm and assured them that help and government assistance is coming.

"Fresh reports are coming from the United States, where the situation is worse. As per an early estimate, about eighty to ninety percent of the population in North and South America have been affected by sleep coma. A small number of people who are awake have reportedly experienced fatigue and sleeplessness. It is believed that they are suffering from wake syndrome.

"There have, so far, not been any significant reports of cases from Asian countries such as India and China, but fear and panic have engulfed the entire world."

Horror-struck, I stood near the TV with my mouth open, listening to every word uttered by the reporter. Each one felt like another iron weight added to the sack suspended from my neck.

I was about to collapse under the unbearable weight of the daunting words ringing in my ears when I heard a ring coming from my phone. It was my mom, calling from back home in India.

"Hello, Mom!" I said, clearing my throat. "Yes. ... I was out, um, walking Caesar ... We are fine, Mom. Is everyone ok there? ... Yes, they are showing it on TV, but it is not as bad as they say. ... Do not believe everything they say, everyone is awake, Mom. Viru is fine. ... Yes, Reva too, and Ryan also. Listen, I've got to go, I will call you soon. Tell everyone that we are fine. ... Bye, Mom."

I kept the conversation brief, lest she found out, for all mothers have this supernatural power of hearing what their children do not say.

I do not know why I lied to Mom, for everything that could have gone wrong had, and nothing was right. Perhaps, this response had entered my reflexes. Despite all the problems, telling her that everything was fine had become my trademark response over the years, as otherwise she would worry a lot and I feared it would deteriorate her health.

Worrying about children and family was something that I had inherited from Mom. She would beat me hands down had there been a comparison between our scale of worrying. In Viru's words, my family specialized in the field of worrying. If mine were in excess, as per Viru's benchmark, Mom's extent of worrying would be unlimited. Mom's day would begin with concern about my brothers and their children and end by worrying about my kids and me.

Amidst the looming hopelessness, I made a firm resolve to bring Viru and Reva back to life. But I had no idea about the nature of action to take in order to achieve the desired objective.

How did Jack know that Ryan was simply sleeping and not in a sleep coma? I thought. *Is it possible that he knows something? Well, he certainly seemed to know a lot. How else could anyone under these circumstances tell so confidently that he could help?*

I must not forget that he is just an illusion and not someone with physical existence. But again, how could he tell me accurately about Ryan? Should I ask him for help?

Engaging with the person in your hallucination and asking for help?

Na. Even the conception of this idea seems idiotic and senseless in my head. But is there anything that has made sense since this morning?

Wait. Doctor Bob warned me to stay away from Jack because he feared that my condition could worsen. But is there anything that can be worse than the situation I am in?

No, no, this is insane. I guess I am overthinking. How can Jack help in a global catastrophe? But again, how come he was spot on about Ryan?

After making breakfast for Ryan and Caesar, as edible as a person with an absent mind and contradictory thoughts could, I set off to find Jack. Leaving both Ryan and Caesar in charge of the house, as I was not sure who would be more compliant, I gave them instructions to stay indoors and look after Daddy and Sister.

He must be in the park. He said I could find him there when I left the park, I thought while hooking the latch of the outer gate of my house.

It felt so strange to run after the illusion of my mind, something that I had been running away from all this while. I walked along the empty street as fast as I could with my tired legs and arrived at the deserted park that would otherwise have been alive with people. I looked around all possible corners of the small park, for there were not many, but did not find Jack anywhere.

Oh well! Now we are playing hide and seek! I thought, sitting on the same old bench. *I always dreaded walking alone on the street, and avoided looking around, as I would get this uncanny feeling that he perhaps followed me, and now, I look everywhere and see nothing. The moment you stop fearing and start seeking their assistance, these hallucinations stop chasing you!*

"I am glad you came back, Miss Mandira. Tell me, how can I help?" asked Jack as he stood a few yards behind me.

"Oh, here you are! You are confident that I came looking for help?" I returned, trying to regain composure after the expected company managed to surprise and shake me with his strong voice yet again.

"I do not doubt it. Why else would you come back to this park and sit on this bench?"

"Well, I have to admit that you are right," I said, still struggling to maintain my composure. "Can I ask you a question?"

"Of course, you can."

"How did you know that Ryan was just sleeping?"

"Oh, that's easy. You know, he never wakes up by himself. This morning, you became so agitated seeing Viren and Reva unresponsive after trying to wake them that you assumed Ryan was also in the same state, while he was just sleeping peacefully like any other day. You forgot to make an effort to wake Ryan."

"I don't understand. How do you know all this?"

"Well, I know a lot of things, and you will find out everything shortly." Jack sported a mysterious smile.

"Wow, it is hard and scary to believe when an illusion tells you all this," I mumbled.

"Umm, Mandira, I would like to correct you again. I am not an illusion, and you are not hallucinating when you see me. You must trust me," returned Jack, who, unlike me, was calm and composed.

"But who are you? How can I trust you when I do not know who you are? Are you a ghost?"

"Ghost? Oh, you mean the dead who come back and haunt the living people? No, I am not a ghost either. I am a manager."

"Manager? What kind of manager?"

"Manager of a state."

"A state? What kind of state?"

"Ok, Mandira. I promise you will find out everything about me soon. But before that, I need you to listen to a story."

"A story?"

"Yes, a story, and do as I say. And most importantly, you must trust me."

"Ok, but you said that you could help me. Can you really help in waking up my husband and daughter?" I asked anxiously.

"Of course, I can and certainly will. You will play a big role in that. In fact, you will be able to wake up everyone around you. But you must hear my story first."

"Alright. I will listen to your story. Go on."

Without further ado, Jack began to tell his story. "Once upon a time, there was a large organization."

"What kind of organization?"

"A law-and-order management organization. The organization had three branches. Let us call them A, B, and C. The CEO was a noble and upright gentleman. He made sure that the organization was run according to strong morals and ethics and not once allowed any negligence in the way of its mission and vision.

"His son headed Branch A. As I mentioned, the principled CEO never offered any undue advantage to his son. His appointment was made through a selection process in a democratic way of voting by members of the working committee of Branch A, and the CEO abstained from voting to ensure fairness.

"Now, the son was poles apart from his father when it came to moral conduct. He was unscrupulous, manipulative, and wicked. He dreamed of taking his father's place one day and ruling the organization according to his will.

"When the CEO found out about the unethical practices of his son, he decided to remove him. He also declared, without disclosing their identity, that a person from Branch C would be his successor.

"This made the working committee of Branch A upset. Being an influential branch, it was always expected that one of the members from Branch A would succeed the CEO.

"Taking advantage of the insecurity of the committee members, some of them being his close allies, the son gained adequate support by manipulating them. Thus, the CEO could not remove him, and the organization was split into two factions, the old and experienced loyalists of the CEO, and the young and aggressive supporters of his son."

I began to realize that I had perhaps wasted my time

expecting help from this strange man, who called himself a manager and told some irrelevant and nonsensical story about a CEO of a company. I would rather have focused all my energy on taking Viru and Reva to the hospital despite the slight hope of finding any help there.

I do not know if he intended or even noticed my lack of interest, for I had bigger problems to deal with.

Jack ended his narration and said, "I think, Miss Mandira, that is enough for you to know at this point. I would now like you to go home—"

"And do what?" I asked anxiously, cutting him short.

"And do as I say. Now listen to me carefully. Go home and lie down with Ryan on his bed, with one of your arms under his head, supporting him like a pillow. Your other hand should gently hold his hand, and both of you must close your eyes."

"Why? What do you mean? What do you want with Ryan?"

"Well, Ryan is the key person in our mission."

"What mission?"

"The mission to bring your husband and daughter back."

"This is absurd. Your mission to wake Viru and Reva from sleep involves me going back to sleep with Ryan and us holding hands? I should not have trusted you and come here in the first place. Why can't you help me take Viru and Reva to the hospital?"

"Hospital? Do you really think the hospital can fix this? Miss Mandira, the entire world is affected right now. No hospital can help you."

"See, I caught your lie. I saw on TV that not all countries are dealing with this problem. I talked to my mom back in India, and everyone is fine there."

"I am afraid, my dear, that is not correct. All the people who are awake cannot go back to sleep. Your mom and others in India will not be able to sleep at night. I repeat, the entire world is affected."

"I don't believe you. Whatever you have said until now,

including your story of the CEO, has no meaning. You are a mysterious person asking me to do ridiculous things. And you want to involve my son in your silly whims and fancies? That's not going to happen, Mr. Jack," I declared angrily as I rose from the bench, meaning to storm off, but sitting back in the next moment, realizing there was nowhere to go. "Why? Why would you involve Ryan?" I asked.

"Ok, Mandira, I was not completely honest when I said the entire world was affected. There is one person who is not affected. His name is Ryan. Your son, Ryan."

As always happened, anything remotely positive attached to the mention of Ryan hooked me back to this failing conversation.

"How can you say that Ryan is not affected?"

"Well, he slept last night normally and woke up this morning like any other day."

"I hear what you are saying about Ryan. Perhaps you are right. But I am not affected by sleep coma either," I returned, now in a mellowed tone.

"Oh, I like the term "sleep coma," if that is what you call it. But you are very much affected like others. There are two categories in this situation—those who cannot wake and others who cannot sleep. You lie in the latter. You could not sleep last night and will not be able to sleep tonight."

Seeing me silent and paying attention, perhaps for the first time during this conversation, Jack continued, "Listen, Mandira, I know this is overwhelming, and many things do not make sense to you right now. But I promise this calamity will be over soon, and so will be your trouble. I need you to go home and think it over and consider doing as I said. Remember, only I can bring your husband and daughter back to life, and to do so, I need your cooperation."

I returned home, wishing to find my husband cracking unfunny jokes, my daughter finding amusement in them, my son showing the usual indifference to their fun, and my dog running around eagerly, trying to seek his attention.

But when did I ever have the good fortune of my wishes

coming true?

The state of affairs of my house had not changed. Viru and Reva were lying in their beds, motionless, whereas Ryan and Caesar were in constant motion, running after one another.

As I settled on the easy chair in the living room, I realized for the first time since that morning how much my feet hurt and eyes burnt, as, until that moment, the shock had perhaps eclipsed all other senses. The fatigue had entered every piece of my body, and my mind was not at peace.

It was well past two in the afternoon, and with effort, I tried to recollect everything Jack had said.

How could Jack be so certain in claiming that Mom will not sleep tonight? I thought. *She usually sleeps around 9 p.m. It must be about midnight in India. Shall I check if she is awake?*

I called my mom on her mobile. As she did not pick up after several rings, I breathed a sigh of relief, thinking that she must be fast asleep.

So, he lied. Why would he do that? What does he want? I was pondering over these questions when mom returned my call.

"Hey, Mom, sorry, did I wake you? … In the kitchen? Why were you in the kitchen? … Fetching water? Why? Are you thirsty? It's midnight. … You can't sleep? Did you take your pills? … Hm. … Nothing, Ma, I was just checking if everything was fine with you. … Yes, we are alright. … Mom, we are all ok! Try to get some sleep. I will call in the morning. Bye."

Oh God, Mom is awake, I thought, as wrinkles of concern returned on my forehead, *Jack could be right in stating that the entire world is affected. Does that mean what Jack said is true, that everyone sleeping is in a sleep coma, and that all the others suffer from wake syndrome? Sleeping people cannot wake up, and those who are awake cannot go back to sleep!*

And he said that this condition does not affect Ryan, that he is the only one in the entire world who is unaffected by this disaster. What does that mean? No matter how pleasing that may sound, why only him?

What do I do now? Jack says, "Do what I say." But who is that man? How can I trust him? But then, what is my other option? He said he could bring Viru and Reva back to life. But why does he want to involve Ryan in his so-called mission? What is this mission? Does it pose any risk to his life?

Oh, God. Please stop testing me and guide me on the right path.

The most challenging thing is to make a decision that is entirely guided by hope and not based on logic. I invoked my tired brain to supply the appropriate logic attached to Jack's abstract story and the direction he gave me, but in vain. My decision thus depended upon the hope that he had ignited in me.

After a few hours of pondering nervously, I made my decision.

Chapter Four

I gave a lot of thought about the odds in favor of Jack's claim of bringing Viru and Reva back from sleep coma, and all I could gather was that he seemed to know about the situation better than I did and was the only one who had offered help.

I also contemplated Jack's strange instructions of lying down with Ryan on his bed. The worst-case scenario I could think of was the possibility of us never waking up, like others. But then, what good were Ryan and I being awake and helpless?

After a warm embrace and my long teary-eyed gaze, the familiar blank expression returned on Ryan's face that seemed to pose questions without uttering a single word.

I answered the question that Ryan did not put into words, but that I had heard, "Ryan, my son. Look, Daddy and Sis have been sleeping since this morning. Mommy tried, but they did not wake up. Now I need your help. We will lie down and take a nap. And then, who knows? Perhaps all of us will wake up together. Tell me, will you help Mommy?" I asked, and Ryan nodded.

I do not know what was in that nod, but it felt different from all his previous nods. It was not simply a nod of agreement, but it seemed like a nod of conviction. In my interpretation of his nod—a superpower that only mothers possess about their children—he did not simply say, "Ok,

Mommy." He seemed to convey this message, "Don't worry, Mommy. I am there for you. You can count on me."

Ryan followed me to his room. As we slipped into the small bed just big enough to accommodate the two of us, I stretched my arm under his head to support it like a pillow and clasped his hand with my other hand, exactly as per Jack's instructions.

Caesar seemed to wonder what the fuss was all about, but he was also eager to be a part of it. He hopped on the bed and took the space next to Ryan that was so little that his slight stretching of legs or any movement by Ryan could tip him over. Since Jack had not assigned any role to Caesar in our escapade, I tried to move him out of bed but gave up shortly, seeing his reluctance to part with his master.

I waited for Ryan to close his eyes and for Caesar to imitate his master before I closed mine. If Jack were to be believed about Ryan being unaffected by the sleep disorder, he would fall asleep soon, for Ryan was a gifted sleeper who could sleep at the drop of a hat at any hour of day or night.

About a minute passed with our eyes closed, and every second felt like eons. I began to wonder how I could involve my son in this preposterous stunt.

A sudden jerk whisked me off the bed, and I felt I was about to fall when I opened my eyes.

The bed was still there. I had not moved, nor had Ryan or Caesar. A freezing chill went down my spine as I wondered what had just happened. Ryan had fallen asleep by now, and I was terrified to close my eyes again.

I tried to wake Ryan up, but he would not respond. Now that I had introduced Ryan to something unknown and horrifying, there was no way I could leave him alone with this and risk his life.

Taking a deep breath, as if getting ready to plunge into the deep sea, I closed my eyes. A few uncomfortable seconds passed quietly, which felt like the calm before the storm.

Then, the jerk happened again. The bed slipped away, and I felt like I was falling freely off a great cliff. I felt a strong desire to open my eyes again and perhaps find myself on the bed like before, but then I would be stopping something that Ryan and I had started together, and Ryan was already deep into it.

I do not know if it were a few seconds, a few minutes, or hours, for that matter, for it seemed so long that I felt I would soon be hitting the center of the earth. But I kept my eyes closed the entire time, dreading opening them.

At last, the free fall ended, not with an abrupt strike, hitting the surface, but with a smooth landing like that of an elevator halting at the ground floor.

After a few seconds of being stationary, I opened my eyes, hoping to find myself on the little bed with my little warriors. Instead of the well-crafted, brown-colored, rectangular wooden ceiling, my eyes witnessed a strikingly plain, blue-colored space of no particular shape that stretched as far as my field of vision. Startled, I sat up in haste, felt an intense head rush, and looked about me as soon as it settled.

I was sitting under the blue sky, bluer than ever, without the slightest patch of cloud. It spread far and deep like an infinite blue dome and merged at some point with a deep blue sea. I could not tell where the sky ended and the vast sea began, for both were equally blue, so much so that the only time I noticed the distinction was when ripples appeared near the shore, a few yards away from my feet.

I felt the soft sand with my hands and took a fistful to examine closely what looked like powdered white gold.

Imagine the shining snow in your hand, which is neither cold, nor does it melt when you clench your fist, but trickles through your fingers and spills over.

The pebbles scattered around the shore were precious gemstones, or at least they looked like ones of different varieties and colors, like shining yellow topaz, gleaming red choral, twinkling pink ruby, glittering blue sapphire, and beaming green emerald.

I walked on the soft white sand, which appeared about

three to four inches deep, wobbling now and then, blinking my eyes tightly and repeatedly trying to make sense of this wonderland.

I could see gigantic trees with wide branches, sections of which looked very distinct from others. A part of the tree looked young and childish, with fresh leaves sprouting and new flowers blossoming.

Another part of the same tree was strong and healthy, with leaves and flowers and ripened fruits. It was amazing to find all kinds of fruits one could think of in this part of the tree, like apples, mangoes, bananas, cherries, et cetera.

A third section seemed to be seasoned and wise, with dense and large leaves looking stunning in red, brown, and orange colors.

The last section of the tree was old and weak, with bare branches, sans leaves.

It took me some time to realize that every tree with its distinct sections represented all four seasons—spring, summer, autumn, and winter.

So, I was on a magical island surrounded by a vast and perhaps deep sea, where nothing looked real or natural. I could not spot the sun in the sky, but everything was bright and colorful. I wondered if it were a dream, but then how could I be aware of every development, from being with Ryan in the bed, leading up to this place?

The sudden recollection of Ryan ended my temporary euphoria about this place, and I became concerned about his whereabouts. *Oh my God,* I thought, *Did I leave the poor thing all alone by himself sleeping in the bed? What have I done? Where have I landed? How do I go back now?*

Just then, I heard faint but familiar sounds. I walked past the all-season trees, the multicolored bushes, and the gemstones—or gem-rocks, to be precise—in the direction of the laughing and woofing sounds.

To my overwhelming delight, I discovered Ryan and Caesar, merrily playing chase games on the white sand and hide-and-seek behind the gem rocks. My carefree son was having a great time playing with his favorite buddy, oblivious to the fact that he was in some unknown place in inexplicable circumstances. I had not seen him so ecstatic since the incident at his school. It seemed as if Ryan and Caesar had always belonged to this place and found nothing abnormal about it.

Standing there, seeing Ryan radiant, I wept tears of joy until Ryan noticed me and came running, followed by Caesar. A warm hug from my son had a therapeutic effect on my frail muscles and tired bones and invigorated my body.

Our embrace lasted a long time, long enough to make Caesar jealous again, as he stood on two of his feet, leaning on our shoulders, trying to separate us.

"It is a beautiful sight. Isn't it, Miss Mandira?"

I turned around to find Jack standing near me, smiling under his conspicuous nose.

"Jack! How? What...what is this?" I returned with an overwhelming urge to ask many questions but fell short of words to express.

"Well, this is good, Mandira. Thank you very much for acting upon my request. Hello, Monsieur Ryan and mon cher Caesar! A pleasure to see you."

Jack's greeting was returned with an amiable nod by both, and I was amazed to see Ryan's quick reaction, for he would rarely give any.

"Can Ryan see you? And Caesar too?" I asked, surprised, as the very basis of my belief of Jack being an illusion was that nobody else but I could see him.

"Yes, they can see me."

"Every time?" I asked as I wondered if this mysterious place had something to do with their renewed sight, and in that case, it would not count.

"They can always see me, Mandira. Do you remember our last meeting when you stated that only you could see me and I said, 'Technically, it is not true'? Well, this is what I meant by that. So, only Ryan, Caesar, and you can see me. One more thing. Not only can they see me, but they know me very well."

"What? Does Ryan know you? Oh God, I am bewildered. Talking to you confuses me even more. For God's sake, Jack, could you tell me what is going on? How does Ryan know you? What is this place, and why are we here?"

"Of course, you will get all the answers. I will tell you everything, I promise. But before that, I have something to say."

I wondered if he was about to say something unconnected that would confuse me further, like the story about the CEO.

"You see, Mandira, humans only believe what they can see. But humans see very little. So, I bring you to this place so that you can see for yourself and believe. Here you will see all that humans do not get to see in their lifetime. Today, you will embark on a path of discovery. A dazzling visual experience and volumes of information await you on this journey that may seem magical and hard to absorb. But remember, when a newborn opens his eyes for the first time, the visual experience and the perception of the surroundings for him also is nothing short of magic. I also need a promise from you that you will trust me. That is the only way we can help each other."

"I promise, Jack. Now please be so kind as to tell me. The suspense is killing me."

"Alright then. Let us sit on those beautiful rocks near the shore while Ryan and Caesar play with each other. Tell me, how do you want to proceed? Do you have questions, or shall I begin with my speech?"

"There are so many questions that I don't know where to begin. I think you better start. But before that, please tell me what this place is?" I asked as I sat on the pink ruby while Jack rested on the blue sapphire next to it.

"Oh, this place! This place is Jantar."

Chapter Five

"Jantar? Where is it? I don't think I have heard of any such place before."

"That's because it is not in Loka."

"*Loka?* Now what is Loka?"

"I am sorry, I call your world Loka. The world that you know and where you live."

"Why do you call our world Loka? Never mind. So, if this place is not located anywhere in the world—or Loka—then where is it?"

"This place, Jantar, is our second stop en route to another world of which you have little knowledge, or no knowledge at all."

"Another world? What do you mean? Are you trying to say that we are not on Earth?"

"Yes, that is exactly what I mean."

"Then where are we? Are we on some planet? Are you saying that we just closed our eyes and arrived on another planet? Is that what you mean?"

"Well, you are not on any planet that you know of, as that would again be Loka, a part of what you perceive as your world. I am introducing you to a new world."

"A new world! Don't tell me that my life has now become like those sci-fi movies where any crazy thing can be possible." I said, worked up by his answers that I was unable to fathom.

"Ok. I have a fair idea of what movies are, but what are sci-fi movies? I do not get the reference. Is it something that you people watch on those small devices all the time? What do you call that? Telephone?"

"Do you mean smartphone?"

"Yes, smartphone. Well, I am an old fellow, Mandira. I liked the movies back in the days when you people would watch on those big boxes you called a TV. I am a fan of Marlon Brando, Al Pacino, Dileep Kumar, and Raj Kapoor."

One thing I realized was that asking questions to Jack had proved to be futile, as every time I did, his answers would leave me in a state of more confusion than before. If it were possible to quantify confusion, I would say it kept piling up with every new question over a load of confusion of previous questions that remained unanswered. I figured that there should be some comprehension of the topic even to appreciate the answers to my questions, and clearly, I was primarily alien to the topic we were dealing with.

What is the point of asking questions when all I can understand from his answers is the reference to Marlon Brando, Al Pacino, Dileep Kumar, and Raj Kapoor? I thought. *And he could not think of a single female actor! What about Meryl Streep or Meena Kumari, Mister Jack? All men are the same. Even the strange men, like him. But the signs of patriarchal values in Jack are not something that I need to focus on right now.*

I decided to let him go on with what he had to say and hope to get more clarity over time. However, I was not sure about that either, as when I had tried to give him a patient ear last time, he had perplexed me with his vague CEO story, and I was lost in the abstraction.

"Ok, Mandira, I think I know how to explain this concept to you. Let me ask you a question. What do you do when you close your eyes in Loka, I mean, your world?"

"What do I do when I close my eyes?" I repeated slowly, wondering if his method of storytelling or answering my questions had not created enough confusion for his liking, and if he now wanted to crank it up further.

"Well, when I close my eyes, I do nothing. What do you expect me to do?"

"I don't think you understood my question."

"That's exactly what I think, too."

"I mean, what do you say when you close your eyes?"

"I do not say anything."

"No, I mean…what is the word for that?"

"The word is 'close.' Close your eyes. Or maybe 'shut your eyes' if that's what you are looking for."

"Ok, let me put it this way. You people lie down on the bed and close your eyes. What is the word for that?"

"Ah, are you looking for the word 'sleep'?"

"Capital! That is exactly what I was looking for. The word is sleep. You see, Mandira, I am not good with the language that you humans speak."

"I think we have used the word sleep many times in our conversations before."

"We did, perhaps. But I forget words, Mandira. I am ancient."

By ancient, he perhaps meant old, but correcting his vocabulary was the last thing on my mind at that moment.

"Anyways, what about sleep?"

"So, when you sleep, Mandira, you come here, to this place."

"This place? I don't think so. I do not go anywhere. I stay where I am, and when I wake up, I find myself in the same place."

"That is because you perceive sleep as an activity, just like eating or walking. What you do not know is that when you sleep, your body becomes inactive, but your head does not. While your body remains where it was, your head enters a new world."

"What? That is ridiculous! How can my head travel anywhere without my body? It is a part of my body. Do you mean we become headless while sleeping?"

"Yes, you become headless in your world."

"I don't think I get that."

"Head, Mandira, head!" repeated Jack, pointing towards his forehead.

"Oh, wait, do you mean brain? Are you saying that when we sleep, our body is inactive, but our brain is active?"

"Capital! The brain is the right word."

"And according to you, our brain activity transports us into a new world?"

"That is exactly what I said. See, Mandira, you are a smart lady."

"I am, but what you say doesn't make any sense."

After some struggle with the unprecedented nature of the revelation and Jack's choice of misplaced words, I finally managed to absorb some information, though I doubted the veracity of the particulars. According to him, sleep was not simply a recurring state needed to recharge us, but a process of leaving one world and entering another.

He seemed to suggest that while we are awake, we stay in one place, or in his words, in Loka, the world that humans know of, but when we sleep, our mind wanders off to an altogether new world, an unknown world, leaving the body behind.

In this world, one can perceive themselves in the shape and form of the body that can move, which, by the way, is still stationary back in our world.

This new world was as authentic as the world we knew. There were picturesque locations, such as the one where we were talking, and the places had names.

Apparently, humans enter this unfamiliar world when they go to sleep and remain there while they are asleep and wake up back in the world familiar to them, leaving this magic land with almost no recollection of it.

It felt bizarre for me to think that humans were space travelers, traveling regularly to an outer space known as sleep, transported by spaceships of the human mind. If there existed the degree of bizarreness, it was even more bizarre to believe that I was in this world with my child and dog, being made aware of the concept of its existence that was hitherto unknown to me by a man whose identity was still a mystery.

Even if I believed in this bizarre concept of the existence of the sleep world for a moment, there were still many questions begging for answers. For instance, why did Jack bring us here? Why did he choose only me to tell this secret to? How would all this unworldly information help in saving the lives of Viru and Reva?

There were other less significant questions, like Jack's frequent usage of terms like "humans" and calling our world "Loka," which gave the impression of him being alien to the human species.

Another question in my mind, a rather insignificant one, was the reason for the repeated use of the word "capital." I wondered when the last time anyone had used that word for expressing delight.

I continued to refrain from asking questions for fear of getting lost, and instead focused on helping him with his vocabulary to comprehend his account better.

"So, Mandira, now that you have an idea about where we are, it's time to begin our journey. Are you ready?"

"Oh, is there a journey? Are we supposed to go somewhere else in your new world?" I asked, not with the intent of posing another question to start the loop of confusion again but trying to make sure that his usage of the word "journey" actually meant some kind of voyage and was not merely a bad choice of word.

"Of course, Mandira. Well, technically, we are not in the new world yet. We are on the way to the new world. Jantar is the second leg of our journey."

"And what's the first leg of the journey?"

"Oh, that is Antar. You have already covered that part."

"When?"

"Remember what happened in the bed when you closed your eyes?"

"I felt a sudden jerk followed by a free fall."

"Well, actually, you entered Antar."

"That was Antar?"

"Yes, Mandira, that was the first part of the journey, the Antar. This journey begins with Antar. Does that make sense to you?"

Things had stopped making sense to me since that morning when I found Viru and Reva listless in bed, and all I cared about was that they returned to their senses.

"Jack, I just want to say this. This development is overwhelming for me, and I do not know how to respond to it. I am a simple woman, and all I care about is the well-being of my family. My life revolves around my husband and kids, and I can embark upon any journey to some unknown super world with you if that results in the safety of my family—my ordinary little world—and returns our life to normal."

"Mandira, I promise again that I will bring your life back to normal. Your husband and daughter will be alright. You will find all the answers on this journey. Believe me, I need your help as much as you do mine," returned Jack, sounding candid and reassuring. He turned to my son, "Monsieur Ryan and mon cher Caesar! Please come. It's time to leave."

Ryan and Caesar were playing with the most beautiful tortoise I had ever seen, whose shell was embellished with hexagonal-shaped colorful gems, looking like a shining shield of a decorated soldier. Upon Jack's call, they stopped playing with their living toy and ran back to Jack, as if they knew what was to happen next, and that prospect seemed to them more exciting than playing with the dazzling tortoise.

I had noticed new energy in Ryan. He was not reluctant and sad anymore, rather he looked alert, playful, and compliant, especially to Jack's commands. Though this positive change had a pleasant effect on my motherly instinct, it also made me a little anxious—as any sudden change would—and skeptical about its lasting.

As this beautiful little island called Jantar was surrounded by sea, I thought there would be some kind of ship waiting for us to board, since Jack walked towards the sea, with excited Ryan and Caesar by his side and I, a step behind. I began to wonder if he were expecting us to swim next, as I could not spot any ship or other means of transportation that could help us cross this limitless sea.

"Jack, are we going to cross the sea?"

"That is correct, Miss Mandira."

"Ok, but how are we going to cross it?" I posed the question curiously, as we were only a few steps away from the water. I had by now run out of hope of running into a ship.

"We are going to cross it by walking."

"Oh, I see. I think the word that you are looking for is swimming. But how are we going to swim?" I returned promptly, with an air of catching another wrong choice of word.

"No, Mandira, I am not looking for the word swimming. I know what swimming is. I also know what flying is. But here, we are just going to walk."

As soon as Jack stopped talking, Ryan sprinted ahead, followed by Caesar, hitting an oncoming wave that was aggressive enough to sweep them off their feet. My heart stopped beating for a moment, and a helpless cry burst out of my mouth as I was not close enough to protect Ryan from falling.

Then I witnessed something strange. While the wave hit the shore violently, Ryan and Caesar, unharmed by its effect, continued to pace forward into the sea.

And wait. What was that?

I could not believe my eyes when I realized that Jack was indeed right. He did not mistake walking for swimming. To my sheer surprise, Ryan and Caesar were running on the water as casually as somebody ran on the ground.

"Relax, Mandira. Monsieur Ryan is alright. See, I was right. He can walk on water. Not only can he and Caesar walk, but they can also run on water. And by running, I again do not mean swimming. Now come over, you will be fine too," said a visibly amused Jack as he stepped on the water.

I took the first step hesitatingly, followed by a few more

cautious steps when another threatening wave came by, and my eyes closed in a reflex action. When I fearfully opened my eyes, the wave had surpassed without tumbling me or wetting my clothes.

How did walking on water feel? If I had been asked this question before, I would have posed a counter-question: "How can the feeling be described for an act that is not possible?"

In an ideal world, asking such a question or even suggesting the possibility of an adventure like this would be the easiest way of inviting jokes upon oneself. Even a skillful magician would not dare deceive an audience by performing a magic trick of this nature. Any person would make a fool of himself by asking such a ludicrous question in the world known to me, where things could be explained only by logic. He would easily be silenced by smart people with earthly concepts like the force of gravity, the human weight, and the surface tension of water.

But what explanation could be given here in Jantar? Could I say that my weight here was as light as a feather, or that the gravitational force had no role to play, or was it the surface tension of water, strong enough to support the human body?

Walking on water was surreal. It felt like an invisible and infinite glass sheet supporting my weight that was crystal clear, so much so that I could spot the bottom of the sea and visualize the mesmerizing aquatic life under my feet.

Hundreds of curious and colorful fish swarmed near my feet now and then, some of them leaping out of water in excitement and poking my bare lower legs, thereby giving me a gentle tingling sensation. Large colorful dolphins leaped out in groups as if breaking the invisible glass sheet temporarily, splashing water everywhere, and then plunged back in, giving the illusion of a rainbow.

Ryan was exhilarated like never before at the sight of these momentary rainbows appearing all over.

While I walked with Jack, who was smiling the entire

time, glancing now and then at the astonished look on my face, Ryan and Caesar continued to pace ahead with playful nonchalance, as if running on the water was a regular affair for them.

The small islands all around me looked magnificently rich, and I felt like a tiny part of the limitless imagination of Picasso that he would use to create one of his beautiful seascapes.

Then suddenly, the splendid seascape vanished and what I witnessed in front of me was breathtaking.

Chapter Six

The enormous sea that appeared never-ending and the magical water on which we walked vanished suddenly, replaced by the thick mist that seemed to engulf our surroundings so much so that I could hardly spot Ryan and Caesar, who walked only a few steps ahead of me, on the white sand.

Before I could ask Jack, he turned to me. "Miss Mandira, does this place ring a bell?"

"Oh, do you mean if I know this place?" I returned, realizing that this place indeed rang a bell, and I was not sure why.

"Yes, do you remember when you saw me for the first time?"

"Yes, I think at the Christmas parade. I was almost dumbfounded at the sight."

"No, I mean before that."

"Before that? Oh, do you mean in my dreams? Ah, yes. I would see you in those dreams nonstop for a few days with a fog like this all around."

"You are right, Miss Mandira. I used to talk to you from this place in your sleep."

"Really? Like, literally this place? Do you mean there exists such a place from where you can talk to me while I am sleeping? That's crazy!" I said, bewildered.

"Yes, Mandira. This world is crazy. This is the place where Jantar ends. What do you call it? The line where one place ends and the other starts. The stopline?"

"Oh, do you mean borderline? Border?" I asked with a smile, feeling better after my previous attempts of correcting him had failed.

"Yes, border. That is the reason why you could remember everything I said to you. From the border, one can talk to anyone."

"What do you mean? I remembered you because you talked to me from this border? Are you saying that any sleeping person can see and hear everything if you conveyed it from this border?"

"Absolutely right. You learn fast, Miss Mandira. If you think about it, anyone sleeping in Loka is technically present in the new world. And I can communicate with them from this spot."

"Does that mean Viru and Reva are in this new world?"

"Yes, technically, you can say that."

"Can I meet them?"

"Well, technically, it is not so straightforward, Mandira. You will learn."

"Is it possible for me to talk to Viru and Reva? They are sleeping, and based on what you said, we can talk to anyone from this border. Can I do that?" I asked, all in one breath before he could use that annoying word "technically" one more time.

"I knew you would ask me this. Well, Mandira, the answer is yes, you can do that."

The idea of talking to Viru and Reva sounded crazy. But if this were crazy, what could be said of landing on a magical land with colorful gemstones and all-season trees? How could I explain finding Ryan, Caesar, and Jack in this inexplicable world? Knowing the social interaction skills of Ryan with strangers, how could one explain his chemistry with Jack? What was the physics behind walking on water? And I thought I had gotten rid of those subjects—geography, physics, and chemistry—as soon as I finished school.

What could one make of the idea of the existence of a whole new world coming alive when they slept? The word "crazy" had lost its effect on me as soon as I arrived here, and now nothing could give it back its old meaning.

I would not miss an opportunity to talk to Viru and Reva, even if there was a remote possibility of the claim made by Jack being true.

"Would I be able to see them?"

"No, but they can see you."

"Can they talk to me?"

"No, only you can speak. This is a one-way speaking facility."

"Very well. Ok, to whom shall I address first, Viru or Reva? Or do I need to follow any orders?" I asked, with the child-like curiosity of inquisitive little Britney Hayden.

"You can follow any order you like, address one by one, or both together. All you need to do to connect is to say their names, and the hotline will be established. It is called a hotline, correct? Or is it warmline?"

"Hotline. Where should I look?" I asked eagerly, with little interest in correcting Jack.

"You can look anywhere, Mandira. Our cameras will catch you," returned Jack, smiling.

I tried to overcome the slight attack of stage-fright that I had never felt before while addressing Viru or Reva and started to speak, "Viru, can you see…and hear me? Well, I would like you to know…rather, I would like to ask why you are still sleeping. It is late. You must wake up now.

"Do you know that I had to take Caesar on a walk this morning? I know you do not like to walk him, and I wonder if that is why you used to go on those business trips for many days and weeks. You cannot run away from your responsibilities.

"I can see that you are focusing on your job hunt these days, and I am positive that you will find one soon, but you must realize that we need you to spend more time with us. With me, with Ryan, and with Reva. You talk so little to

Ryan, and he misses you. Please spend time with him.

"And I can handle your jokes, but you should also sometimes appreciate my effort, all that I am doing to raise our children, and help me with that.

"One more thing: Always turn off the bathroom light when you are finished. Even Ryan does that without fail, but you forget every time. And for the last time, do not enter my kitchen with your shoes on."

Then I spoke to my daughter, "Reva, my Revu, I do not know what I would do without you. I love you so much. You are the best daughter and sister one could wish for. You are the glue that holds us together. Sometimes I feel that I have neglected you by focusing a lot on Ryan and his challenges. I know how you feel, but you never complain. I promise I will make up for our lost time and have more of those girl talks that we used to have when you were little, you loved them." I finished speaking, teary-eyed.

"Good speech for the girl. But the husband...I am amused that you used the hotline for this. You complained to your husband Viru about how careless he is! You could have waited for him to wake up to tell him that."

"Yes, I thought I would say some nice things to Viru but then changed my mind. How could I miss an opportunity to lecture him without having to put up with his silly jokes and excuses? It is so satisfying to picture Viru gazing helplessly at me with his mouth open, wanting to speak but in vain. I hope the hotline does work as you say. I wish I could see Viru's face."

"You are a funny woman, Mandira." Jack chuckled, noticing the mischief in my eyes. After a pause, he added, "Are you ready for the next stage?"

"Oh, we have the next stage! What is this, a video game? Where are we going now?"

"We are going to Mantar, the third and last stop before we arrive in our world."

"I see, so after Antar and Jantar, we are now going to Mantar. Ok, but I have a question. How did Jantar vanish suddenly?"

"It did not vanish. You crossed it. Remember?"

"Yes, but that's it? We only walked like two hundred meters."

"Oh no, Mandira. You walked on water, not on land. You do not feel it but walking on water is much faster with a quicker time-lapse. A hundred miles on water and a hundred meters on land take about the same time. Yes, it would be about two hundred meters had we walked on land, but on water, we have covered a good two hundred miles."

Now there was no point in asking the logic behind walking for miles in just a few minutes when I did not know the science behind walking on water in the first place. Moreover, I never liked science back in Loka—I didn't know why I was calling my world Loka now—and definitely had no interest or patience to learn the time-lapse theories of another world, even if it was the world of sleep.

Jack's mention of the next stage made me feel like I was a character in some videogame, and that we had just completed the first stage.

The mist lasted for a few steps until it faded away completely. I could not say if we had covered a few meters or many miles, as I had no idea how the concept of speed and time worked in a dense fog.

When the mist faded away, I encountered an unbelievable sight. I saw a bridge. Now, it is hard for me to describe this bridge. If I were to talk about its size, words like "enormous" or "gigantic" that I had used for structures back in our world gave the impression of a peanut when compared to this.

The arc-shaped bridge looked like a monstrous rainbow emerging out of the heart of thick clouds and disappearing somewhere far off in a similar fashion. My neck started to ache while looking at this structure, as it was so high, as if many Burj Khalifas and Eiffel towers were stacked over one another. And do not even get me started on its length.

It was breathtaking to catch sight of such a massive

structure that seemed as if it was connecting Earth to Mars. I wonder which architect could create such a gargantuan structure, other than the Creator Himself.

Looking at my face, which was clearly not difficult to read, Jack asked with a teasing expression, "Looking at that, Mandira? Do you like it?"

"Like it? What is this?" I returned. His question changed the shape of the wrinkles on my forehead, as my eyebrows that had stretched away before were now pointing at each other.

'This is a bridge—like you have in your Loka. It is called the Rainbow Bridge."

"Rainbow Bridge?" I almost burst into ironic laughter as the image of the bridge across the Niagara River—also called the Rainbow Bridge—flashed in my head. "What now? Are we going to walk over this bridge?" I said sarcastically.

"Absolutely, Mandira."

"Really? Because I just asked jokingly," I said, shuddering at the mere thought of such an adventure.

"I know, Mandira, but I am not joking. I look funny, but I am a man on serious business."

"But that looks scary, Jack. And Ryan gets uncomfortable with heights," I said, pointing at Ryan, who, for some reason, was not showing any signs of discomfort.

"I think he is fine, Mandira. Are you ok to walk on the Rainbow Bridge, Monsieur Ryan?" asked Jack, and Ryan nodded promptly with the composure of a grown-up kid, a demeanor that I had not seen before.

"Do not be scared, Mandira. You are safe here in Mantar. You know, everything that lives in Loka must walk on this bridge every day. That is how this thing that you call sleep works."

"Oh, do you mean that there will be people walking on that bridge?"

"Yes, not only people, but everything that moves in Loka."

"Wow, my head starts ringing every time you make a

fresh revelation. I do not know what to say!"

"Say nothing, Mandira. You are with Jack, so you do not have to walk on the bridge. Just enjoy the ride."

"Oh, another ride? What now? Are we going to walk on air?" I asked sarcastically, hoping he would not say, "Absolutely!"

"I like your jokes, Mandira. But I will not astonish you with the usual conveyance of Mantar. I like the way you people travel in those little things in Loka. What do you call them?"

"I hope you are looking for the word 'car.'"

"Absolutely, Mandira. Car it is."

"Very well. Where is your car? Is it parked somewhere around?"

"Yes, it is parked here, in my pocket," returned Jack as he slipped his hand into the pocket of his cloak.

Chapter Seven

Jack slipped his hand in the pocket of his cloak, grabbled a little, and held out something for us to see. It was a small toy car. The red roofless car looked like one of Ryan's favorites, among his fleet of toy cars back home.

"What, this? That's a toy!"

"Yes, it is."

"But aren't we talking about a ride for that bridge?"

"Yes, Mandira, this is our ride."

"But how? It looks like Ryan's toy car!"

"Yes, it is Ryan's toy car. I just grabbed it from your house."

"My house? No, you grabbed it from your pocket. I just saw you do it," I protested, wondering if I had heard him right.

"Yes, what you saw was right. But what you don't see is that I can grab anything from Loka by putting my hand in my pocket."

"Wonderful. So you are a magician, too. You perform magic tricks."

"Magic! Magic is the word I was looking for. But I am not a magician. I can only perform this magic in Mantar. Actually, it is a simple science of tracing your home location in Loka—where you are lying in bed with Monsieur Ryan and mon cher Caesar—and picking anything using the inter-Mantar hand-pick technique. I will tell you more some other time, as we must start now."

"But how? That is still a toy," I returned, trying to ignore the science behind the vague "inter-Mantar pick-up technique" behind obtaining Ryan's toy car and focusing on the task at hand.

"Oh, you forgot. I just told you, Mandira, that I can perform magic in Mantar. See this."

Jack held out his hand and dropped the toy. The moment it hit the white gold sand, it turned into a plush full-sized roofless car with four seats. We hopped in the car, and I did not bother to ask the scientific theory behind the toy turning into a remarkable car. If I had, perhaps he would have told me that it was the inter-Mantar convertible technique.

As I took the passenger seat next to Jack, and Ryan and Caesar settled in the back seats, he started the engine and stepped on the accelerator so forcefully that the speedometer gasped for breath. The car quickly attained the top speed with speedometer display digits steadying. We approached close to the bridge in no time, amidst the excitement generated among Ryan and Caesar by the speed.

What I witnessed now was breathtaking. I had heard people mention the road to Heaven before, but the view in front of me would undoubtedly qualify had there been a literal meaning attached to this metaphor.

I could spot countless dark lines on the white sand that stretched beyond my field of vision, and it seemed as if there were multiple parallel black lines drawn over a blank white sheet with equal spacing, such that no line could meet the other. As we approached, the dark solid lines turned into dotted lines, and in the next few moments, these dots seemed to be moving steadily.

I was waiting for Jack to describe the dots as another piece of the magic of Mantar when I realized, after getting sufficiently close, that these lines were in-fact queues in which people walked mechanically.

As he drove right down the middle of two parallel queues among the sea of thousands, Jack slowed down for the first time, perhaps meaning to show me around.

There were men, women, and children of all ages, oblivious of their surroundings, walking at the same pace and maintaining equal distance from each other. Even infants and toddlers could be seen in the line. None of them talked to others or looked around.

A lady looked amused by something, a girl was giggling by herself, a young man kept a very stern face, another young man was upset about something, an old man was shedding tears, and the infants and toddlers laughed frantically. All these human robots were absorbed in their own little worlds.

I turned to Jack, who was perhaps waiting for a question. "What is this, Jack? Where are all these people going?"

"They are going to the same place we're going, Mandira. All in Mantar go to only one place, and that is Shloka."

"Shloka?"

"Yes, Shloka. Do you remember the world that I talked about?"

"Oh, so that world is called Shloka. That means the people from Loka are going to Shloka?"

"Absolutely."

"But why? What's in Shloka?"

"Well, you will find out soon."

"How often do these people go to Shloka?"

"Every time they sleep in Loka, they come here. There is no other place to go. That is how it works."

"Wow, I have never seen so many people, including children, walking so precisely in this order."

"Order. That is a powerful word Mandira. Order is the basis of everything that happens here and must be maintained at any cost," returned Jack, a grim expression suddenly appearing on his face.

"But what is with these people? Some laughing, some upset, and others crying!"

"Their expression is the reflection of how their day went in Loka."

"So, the humans, when sleeping, come this way?"

"Not only humans but all the minners, Mandira."

"The *minners*?"

"Yes, all the living things that sleep and walk up to Shloka. We call them minners. Wait a minute."

He suddenly took a sharp left and drove fast, crossing the queues, one after the other. So precise was the order in which people walked that nobody got in the way.

Jack slowed down again when the queues of humans ended, and I could see elephants walking in a similar fashion. As he kept driving and cutting the lines, I witnessed lions, tigers, buffaloes, horses, dogs, and cats walking in a similar fashion.

A random thought crossed my mind for no particular reason. If only living beings minded their behavior more often, the world—or Loka—would certainly be a better place.

This reminded me of Ryan's peculiar sketches of people walking in queues in a similar fashion that Ryan's teacher had shown me during last year's parent-teacher meeting. She also showed me similar drawings of animals and joked that Ryan was obsessed with teaching all his animals the human custom of walking in queues.

I wondered if it could be a mere coincidence that Ryan had drawn the sketches of this unique spectacle almost a year ago. How was it that Ryan, who would rarely look about him and barely paid attention to anyone back in Loka, was fascinated by the chains of humans and animals stretching to eternity, and, equally, paying such attention to Jack?

So, I was sleeping in my world, Loka, but *technically*, as Jack would say, I was journeying to an unknown world called Shloka, via magical lands called Antar, Jantar, and Mantar.

However, the best part was that every living being, including me, made this journey from Loka to Shloka and back daily, the difference being that I was conscious of it in my state of unconsciousness, and not alone.

Ever wondered what all questions have in common? And the same with all answers? Well, the answer to the former is curiosity. The answer to the latter is information. Curiosity is the engine driving all the questions in our minds, and information is the oil that keeps it lubricated. We humans thrive on the information that is continually needed to feed our curiosity.

At that moment, my curiosity was far exceeding the information that I had received, and I could only hope that the two matched up soon. Questions were bubbling inside me like boiling water in a pan with a lid, and either the stove needed to be turned off or the lid thrown open.

Apart from all his gifts of magic, Jack also had a great sense of gauging the mood, and before I asked, he began speaking. "Miss Mandira, do you remember the story that I told you, back in Loka, when you were in the park, sitting on the old bench?"

"Ah, the story about the gentle CEO and his wicked son? Yes, I remember that. You also said that the CEO heads three branches of the organization and the son is in charge of one of them. Is that correct?" I asked, pleased by my memory that was still intact in my state of sleep.

"Absolutely. The name of the CEO is Joseph, and his son is called Hogdon."

"Oh, I thought it was a fictional story. Do you mean these people are for real?"

"Yes, absolutely," Jack continued. "Joseph is a man of honor and puts his duty above everything else. He is responsible for keeping the organization in order and does that work with great passion. This organization is known as Kendram. As Joseph is getting old, he wants to retire soon and ensure a successor worthy of the top position and capable of keeping Kendram in order.

"Hogdon, on the other hand, is dishonest and manipulative. He aspires to be the next CEO and has tactfully managed to win the confidence of the majority of board members of Kendram. These board members are mainly the ex-CEOs and ex-chairmen, the old and experienced people of Kendram, and they play a vital role, along with Joseph, in the selection process of the new CEO, who will head the three branches. Any guesses what those three branches are?"

"No, how can I guess? I barely know your story."

"I asked because you are part of this story."

"What do you mean?"

"The three branches, my dear Mandira, are the three worlds, the Loka, Shloka, and Parloka."

"Wait, what? Did you just say Loka?"

"Yes, Mandira. I said Loka. Your world Loka."

"But how? How is such a thing possible, that our world is managed by an organization called Kendram, that has a CEO?" Rattled, I could not believe my ears.

"Yes, not only your world, but the other two also, Shloka and Parloka. You will find out about Shloka soon, and I will tell you more about Parloka at the right time."

"Oh, God," I said, bewildered by the wild turn that Jack's story had taken. After a long pause, I continued, "Of all the theories or stories that I have ever heard, this one has blown my mind. There are two more worlds apart from the only world I know, and these three worlds are managed like a company by a CEO called Joseph!"

"Well, nothing can operate on its own, Mandira. The worlds must be governed to keep them in order."

"Tell me one thing, Jack. Who exactly is Joseph? Is he God?"

"God? Do you mean the Supreme? No, Joseph is not the Supreme. Nobody has ever seen the Supreme. Some say that Joseph has met the Supreme once, but nobody can tell for sure. Joseph is a keeper, or, you could say, the head of the keepers."

"The keepers?"

"Yes, all the employees that work for Kendram are called the keepers. Like me; I am also a keeper."

Chapter Eight

On our way to Shloka, Jack explained to me the functioning of the largest organization called Kendram (not known to mankind) responsible for managing Loka, Shloka, and Parloka. In the meantime, the state of affairs of Loka was in topsy turvy.

Viru, Reva, Elena, Britney, and everybody around had been sleeping, and so had Ryan, Caesar, and I. Though not very confident, I was kind of aware of where I was, along with Ryan and Caesar, and what my sleeping meant. However, no such thing could be said about the others.

There was nothing normal in Loka. While half of the world was paralyzed with sleep, having no hope of waking up, the other half panicked upon realizing their inability to perform this natural act.

The sleep coma had shut down the West, causing irreparable damage that no pandemic or war or any other historical event had hitherto managed to do.

The small fraction of the total population that was awake went berserk with sleeplessness and cluelessness. The hospitals were flooded with patients in a deep sleep, brought in by their awake relatives, but in vain, as the overcrowded hospitals were severely understaffed due to sleeping.

The roads and highways were empty, the shops closed, and houses looked as if they had been abandoned. One could not believe that this beautiful part of the world, once abuzz and happening, where people carried on their daily work and children played in the yards, would suddenly come to a standstill.

The Eastern world, on the other hand, after receiving scary news from the West, had started to realize that they had been hit with wake syndrome. The day did not begin as usual for anyone. Not only did the fatigue from a sleepless night hamper the daily activities, but also the fear of uncertainty caused by the distressing news gripped the common man.

The hospitals were flooding with weary, confused, and sleepy patients, and the weary, confused, and sleepy staff struggled to attend them. The heads of governments and the officials tried hard to calm down the people and hide their nervousness.

While some angry people marched down the streets shouting slogans against the authorities, others were outraged on social media about the mismanagement. The debate of civilization being doomed picked up amidst chaos, with scientists struggling to provide a credible phenomenon to reject this belief, while astronomers, on the other hand claimed the unique positions of planets and the moon in its support.

The same could be said about animals and every other living thing, but the situation was akin to the announcement on airplanes about oxygen masks in case of an emergency, that one should protect themselves first before looking after others, and hence the plight of animals was forgotten.

Loka was now controlled by only one state. A state that was more horrible than the worst authoritarian state. The state of fear. A great civilization of thousands of years was knocking on the door of extinction.

*

"Ok, Jack. So, you work for this organization. What is it

called again?" I asked, trying to grab the opportunity to finally get to know him better.

"Kendram," returned Jack, as he drove amidst the sea of humans and animals that marched like robots along the rainbow bridge.

"Kendram. And the employees of Kendram are called Keepers.

"Absolutely. I am a keeper," he replied, smiling with a hint of pride.

"What does your work in Kendram entail?"

"I am a manager. Remember, I told you? I am responsible for keeping the order of the route that connects Loka to Shloka. I am in charge of Antar, Mantar, and Jantar."

"Oh, so you look after the route that leads to Shloka, the one we are taking?"

"Well yes, this, and hundreds of other routes in Antar and Jantar, and of course the four rainbow bridges in Mantar."

"Four rainbow bridges! Do you mean there are three more bridges like this?"

"Yes. This bridge is the smallest one. Antar, Jantar, and Mantar are quite large."

"That's crazy. And all the sleeping people must traverse Antar, Jantar, and Mantar!"

"Absolutely."

"But I did not see these people in Antar and Jantar!"

"They have a well-defined route. You entered Antar via a secret route that is not used by minners. As I said, there are many routes. I am taking you through, what do you call it…a short path?"

"Shortcut?"

"Yes, shortcut. My team works hard to keep things in order here."

"Oh, so you have a team here?"

"Yes, Mandira. A team of keepers. I have a tough job to do here. I also work on the special projects assigned to me by Joseph."

"Joseph, the CEO? Does he assign you projects?"

"He does. I am working on an assignment right now."

Surprisingly, Jack and everything else I saw and heard, which had seemed like an illusion far from the truth before, was now looking like a possibility. Though the miraculous grandeur of the visual experience looked nothing short of a fairytale, Jack's conviction about the existence of this alien world was somehow alluring me to believe him.

It was not tough to guess that there was a reason for Jack introducing me to this uncharted territory. That it was not simply a fun ride into a hidden, magical land. Jack perhaps needed something. He needed some favor from me, and in return, being a keeper with magical powers, maybe he would bring Viru and Reva back to life.

But what could I, a mere mortal of Loka, possibly do to help a keeper who claimed to manage the worlds? And what had I done to deserve preferred treatment when there could be smarter and more qualified people of Loka in my place?

I guessed that the answers to my questions lay in the story of the tussle of power between the father and son, that this faithful keeper of the father had chosen to share with me.

"Jack, is there any reason why Joseph does not want his son to be the chief? Did Hogdon do anything bad that the keepers are not supposed to?" I pressed.

"Hogdon is not a true keeper. We, the good keepers, call him and his followers daggers. We cannot trust daggers with keeping the order of Kendram. And becoming a chief is a huge responsibility, Mandira. And speaking of bad, what will you say if I tell you that all the troubles that Loka is going through right now are caused by that dagger Hogdon?"

"What? Do you mean sleep coma and wake syndrome?

"Yes."

"Are you serious? Are you saying that all the chaos happening in Loka is caused by one man...dagger. I mean…Hogdon? How is that even possible?" I returned, unsettled at the mere thought of such a possibility.

"It is possible, Mandira. Your husband Viren and daughter Reva are in trouble because of Hogdon. You can guess how bad he is."

"Really? But sleep coma and wake syndrome are diseases. That is some sort of pandemic we are facing in Loka. How can a person inflict that disease on millions of humans?"

"Well, Mandira, humans only believe what they see or know about. And believe me, they have seen and known little. You human-minners think that everything wrong with you is some disease. You think it's a disease because you only know about diseases. And I don't know what that other word means. P…Pandem, is it?"

"Pandemic. It means a disease that affects people globally."

"Oh, so *disease* again. Anyway, you will find out very soon how that dagger started this mess. Shloka is not far from here."

According to Jack, we were soon to arrive in Shloka, the mysterious world unknown to mankind, but all I could spot ahead was our gigantic bridge that carried the burden of living things, the minners as Jack would call them, vanishing into the dense mist.

Now I had no idea which one was thicker; was it the mist that filled the space in front of me, or the fog that clouded my mind thanks to Jack's latest revelation?

Suddenly the fog disappeared. Not the one clogging my mind, for that was only going to grow thicker, but the one ahead of us that was seemingly swallowing the monstrous bridge.

It looked as if we were close to the other end of the bridge, as we were now sloping slightly downhill, and there seemed to be some commotion at the far end, but we were not close enough for me to figure out what it was yet.

"Miss Mandira, we are near the border of Mantar," said Jack as he pulled over.

"Oh, are we getting off?"

"Yes, I want to show you something, and this car will not be suitable. You need a better view of this," returned Jack, as we all hopped out of the car.

Jack held out his hand, pointing towards the car, and with a flash, it turned back into the toy car sitting on his palm.

"We need Monsieur Ryan's helicopter now. Let me see…" he grinned as he slipped the toy car back in one pocket and rummaged in the other pocket of his cloak.

Jack took out a green toy helicopter, looking exactly like the one that Ryan would always use during playtime as a standby behind his fleet of toy cars.

Jack again performed the magic of turning the toy in his hand into a large military helicopter by dropping it.

I could not contain my curiosity this time and inquired how he did it. He said that he applied the law of total transformation by Dr. Ramanujan, a renowned mathematician and keeper from Parloka, and I did not bother to press him further.

We hopped on the four-seater helicopter, with Ryan and Caesar thrilled more than they were on the last ride, and Jack flew us right over the site where the rainbow bridge ended.

From the top view, I could spot the wide road ahead branching off into two, a large one going straight and a smaller one at an angle of about twenty degrees, looking like a giant Y. Perhaps Jack's mention of the mathematician keeper had rubbed off on me, as I guessed the angle between the roads accurately.

Shortly after hovering over the spot where the bridge ended, Jack carried on, slowing again over the site where the roads split. While the majority of the minners followed the wider road, a small fraction took the other one.

There stood two monstrous gates at the end of the roads, beyond which nothing could be spotted due to thick mist. The queues that had looked so organized on the bridge were not to be seen any more on the wide road.

Like highway congestion, this wide path became more

and more crowded nearer the gate, thus converging all the dotted lines (that were parallel before) into one large full-stop.

I noticed that the grand-looking cast-iron gate was closed, thus preventing all minners from moving any further. I also noticed that the gate at the end of the other path that branched off from the original was open. The few people and animals that had turned to this path walked freely and disappeared through the open gate.

"Jack, what is going on here? What is this place?"

"Miss Mandira, this is the place where you will find all the answers. Do you see that path? That is the way to Shloka."

"Ok, but why is it so crowded? And why is that gate closed?"

"Well, your second question is the answer to the first. The path is crowded because the entrance gate to Shloka is closed. The order of the world is disturbed. Mandira, when the minners of Loka enter a trance—the thing that you humans call sleep—they must travel to Shloka and return. This order has been followed since the conception of Loka. Now that the gate is locked, the order has been broken."

"So, you are saying that people must travel to Shloka. What happens if they don't?"

"Exactly what is happening in Loka. All those people who cannot wake up—what you call sleep coma disease—are trapped in Shloka. They cannot come out of the locked gate and go back to Loka, so they will not wake up.

On the other hand, all the others crowding here cannot enter Shloka and hence cannot complete the cycle of trance. In other words, these are the people who, according to you, have wake-up syndrome disease, and hence cannot sleep."

"Let me see if I've got it right. Viru and Reva are in endless sleep because they are trapped in Shloka. And my mother is unable to sleep because she cannot enter Shloka. And all this because of the gate that was open before but now is locked. Those who are inside the gate are sleeping in Loka. Am I right?"

"Absolutely."

"And the others outside of it are wide awake?"

"Those outside the gate may get a slight feeling of mild sleep, but they cannot sleep well until they complete the cycle. After waiting here for a while, these minners will return to Loka and come back again, hoping to cross the gate. This back and forth will go on for some time."

"That's the most ridiculous theory I have ever heard," I said, gesticulating to emphasize my disbelief, "The world is a mess and people are dying because of this locked gate in the sleep world? How can such a thing be possible?"

"I don't blame you for thinking that, Mandira," returned Jack with a composed smile. "This is the first time any minner has been exposed to this information. Minners cannot quickly process such incredible information. Minners are slow."

"Oh, wait, Mr. Einstein. Let me prove you wrong," I said, hurt by his patronizing remark about my minner clan. "The sleep coma and wake syndrome have affected people differently based on their geographies. How do you explain why people in the West are sleeping, and those in the East are awake because of this gate?"

"Good question, Mandira. I like the way you challenge me. Ok, let me try it another way. When you are in the state of deep sleep in Loka, it means that you have entered Shloka, a temporary residing place for minners. Your world, Loka, operates in different time zones. When it's night in one region, it is day in the other. So minners sleep at different times in different places.

"Now, when this gate was locked, it was midnight in the place that you call the West. So, most of the minners of the West had entered Shloka, except for some, like you, who were awake in their bed or still in Antar, Jantar, or Mantar. So, those who entered Shloka were trapped and continued in a state of sleep.

"On the other hand, since it was daytime in the East, those minners had not started their journey through Antar,

Jantar, and Mantar. And when the night fell, they tried to sleep and arrived here but found the gate closed and hence could not complete their sleep cycle. So, they are awake. Phew, that is the best explanation a keeper can give to a minner. I am so proud of myself."

It took me some time to register this unworldly information in my brain, much like Jack had proclaimed in his remarks about minners' poor processing capability. With that confidence backed up by particulars that I was clearly lacking, it was futile to argue with him. So, conceding with his account, I began after a pause, "Why is this gate locked then? Who locked it?"

"Who do you think? Take a guess."

"Now, how can I guess? Wait. Was it Hogdon?"

"You guessed right."

"Chief Joseph's son Hogdon? The one who wants to become the next chief? But why?"

Chapter Nine

As Jack's fairytale took an unpleasant turn, the journey of the magical lands lost its attraction.

"Why doesn't anyone fix it? Can't you open this gate, Jack? You know all the magic!" I inquired impatiently.

"I am an ordinary keeper, Mandira. I do not have the power to restore the order. The order has never been disturbed before. To fix it is complicated."

"But all you keepers are supposed to maintain the order. How can Hogdon disturb it? Why don't you punish him? What's your chief doing?"

"Chief cannot punish Hogdon as there is no way to prove that he has locked the gate. Hogdon has done it...umm...what is it called, sur...surreptitiously. Phew, I am getting better at your language. That dagger Hogdon is wicked, Mandira. He holds a responsible position in Parloka. He has a following of many other daggers and is well connected within the committee of Kendram. Many keepers believe that he was behind this act, but no one will speak of it. Hogdon will not admit that he disturbed the order."

"What will happen to Loka if this gate doesn't open?"

"Loka will be destroyed forever. Do you see that open gate?" Jack pointed in the direction of the sparsely occupied path that I had almost forgotten in the heat of the moment, "That is the entrance to Parloka. Let me tell you more about Parloka. It is the mother of all worlds. When minners complete their time in Loka, they go to Parloka."

"Complete their time? Do you mean when they die?"

"Absolutely. *Die* is the word. When minners of Loka die, they arrive at Parloka."

"Oh, are you talking about life after death? Is Parloka heaven?"

"Yes, if that's what you minners call it. Parloka is heaven. And these minners are so tired of waiting at the gate of Shloka that they run out of patience and begin stepping into Parloka before long," said Jack, pointing at the minners heading towards the open gate. "Soon all the minners waiting outside will be exhausted. Rather than going back to Loka each time, they will head towards Parloka through that gate. Also, the minners who are trapped in Shloka will soon exceed their time of stay and eventually head to Parloka."

"Is there another way to Parloka when you get inside Shloka?"

"Yes, there are many shortcuts to Parloka. So, the minners will disappear from Loka soon, and it will become a barren land like the ones you call planets. Problems have happened in the past but not on this scale. Before, notorious daggers faithful to Hogdon would venture into Jantar or Mantar and obstruct the journey of random minners, thereby preventing them from entering Shloka. Disguised as minners, they would join the queue and turn some innocent minners back to Loka from Jantar itself or forcefully set forth a few from Mantar into Parloka instead of Shloka. Once those minners entered Parloka, they would never return to Loka."

I wondered if that explained those intermittent cases of wake syndrome and sleep coma that had been going on for a while.

Does that mean that wake syndrome and sleep coma were nothing but people turned back to Loka or set forth to Parloka respectively by those awful daggers? I thought. *Perhaps Elena's ex Jim also died in such circumstances.*

"We recently found about these shameful activities that

had been going on for a while and increased the surveillance of this zone since then," continued Jack, "but this latest ploy of Hogdon's has rendered everyone clueless."

"That is horrible! Are we all going to die? But why? Why is Hogdon destroying Loka? What have we done to him? We are innocent people. We poor people do not even have any knowledge of your world's Shloka, Parloka, and whatnot."

"Well, the reason why Hogdon wants to destroy Loka is that he hates it. Ever since Chief Joseph announced his successor, Hogdon had felt threatened by the existence of Loka."

"But why?"

"Because Joseph has announced that the next chief of Kendram, the largest organization ever existed, will be from Loka."

"What? From our Loka? Do you mean a person from Loka will manage these worlds?"

"Yes, you heard me right, Mandira. This is the first time in the history of Kendram that there will be a contender from Loka for the position of chief and, since the chief himself is backing that person, Hogdon feels threatened. Also, many of the old chiefs and ex-chairmen of the committee of Kendram do not like the chief's idea. So they secretly support Hogdon. By closing the gate of Shloka, Hogdon intends to bring all the minners of Loka over to Parloka where he has a good hold."

"But why does chief Joseph want his successor from Loka?"

"That is destiny, Mandira. Chief Joseph is blessed with some unknown powers. Senior keepers believe that the chief can connect directly to the Supreme. And it is His wish that the next chief should be from Loka. Chief Joseph must execute the wish of the Supreme."

"The Supreme means God, correct?"

"Yes, you could say that."

"What now? There must be something you can do, Jack. You cannot let the people of Loka die like this. Please tell me what can be done," I said, making an earnest appeal.

"There is only one person who can fix the order," he returned.

"Who, the chief?"

"No, not the chief. It is the person who will succeed the chief. That brings me to some important news. Do you know who that person is?"

"Do I know that person?"

"Yes, you do. That person is here, Miss Mandira."

"Where? Among that crowd? Do I know them?"

"No. With us. That person is Monsieur Ryan."

"What? Say again?"

"The next Chief of Kendram will be Monsieur Ryan."

After witnessing the developments of the day, which felt like they should only have happened in either wild fantasy movies or kids' video games, I would have believed Jack had he named the man who loaded the garbage bins into his truck every morning, or the one who sold candies at the subway station, for that matter…but *Ryan*?

"Jack, are you kidding me?"

"Kidding? I do not know what that means, Mandira."

"Is this a joke?"

"It's not. I look funny, but I have no sense of humor."

"Do you even know that Ryan is a nine-year-old boy, and he…" I hesitated as Ryan was listening to our conversation in the backseat of the helicopter, "Life is already difficult."

"See, that's the problem with minners of Loka. If a minner does not act like them, they think he is no good. Miss Mandira, Monsieur Ryan is the only boy who has the heart of a minner and the brain of a keeper, an unmatched combination. His evolved brain is way beyond the comprehension of the minners of Loka. Monsieur Ryan is, what you do you call them…a gennie?"

"Genius?"

"Genius! Yes, he is a genius."

"But Jack, he has difficulty in speaking and learning."

"What, speaking minner language and learning minner

ways? Minner language is foolish, and do not even get me started on your math and science. You cannot expect good results by running outdated software on a supercomputer, can you?"

All these years, I had longed to hear a single positive remark about Ryan's cognitive ability from his schoolteachers, therapists, or anyone else, and now, as Jack called him a genius, my heart took a giant leap of pleasure, but my mind found it hard to process.

"Mandira, Monsieur Ryan is a gifted boy. He was not born in Loka to follow minner ways. He is destined for greatness. Joseph, the Chief of Kendram, is a wise man, and one cannot doubt his vision. If he believes Monsieur Ryan is the one, he is the one."

"Jack, I think you have made some error. Joseph must be looking for someone else, perhaps some other boy named Ryan," I returned, shaking my head in denial.

"Keepers do not make mistakes, Mandira, and certainly not the chief of keepers."

"But he is just a kid," I said, looking at Ryan, who was beaming with confidence that I had not seen before. "He does not know anything about your worlds and the functioning of your Kendram."

"That's what you think, Mandira. But this journey to Shloka that every minner makes without any knowledge of its existence and that you are discovering for the first time is no secret for Monsieur Ryan. He is the only minner capable of making conscious trips to Shloka every day.

"He knows about every place here. He has explored all 130 routes of Jantar that lead up to Mantar, something that even I, being the caretaker of this place, have not done. He has walked over all the four bridges of Mantar to enter Shloka, something that no minner has done before."

"But he is just a kid."

"That's what the board members of Kendram said when the chief proposed Ryan's name as a contender. Do you know what he said to them? 'It takes nothing to find the right age but takes ages to find the right one.'"

It was hard for me to understand the significance that Jack attached to Ryan's wandering around this place, and all I could think was that this was perhaps the reason why he had always been reluctant to wake up. However, Ryan's awareness of the world we humans knew as sleep and perceived as a suspended consciousness was unnerving, yet remarkable.

"Mandira, this is hard for you to understand, and I get it," continued Jack, "but think of it like this: You spent a sleepless night in Loka, and your daughter and husband could not wake up. Half of the minners of Loka are becoming deranged from lack of sleep, and the other half are lying unconscious. But did you notice that Monsieur Ryan slept peacefully and woke up like any other day? Even the closed gate could not stop him from entering and leaving Shloka. He is special. He has a rare brain. Even the keepers do not have such strong mind power."

"Really?" I asked, full of delight.

"Yes. Perhaps that's the reason why the chief chose him."

"But didn't you say before that it was the wish of the Supreme?"

"Oh, I did? Yes, that also. What do I know about big shots? I am just a small manager here."

This was the first occasion where someone had showered my son with praise, and my motherly love—without caring for the authenticity of such claim or any evidence in its support—wished that Jack would go on and on.

I had spent all these years trying to make Ryan independent, helping with routine activities that Jack called "silly minner ways" and that any other child of his age could carry out without supervision. And here was Jack telling me that Ryan was an extraordinary human with powers that even the keepers did not possess, let alone human beings. That was no ordinary claim, and the mere thought of it gave me palpitations.

Jack landed the helicopter on the patch of land across the shoulder of the road, and after we got off, the helicopter landed right into his pocket, just like the red car before it.

"What do you want from us, Jack? What do you want from Ryan? I can see now why you brought my son and me here and disclosed the secrets that nobody knows. Now I am scared. Tell me, what do you want?"

"Don't be scared, Miss Mandira. I just want you to give your blessings to Monsieur Ryan."

"Give my blessings? Blessings for what?"

"See, Mandira, your love binds your son. A mother's love is a strong emotion of Loka, and her belief has unlimited powers. Even the best scientists of Parloka have failed to calculate the depth of mother's love. You protect your son because you think that he is weak and frail, when in fact, he has the potential to protect the entirety of Loka. Unless you have faith in his potential and instill that belief in him, Monsieur Ryan cannot become the legend he has been chosen to be. Only your blessings have the power to make him the guardian of the worlds."

"You want me to give him blessings so that you can set my poor child up against that cruel dagger Hogdon? The Hogdon who caused all this mess? You want to involve my son in your politics of Kendram and put his life in danger?

"Look, Jack, I am flattered by your comments about Ryan, and you may be right about everything you said, but we are ordinary people. We do not want this. All I want for my son is to lead a normal life and have a childhood that every child deserves. I do not want him to be the guardian of the worlds."

"Miss Mandira, there is a saying in Parloka that I will interpret for you to understand. It goes like this, 'The choice made to stay in the dark for fear of discovering the unknown had you turned on the lights is never the right one.'

"Monsieur Ryan can never become the ordinary boy that you want him to be. And why settle for ordinary when you can be extraordinary? You must understand, Mandira, that he is like a bird trapped in a cage called Loka. He does not belong there. Only your love can give him the wings to fly and carve his path," returned Jack, with an air of someone who had shared the precious jewel of foresight out of his treasure of wisdom.

"I am sorry, Jack. No matter how hard you try, you cannot convince me. Ryan is my most precious possession, and I cannot let you risk his life," I returned with firm resolve.

"I see you care for your son, Mandira. According to the guidelines of Kendram—that the chief and the keepers follow diligently—a mother has the right to decide for her minor child, and nobody can challenge her decision. I can do nothing against your wishes. I hate to push you, but you must realize that the fate of Loka depends on your decision. The order must be fixed, and only monsieur Ryan can do that. Else, all minners of Loka will die. If you want to see your Viru and Reva alive, then you must make a decision."

A long silence followed. The firm resolve that I had taken a few moments ago was now shaking at the mention of Viru and Reva.

"Look, Mandira," continued Jack, "your blessings will untap great powers in Monsieur Ryan that he has not known or felt until now. He can take care of himself and Loka, and nobody can harm him. Moreover, the army of keepers will always be there to protect him."

The moment I made the resolve to not expose my precious possession Ryan to any danger by giving in to Jack's appeal, I had forgotten that my other two precious possessions were lying at the door of death. According to Jack, only Ryan could save my family, my friend Elena's family, and all the other families of Loka, although I had no idea how he would do that.

Noticing that my resolve was on the verge of breaking, Jack made the final attempt to shatter it into pieces.

"Miss Mandira, have you ever wondered why Caesar is so fond of Monsieur Ryan?"

"What do you mean? Caesar is like my third child, and Ryan is like his brother. They both are fond of each other. They are always together, perhaps, that's why."

"Certainly. You treat him like your child, and he loves you all. But Ryan is his master. You will be surprised to know that Caesar is a keeper."

"What? A keeper? How?"

"Yes, Mandira. Caesar is a keeper deputed in Loka to protect his master and future Chief of Kendram, Monsieur Ryan."

"No, he's not." I returned with disbelief. "How is this possible? We got him from the dog shelter. I remember my conversation with Mrs. Danielle Silver from the dog shelter vividly, about how a wild bear killed his pregnant mother."

"She was right. That bear who killed Caesar's mother was a dagger."

"What? A dagger? I don't get it. Why would a dagger kill her?"

"Look, Mandira. That is another story, and I promise I will tell you more about it when the time comes. The point I am trying to make is that we have our best keeper dedicated to protecting Ryan. So nobody can cause him any harm. We must hurry now. Every second we waste means more and more minners entering that gate," said Jack, pointing at the open gate of Parloka.

I gazed at young Caesar, whose sagacious eyes were full of reassurance as if telling me, "Do not worry, Mom, I am there for my brother, Ryan. As long as I am alive, nobody can touch even a strand of his hair."

Taking a deep breath, I inhaled the air of reassurance and exhaled the last traces of my weakened resolve.

Chapter Ten

"Alright, Jack. A woman can be weak sometimes, but a mother is always strong. I will not choose to stay in the dark. I will let my son shine under the light of new hope. Tell me, how can I help?"

"Very well, Mandira. You have made an excellent choice," replied Jack, as if he was already positive about the choice that I was going to make. "Let me see here…" he said, rummaging through his pocket just like he had on previous occasions.

"What now? Are you getting another vehicle from Loka? Like a ship or train this time?"

"Not Loka. I am getting something from Parloka this time. Here it is," returned Jack, holding out his hand. A beautiful round locket with a silver chain rested on his palm. The glittering locket emitted all the colors of the rainbow.

"What is this? A locket?"

"Yes, Mandira, this fine piece of art is designed by Suzanne Belperron, only for Monsieur Ryan."

"Suzanne Belperron? The legendary jewelry designer? Didn't she die like forty years ago?"

"Yes, she did. Dying in Loka means nothing but moving the base to Parloka. Belperron has received a place in the hall of fame of top jewelry artists, a rare feat in Parloka. She is a big name there. I need you to put this around Monsieur Ryan's neck and bless him with all of your motherly might."

I had no clue what Jack meant by my motherly might. I felt like one of those mothers of ancient times who would anoint their young sons with sandalwood paste on their foreheads as a good luck charm before they set out for the wars and battles.

Holding his hands, I spoke to him, "My precious Ryan. I have always believed that you are the best thing that ever happened to me, but it occurred to me today that you are also the best thing that happened to this world. I always intended my love for you to become your strength, not weakness. It makes me so proud when Jack calls you the guardian of the worlds. So go on, my little wonder. Guard the worlds. Protect our Loka. Bring back your Daddy and sister. Your mommy is with you," I said with tears in my eyes as I put the shining locket around Ryan's neck.

His eyes twinkled, momentarily outshining the sparkle of the locket.

"Thank you, Mandira. We are ready to save your Loka now. Alright, Monsieur Ryan," said Jack, smiling at Ryan, "let us fix the order. You have a fairly good idea about how things work here, but you don't know how things are fixed. Let me show you something," Jack slipped his hand in the pocket of his cloak again, and this time took out a key. This old and uniquely designed key, perhaps made of brass, was about the size of Jack's hand.

"A key!" I whispered, but perhaps it was loud enough for Jack to hear.

"Yes, Mandira, a key. But not just any key. This is the royal key designed by Sir Lockman Keyhole, a blue-ribbon awardee, legendary key maker," said Jack. "This key can open any gate or lock. Only the chief is authorized to keep and use this key, and I have secured his approval to use it. There is another copy of this key that is missing. Chief and I believe that Hogdon stole it, and he used it to close the gate of Shloka. It is Chief Joseph's wish that Monsieur Ryan uses the key to fix the order of Loka.

"Now, Monsieur Ryan. Listen to me carefully as I am

going to tell you an important feature of this key. Sir Lockman has designed this key by keeping advanced security measures in mind, and its limited use is one of them. It was designed to be used a maximum of four times—two to close and two to open. After the four chances are exhausted, this key will become a useless piece of metal.

"Due to an unprecedented situation that happened a thousand years ago, which I will not get into now, one chance to open a lock was exhausted. With that, this key, or its copy, was left with three chances—two to close and one to open. Okay?

"As you can see, Hogdon has used the copy of this key to close the gate of Shloka, meaning he exhausted one chance of closing the gate. So how many chances are left? Two. Your key can open and close the gate only one time. So, you have only one chance to open the gate. Do you understand me?" asked Jack.

Ryan nodded his head.

"So, Monsieur Ryan. All you need to do is this: walk alongside the shoulder of this road up to the gate of Shloka, find a keyhole, insert this key, and twist it around, like this…" said Jack, rotating his wrist twice.

"Anticlockwise direction to open," I prompted excitedly and added, "Ryan knows that very well. He is fond of locks and keys."

"Very well, then. Anticlockwise to open," returned Jack, again rotating his wrist.

I was relieved. It was just a simple task to open the gate with a key and not some act of daredevilry, the possibility of which I had feared when Jack declared Ryan as the potential guardian of the worlds.

Ryan took the royal key from Jack, which was designed by sir Lockman Keyhole, a name undoubtedly indicative of his profession, and started to walk. I wondered if all these people really existed, or if Jack had simply made up stories like a skillful salesman going the extra mile to sell engaging stories before he sold his products.

Jack mentioned that the key was used for the first time a thousand years ago. I wondered, by that logic, how old Sir Keyhole was, or even how old Jack was, for that matter.

Anyways, Caesar joined Ryan, often taking enthusiastic steps ahead of him and then returning, acting as a perfect guide and companion. As he walked, Ryan looked confident and thoughtful, his demeanor quite different from his usually shy and lost one.

A few steps later, Ryan stopped at the spot where the road split into two. He stood there for a few seconds, looking undecided, and instead of walking straight, took the path that headed towards Parloka. Realizing that his master was not following him anymore, Caesar, who had already taken a few enthusiastic steps forward, sprinted back to catch up with him.

My motherly protective instincts, which I had boldly proclaimed to relinquish a few minutes back, returned within no time. "Ryan!" I shouted, "not that way, honey! You—"

Jack cut me short before I could finish, "Sorry, Mandira, but I think you should let him decide."

"But he is walking towards Parloka. He clearly does not know what he is doing. What if he enters that gate? I cannot lose my child."

"I think he knows very well. Please let him do what he wants. Trust me, Mandira, you will not lose your child."

Ryan kept walking along the road to Heaven. He stopped at the threshold, beyond which there was a thick mist. Ryan carefully examined the cast iron gate protruding through the wall at one side.

I held my breath.

A minute or two passed that felt like ages. Then he did what looked like a maneuver with the key. The very next moment, the giant gate of Parloka began sliding. As the gate closed by sliding into the wall at the other side, it made a loud sound, like closing the garage of a warehouse.

Standing next to Jack, I wondered why Ryan closed the gate of Parloka and how the two closed gates would help in restoring order. Also, I could not understand why he did not follow the simple instructions given by Jack and why Jack was smiling despite that.

Before I could ask Jack, I saw that Ryan was coming back. He again stopped at the spot where the roads branched off and started walking along the shoulder of the main road crowded with minners. Caesar simply followed his master, not attempting to lead this time.

They disappeared into the crowd, and I had no way to see what followed. A few minutes passed, and I became anxious. But Ryan's action amidst the crowd did not remain a mystery for long as the gate of Shloka soon slid open.

"Bravo! Bravo, Monsieur Ryan! See, I told you. I told you, Miss Mandira," said the ecstatic Jack, clasping his hands as we watched the gigantic gate of Shloka sliding open.

I heaved a sigh of relief, and renewed hope twinkled in my eyes. It was clear with Jack's excitement that Ryan had delivered the expected results.

Soon, Ryan and Caesar appeared in the crowd that was now showing signs of movement. After performing the deed that no human had ever done, Ryan walked towards us in a manner that he never had done.

I was not sure if it was for real or in my imagination, but I felt like music was playing in my head as Ryan walked towards us, like in the movies when the background score synchronizes with the victorious walk of the protagonist.

While Jack continued to shower him with praise, I hugged Ryan and made Caesar jealous again.

"The key, Jack," said Ryan, handing over the key with a sense of accomplishment. His newfound confidence and clarity in speech elated me immensely.

"Thank you, Monsieur Ryan. I knew it! Chief Joseph is never wrong. Miss Mandira, this is because of your blessings."

"Thanks, Jack. I am glad I could be of help. Although it sounds evident from your reaction that I still need reassurance. I am curious to know if Ryan was able to fix the problem in Loka."

"He certainly did. The situation in Loka will be back to normal soon."

"And Viru and Reva?"

"They will wake up in Loka, and you will see them."

Jack's words brought a joyous sensation to my body. The thought of reuniting with my family, which had seemed a distant reality at one point, brought back the nostalgia of our ordinary days. I longed to get back to the mundane life that now seemed like a luxury to me. I did not attempt to hold back my tears, which mingled with my happiness.

After taking a few moments to let the blissful feeling sink in, I asked Jack, "There is one thing I do not understand. Why did Ryan close the gate of Parloka?"

"Hmm…That's the real masterstroke," returned Jack with a grin. "Ok, let me explain. Do you remember when I told Monsieur Ryan that this key could be used only three times on any of the gates—two times to close and one to open?"

I nodded, and he continued, "Hogdon has the copy of this key, and he used it to close the gate of Shloka. Now Monsieur Ryan has used the remaining two chances, by closing the gate of Parloka and opening that of Shloka, thereby rendering the key ineffective for further use.

"Had Monsieur Ryan only opened the gate of Shloka, there would be one chance left for the key to close the gate. That means there would be another chance left with Hogdon to again close the gate of Shloka with his copy of the key. Imagine if that had happened; there would be no chance left to open the gate, thus leaving Loka in serious trouble."

"Oh my God, that is scary. I did not think anything beyond the opening of that gate. How and when did Ryan think this through?"

"Well, when I told him about the key. Do not forget, Mandira, that monsieur Ryan is no ordinary boy. He has lived in this place longer than he has in Loka."

"I have no words to describe how happy I am for Ryan.

But what about the other gates? Didn't you say there were more bridges like the one we crossed leading to gates?" I asked promptly, as my curiosity knew no bounds.

"Good question. There are three more rainbow bridges that lead up to similar gates of Shloka. The action made on one gets replicated on all the other gates. Right now, all the gates of Shloka are open, and those of Parloka are closed."

"Hmmm."

"I think you have more questions. Go ahead and ask them," said Jack, noticing that I was thoughtful.

"This looks so obvious to you people. You knew the way, and you had the key. Why would you want Ryan to open and close these gates? Your chief keeps this key and is authorized to use it. I wonder why he didn't do this himself?"

"Order, Mandira. Order. This was a tricky situation where even the chief was clueless. Chief Joseph has resolved to protect the order and never break it. But to fix the order, you need to break one. Chief could certainly open the gate to Shloka but closing the gate to Parloka would mean breaking one of the access points, hence breaking the order, and our principled chief could not have done that.

"Moreover, the chief needed to prove to everyone in Kendram that by fixing the order, Monsieur Ryan was a worthy choice. I had clear instructions from the chief to only tell Monsieur Ryan how to open the gate of Shloka and not to make any other suggestion to break the order. Sadly, I am a good keeper who must follow the chief's orders and the rules of Kendram, but Monsieur Ryan has no such obligation. I know the chief does not approve of breaking the order but deep down inside, he will be pleased. Now the key with Hogdon is useless, and he cannot do further damage."

"I see, that makes sense. So, what is the effect of closing the gate of Parloka? Have we become immortal?"

"Immortal?"

"Immortal means to live forever," I replied, glad to realize that at least there was something I was better at, even if Jack considered it as mundane minners' vocabulary. "Does it mean that the minners of Loka will never die?"

"It does not. What you minners call death is nothing but a natural progression from Loka to Parloka, just like you remove old clothes and wear new ones. There are many routes for this progression, and I will tell you about that some other time. The closed gate here means that there will be no progression, whether natural or forced, of minners from Loka to Parloka in Mantar."

"No progression in Mantar…" I repeated, scratching my head.

"Ok, here is a simple explanation that you will understand. Hereafter, the minners will not die while sleeping."

"Wow, no deaths during sleep!" I said, amused. "That is good news. Why was this gate even open? It seems funny to think that nobody will die of a heart attack in their sleep because a locked gate blocks the way that leads to death. Many proven medical facts have been tossed out, thanks to this gate. It is certainly going to baffle the experts of medical science for years to come."

"Hmm…medical science of minners," returned Jack condescendingly.

"I know you consider it lame, but it works in Loka. We don't do magic in the name of technology as you do, but we are fine," I said, trying to defend the honor of Loka.

The feeling of a sense of responsibility toward Loka had never occurred to me before. The closest I came to representing anything ever was my school in an inter-school sack race competition when I was a little girl, and here I was, representing the entire world, thanks to Ryan.

"Apologies, Mandira. I did not mean to offend you. Sir Lockman Keyhole is re-designing the security system here. When the new systems are ready, that gate will be opened again, and then your medical science will work like before."

"Never mind, Jack. I think I am overreacting. I should rather thank you for saving my family and the entire Loka and helping me realize the potential of Ryan."

"Likewise, Mandira. Kendram could not have saved Loka without you and Monsieur Ryan."

"May I ask the reason why you call him monsieur?"

"Monsieur is the French word for sir. I learned little French from my good friend from Parloka, Isabelle Bergeron. How else would you address a legend?" returned Jack, making my heart swell with pride.

"Can I ask one question? How is it that only Monsieur Ryan remained unaffected when the entire Loka had trouble either in sleeping or waking?"

"Good question. As I said before, Mandira, one must complete the cycle of entering and exiting Shloka to remain unaffected. Monsieur Ryan did that."

"But how? How did he manage to get past the closed gate?"

"Well, he is not a legend for nothing. There is a secret passage in Mantar leading to Shloka. Only keepers know about it and use it when needed. As I told you before, Monsieur Ryan has explored this place so thoroughly that he discovered the secret passage long back. So, when he found the gate to Shloka closed, he used the secret passage to complete his cycle."

"Wow, that is unbelievable."

"Yes, but true. You have seen that minners walk here in queues along a well-defined path, but Monsieur Ryan stopped following the queue when he was just a toddler. He would break out of the line and wander off. It was unusual as no minner would break the line. I had to appoint one keeper just to watch him and bring him back to the line. I intuitively knew that he was not an ordinary minner.

"Later, the chief ordered me to let him roam about anywhere he wanted to. It was clear to me that he was special as the chief had never given much attention to any minner before. Monsieur Ryan is curious and pays attention to detail."

I could relate to the attention to detail part, as Ryan

would spend hours staring at his toys from different angles that I would find abnormal, but knowing he was curious came as a gratifying revelation.

God is the master of timing. He bundles our wishes in such a manner that the moment a long-standing desire gets fulfilled, fresh desire manages to eclipse the joy. I had not expected a situation where my eagerness to see Viru and Reva would take precedence over the joy of praise for Ryan, something that I longed to hear for eternity.

"Jack, talking to you is comforting," I said, "and I still have so many questions to ask, but I cannot wait to see Viru and Reva. Could you please drop us back in Loka?"

"Sure, Mandira. But you must not forget one thing. You have not crossed that gate in the last two days. Unless you complete your cycle, you will not be in good shape when you get back there. Even if you get back right away, you will need to wait for Viru and Reva to wake up. It will take some time for the crowd at the gate to settle down and for things to normalize here. So, let us proceed to Shloka, the confluence of two rivers."

Chapter Eleven

As we walked past the entrance, the dense fog, which almost blinded us momentarily, whisked away with a blink of an eye, leaving us in a sprawling desert. The reddish-yellow sand that spread in all directions as far as the eyes could see shone brightly under the scorching sun, with the tiny particles twinkling here and there.

I could see children who looked about the age of Ryan racing barefooted up and down the highest dune. Only their hysterical laughter broke up the otherwise dead silence of the desert.

The most intriguing part was, it rained at the top of the dune. I looked up at the sky and found one small, dark cloud patch right above the dune. It looked as if somebody had placed it above the dune on purpose as it was the only cloud in the clear and bright sky, and it showered heavy drops, thus exhilarating the children who went up to get wet and came down to dry.

"What is this place?"

"Well, this is oo…ee…aa…" As Jack tried to speak, his voice started breaking. The desert was suddenly engulfed in the limitless fog again. Jack, who spoke from about a meter away, became almost invisible, and his voice sounded hoarse and distorted, like an audio playing in slow motion from a broken radio.

The fog did not last more than a few seconds, and by the

time it had vanished, the sprawling desert was no more. To my utter disbelief, the limitless bed of reddish-yellow sand had been replaced by a vast blue sea, and the dune by a gigantic cliff. It felt like somebody had replaced one landscape picture on the wall with another, and I could observe the switching pictures while being inside those pictures.

Jack, Ryan, and Caesar were standing close to me. Jack was still talking, but his speech continued to lag behind the movement of his lips, making it impossible to follow him.

I noticed three men and a woman standing at the edge of the cliff. Through their gestures and movements, it seemed that there was a heated argument going on over something.

The majestic sun setting in the calm sea made it seem as if a radiating orange ball dropped by a mischievous child was floating in the water.

Suddenly, one of the men pushed the woman off the cliff, and I wailed in horror. I witnessed the free-fall with my half-closed eyes and full-opened mouth.

As she was about to plunge into the sea, I noticed something strange. Her hands turned into large wings, and she alighted momentarily on the water before flying up and away like a large bird.

How can a woman turn into a bird and fly?

Before I could process the scene that had just unfolded in front of me and the extent of bizarre turn it took, the mist once again clouded my vision as if I were wearing spectacles, the lenses of which had just fogged up. As expected, the fog cleared soon, except for the one that clouded my mind, introducing me to a new setting altogether.

This time we found ourselves in a jungle covered with snow. Clad with snow accumulated over time, the branches of the giant deodar cedar trees drooped downwards with the additional weight. The chunks of snow occasionally slipped through the branches here and there, thus breaking the dead silence of the darkest night.

I noticed a large black bear sitting on a rock, staring at

me. His fuming red eyes reminded me of the one that I had seen back in spring when we were driving on our way back from the tulip gardens with Elena and Britney. Perhaps it was the same bear.

Suddenly, it roared at me, and I shrank back in fear. In the next moment, the angry bear pounced on me.

Before it could rip me apart, the fog saved me and transported me to yet another location.

More inexplicable scenes kept blowing my mind for a while. It felt as if I was inside the TV and some invisible person with the remote control kept switching the bizarre channels every minute, and I found myself being part of each one of them. Or perhaps I was time traveling into the future where words like "miracle" and "impossible" did not hold any meaning.

At last, I found myself in a village that was familiar to me. The gravel road that led to an old house, primarily made of wood, brought back my childhood nostalgia. Amazed, I looked to my right hoping Jack would clear my confusion, but I noticed he was nowhere around, and neither were Ryan and Caesar. I was alone in this place.

As I pushed the slightly ajar door open to enter the living room, the smell of old teakwood teased my nostrils. A large part of the wooden floor was covered with a soft grey carpet with a green striped border. A large red couch, the side chairs, and the rectangular wooden table rested comfortably on the bushy rug. The crystal chandelier hanging right in the middle added to the aesthetic appeal of this cozy, warm room.

It felt like I had opened the door to my childhood memories, every piece of furniture preserved. It was my Grandma's house. There was a small rocking chair lying in the corner. Grandma had had it made for me by the house's construction workers when I was a little girl.

Out of instinct and familiarity with this house, I headed straight to the kitchen. Sitting on the slightly elevated wooden platform, I saw a woman slipping a small log through the opening of the clay stove into the fire, and two boys (about nine and eleven) next to her, giggling and jostling occasionally.

The woman turned around and smiled at me, "Munni, what are you doing out there? Come here. Look, what I am doing. Roasting the potatoes in the fire, just the way you like. Come quick, or else these two monkeys will finish everything."

"Munni, come sit here. I saved a place for you," said one of the boys in a familiar, high-pitched voice.

The woman was my Grandma, with fewer wrinkles on her face than the last time I saw her before she died. The two monkeys she referred to were my older brothers, Ajay and Arjun. They had looked like that about thirty years ago.

That was not the only strange thing, though. Grandma and my brothers acted as if I was a five-year-old.

I sat next to Ajay in the place he had saved for me. I was dumbstruck by the presence of Grandma and my brothers and kept staring at them.

I gazed at the clay stove, which had been regarded as a sacred thing by everyone in the house and a fascinating piece of art by me when I was a little girl. Grandma would bow before the stove with her folded hands first thing in the morning and then polish it with a fine mud-water paste. She would say that the stove was the provider of the family.

She would then light a fire with the help of dry twigs and fuel it with chopped wood pieces. Consuming the firewood set aside for the day, the stove would burn throughout the day, with the chimney acting like its faithful companion, forcing the smoke out of the house and through the roof.

I would ask so many questions about the stove, and Grandma would answer patiently with a smile. The modern gas stove in the other corner simply adorned the kitchen; Grandma would barely use it because, like other people her age, she disliked technology.

With the help of the tongs, Grandma took the blackened potatoes smeared with ash out of the red-hot logs burning in the broad clay stove and dropped them on a round brass plate.

She peeled the potatoes one by one and broke the soft pale yellow-colored flesh into smaller chunks with her bare wrinkled hands. To add a savory flavor, she sprinkled powdered black salt over the steamy potatoes.

"Here!" said Grandma, "Grab the big one, my little munchkin. Your Grandpa used to like it...Mandy...so much...Mandy..."

Suddenly, the soft honey-like voice of Grandma started breaking and sounding hoarse, just like Jack's had. I guessed it was time for the invisible power to switch the extraordinary channel by bringing back the clouds of mist and transporting me to yet another incomprehensible site.

I waited, but the cloud of mist did not fill my surroundings this time. The images of Grandma and my brothers became a little hazy. I also felt that there was another voice reaching my ears, eclipsing that of Grandma's. This familiar voice became louder and louder.

"Mandy...Mandy!"

I opened my eyes and saw the bright and boney features of Grandma replaced with the tired and confused face of Viru.

It took me a few seconds to realize that I was in my house with Viru, and he was awake, right in front of my eyes. When I did, I wrapped him tightly in my arms and planted kisses on his mouth and all over his face.

"Oh, Viru! Honey, you woke up! I don't know what I would do without you."

"Are you ok, Mandy? I was just sleeping," returned Viru, taken aback by my sudden showering of affection and display of overwhelming emotions. He was perhaps wondering what he had done to deserve my barrage of kisses. "Why are you sleeping in Ryan's room?"

I would have held Viru in my arms for hours had my motherly instincts not kicked in at the mention of Ryan. I was relieved to find him awake, lying next to me, and Caesar just getting off the bed.

"Ryan! Are you ok, sweetie?" I asked, moving my fingers through his hair, and Ryan nodded.

"Why are you worked up, Mandy?"

"Where is Reva? Did she wake up?" I enquired, without caring to answer Viru's question.

"She is in the kitchen, making coffee. Why, what is wrong?"

"Nothing is wrong," I heaved another sigh of relief, "everything is right. Now, everything is right, Viru."

Viru studied my face carefully with confused eyes.

"I am fine, Viru. How are you feeling?"

"My head is ringing as if I have a hangover. I do not know how I overslept. It is 9 a.m. already! And you were sleeping too!"

"How does it feel?" I asked, realizing that Viru had no idea yet.

"My entire body is stiff. Last night was weird. I've never had so many dreams in one night. I don't have that many dreams in a month! It was like a courier guy piled up a stack for one month and delivered all the parcels in a big package on one day," replied Viru in a strange analogy.

"What kind of dreams?"

"I don't remember anything in particular. I just feel I had a lot of them. Except for the one where I saw you."

"Me? What did you see?"

"You were in some strange, foggy place and saying something to me. You were mean to me and complained a lot."

"Really? Like what?

"Like, I don't help enough in the household chores. You said I should turn off the bathroom light when I am done using it and must not enter the kitchen with shoes on."

"And that was mean to you? What did you say to me?"

"I did not say anything. Like a docile husband, I listened to you, just like I always do."

"Oh really! Like you always do? Great. Of all your

dreams that you think you had, you remember one and claim I was mean and complaining?" I returned with a mild chuckle, recalling the speech I made at the border of Jantar.

Reva appeared at the door holding the tray of warm coffee. She looked tired and anxious.

"Mom are you ok?" she asked, gently placing the tray on the side table. I hugged her. "Do you know it is Sunday today?"

"It is Saturday, Reva."

"It is Sunday, July 1st, Dad. We slept for two days."

"What nonsense! Don't talk silly," returned Viru, irritated.

"I swear, Dad. I just watched the news. Something crazy happened. They say a lot of people slept for two days straight. Many are sick, and some died."

"Kid, you better not be kidding. I don't like pranks in the morning," said Viru as he hurried out of the room.

"No prank, Dad, you can see it for yourself," returned the Daddy's girl, following him down to the living room with cups of coffee in both hands.

I heard the loud sound of the TV from the living room with channels switching in quick succession that oddly reminded me of the feeling of being part of each of them.

Equally loud was Viru's voice, expressing shock in phrases like, "What the hell?" and "Oh my God!"

I had no interest in joining them in watching the news of the disaster as I had lived through every part of it in the last two days. There was nothing that could surprise or shock me anymore. From now on, the words "unbelievable" or "impossible" would not have the same effect on me as before.

I gazed at Ryan affectionately. His sleepy eyes and innocent expression made me wonder if he really was the boy who thwarted the cruel intentions of the most powerful enemy.

Was it possible that I had not only witnessed an unimaginable and inexplicable course of events in my sleep, but also played an active role in it?

Was it possible that my helpless boy, who was cuddling up to me, had proved helpful to the entire world, our Loka, by averting the risk of extinction?

Was it possible that my son, who still found it difficult to wipe himself, had protected the entire species of living things from getting wiped off of the earth?

Was it possible that this nonchalant dog jumping up and down on the bed was a good Samaritan alien who carefully guarded my son against any danger?

Was it possible that the impossible was accomplished?

As I gently stroked Ryan's hair and lovingly moved my fingers along his face and down to his neck, I recalled how I had put the magical locket around his neck upon Jack's request.

It made me slightly uncomfortable when I did not find the locket around Ryan's neck.

Autumn

"Colorful trees in the fall, before their leaves fall,
like candles burning brightest before they flicker out.

Nature, the showman, saves her best act for last."

Chapter One

"That's the reason why I was hesitating to see you, but you insisted. I didn't want to tell you about my experience either because I knew you would think I was making up a crazy story. Nobody can believe that I had such an experience."

"Mandira, I think you misunderstood me. Firstly, I am glad that you came to see me upon my insistence and opened up to me. Sharing is an important step. I am in no way suggesting that you are making up a story. And I completely believe you when you say you had this experience. What I am trying to say is that your experience is that of perception."

"Perception? Of what?"

"Perception of something not present, something that did not happen for real. I can prove that to you."

"Oh, you can prove it! How? Are you saying that the C-cat that shook the entire world for two days was my perception? It did not happen for real?"

C-cat, short form of celestial catastrophe, was the fancy term given to the ugly disaster.

"I did not say that, Mandira. The C-cat did happen, but…"

"How do you think it happened?"

"Haven't you watched the news lately or read any newspapers? Don't you know what our scientists have to say?"

I was amused by Bob's mention of scientists as it reminded me of Jack's remarks on minners' science, which he believed was medieval.

"Ok, hear me out first and then decide for yourself. Have you heard of J-rays, Mandira?"

"Kind of. I have heard them talk about it on TV."

"Wait, let me show you a short documentary I recently watched on YouTube," continued Bob, "that will help you to understand perfectly."

Bob slid the drawer under his table open, reached out to the remote, turned the TV on, and sank back into his chair. The voice sounded like Sir David Attenborough and was supported by animations and visual graphics of outer space, that went something like this:

"The scientists at the Orbit Science and Technology Research Center have discovered traces of a new type of ray in the atmosphere, called J-rays. They observed that the concentration of these harmful rays on Earth was unusually high on the 29th of June, the fateful day when the biggest crisis known to humankind occurred. The scientists believe that these radiations were generated from a celestial activity called a supernova.

"To be more specific, it was a type 1a supernova. Let us understand more about this type. Type 1a supernovas occur between two stars orbiting one another in which one of the stars is a white dwarf.

"What is a white dwarf? White dwarfs are the hot, dense remnants of long-dead stars. They are thought to be the final evolutionary state of stars that no longer undergo fusion reactions.

"Now, when the orbiting companion star comes close enough to the white dwarf, entering the red giant stage, its outer layers are pulled off by the white dwarf. The mass of the white dwarf continues to increase due to the matter transferred from the other star until it reaches a critical mass. At this point, the white dwarf, that is too massive to be stable, explodes violently, causing a supernova.

"Supernovas are known to release tremendous energy, radiations like ultraviolet and gamma rays, and a huge number of subatomic particles in space. However, the discovery of the new J-rays came as a big surprise to the scientific community.

"This supernova happened 200 light-years away from the earth, and usually anything beyond 50-100 light years is considered a safe distance. But what is unusual is how these invisible rays managed to travel so far and penetrate the ozone layer and the earth's atmosphere for the first time ever known to humankind. But then, many things are unusual when it comes to celestial activities, and we humans have so much to learn.

"Early studies have shown that these rays are dangerous, and that their exposure causes extreme fatigue. High levels of their concentration can affect blood supply, which carries oxygen to the brain cells."

"Did you get it, Mandira?" said Bob, as he paused the video. "The reduced amount of oxygen supply to the brain causes unconsciousness. The severe impact of the radiations aided by the dropped levels of activity due to sleep caused unconsciousness in people in this part of the world. Many of them died due to cardiac arrest or stroke."

"Hmm, ok. First, I do not even understand how those J-rays dropped out of the blue. No scientist has talked about them before. Ever."

"Well, Mandira. These are not regular ultraviolet rays emitted from the sun that we all know about. They are generated from the explosion of stars. Supernovae are rare events, perhaps occurring two or three times in a century in galaxies like our own milky way. And they say, this one was the mother of all. You cannot know everything about such rare and enormous events."

"Ok, let us assume for a moment that those rays are for real and caused unconsciousness in this part of the world. What about the other part of the world? Why did people suffer sleeplessness there from the same rays?"

"Well, you must listen to our astronomers carefully. The extent of exposure to the rays is different in the daytime when you are out and about as compared to the night when you are in bed, and so is the level of human activity. The human body responds differently to the degree of fatigue. It depends upon the exposure to radiation and the vitals of individuals.

"In the eastern region, where people were up, most of them at work, the exposure to radiations catalyzed with the high level of activity caused extreme fatigue. Moreover, people panicked due to the news from the West, and the stimulated nervous system activity led to sleeplessness in most people. Many cases of deaths and unconsciousness were also reported. Thankfully, it did not last long, and the radiations soon diminished and dispersed, helping things to normalize."

"So, you believe that mere radiation turned the world upside down?"

"Of course, I do. What is there not to believe, Mandira? Ten years ago, we did not believe that a mere virus could cause a global pandemic and turn the world upside down. Now we do. Our outlook changes with the experience. Unbelievable things do happen."

"If you agree that unbelievable things do happen, why don't you believe in my experience?"

"Because there is no evidence in support of your experience. Your experience is nothing like a discovery of J-rays backed by the logic of the top scientists around the world. Nobody other than you can corroborate your account. Tell me, what does your husband have to say about your account?"

"I did not tell him," I returned hesitatingly.

"And why is that?"

"Well, I did not want to distract him. He has finally got a job after working so hard for the past few months. Besides, I don't think he will believe me."

"That's exactly my point. You are skeptical about telling your husband, the person whom you trust the most. Ok, forget your husband. You say your son accompanied you on that mysterious adventure. Does he recall this account exactly the way you do?"

"He would, but he has limited speech and difficulty in social interaction. You know that."

"I do. I am not expecting him to narrate the incident

exactly the way you do. But have you tried bringing the topic to his attention and getting his reaction? Does he give you any indication or express any knowledge that it happened? You are his mother. I am sure you can find out if he has any idea about the experience that you both have shared."

"I have not talked about this topic to him. It was an overwhelming experience for both of us, and I do not want to stress him out by mentioning it."

"Well, in that case," said Bob, not pursuing his point about Ryan further, perhaps realizing that I was sensitive to it, "the only other individuals who accompanied you on that expedition are the mysterious man that only you can see and your dog. I guess there is no way to get their confirmation," returned Bob with a tinge of sarcasm.

"What's your point, Bob?"

"I think you understand my point very well, Mandira. My point is that you had this experience all by yourself. Even the individuals you claim to have accompanied you cannot attest to it. What do you think it means?"

"What? You think I hallucinated all that time?"

"Yes, you did. I apologize for being blunt, but it is what it is. There is no other way to explain this. Here is what I think happened. You were one of those lucky people who woke up that morning while your husband, daughter, neighbors, and others in the town, including me, had long fallen unconscious in sleep. As I said, those radiations affected individuals differently.

"You took Caesar, another lucky chap who was awake, for a walk, thinking that your husband was asleep. You felt something unusual about the lonely walk.

"Upon returning, you tried to wake Viren and Reva but forgot to wake Ryan, who was fast asleep but not unconscious. You checked at your neighbors'. They did not wake either. Panic-stricken, you ran down the deserted street.

"So far, you were responding very well to my medications, but, at that time, due to excessive stress and perhaps the fatigue caused by the exposure to radiation, the hallucinations were triggered. And you saw that man you call Jack, which is nothing but a sensory experience created by your mind. I had also warned you against talking to Jack or any other stranger, but you ignored it."

"Ok, here's a question for you. You think Jack does not exist. Then how did he know something about Ryan that I did not? How did he know that Ryan was sleeping and had not passed out?"

"That is simple. It was not him. It was you. When you tried to wake Viren and Reva, your conscious mind, in a state of panic, did not register that you forgot to wake Ryan, but your subconscious mind did. The subconscious is the most exhaustive register of the activities of the human brain. 'Subconscious' refers to the domain of experience hidden from our awareness but impacts our behavior by manifesting habits, desires, fears, and attachment. Hallucinations can often be a reflection of what goes into the hidden box of our subconscious mind. So, your subconscious had already registered that you forgot to wake Ryan, but your conscious mind, impaired by hallucination, gave you the impression that a man with magical powers revealed it. A man who is a creation of your own mind."

"I think you've lost me."

"Ok, Mandira. To put it simply, you think Jack told you that Ryan was sleeping and had not passed out, when in fact, this thought was already seeded in your subconscious in the form of belief. In other words, Jack only told you what you believed to be true about your son. It is a coincidence that your belief about Ryan came true."

"So, according to you, I believed Ryan was fine, and it was a coincidence finding out that Ryan was sleeping and had not passed out."

"Yes."

"And Jack is my hallucination, and he tells me exactly what I know or believe."

"Yes, generally."

"Not a great argument, Doc, if it finishes with words like 'coincidently' and 'generally.'"

"Well, Mandira, the human brain is a mystery, like an infinite universe that we humans cannot claim to have tapped partially, let alone fully."

I felt the contradiction in Bob's remark, that on one side, he claimed to have figured out my brain, or rather, what he believed to be an impairment of my brain, and on the other side admitted that humans knew little about the mysterious brain. But I could not ignore an expert who had a Ph.D. in Psychiatry, whose arguments were backed by logic, whereas my experience lacked logic. I could not even have Ryan back it up.

"Now, when Ryan woke up," continued Bob, "all your doubts about the existence of Jack withered away. You began seeing him in a new light, as an extraordinary creature from an unknown world with magical powers who knew everything about this catastrophe. You believed that only he had the power to normalize the situation, or as you say, bring back the 'order,' a word you have repeatedly used while narrating your experience.

"A series of hallucinations and delusional events followed, perhaps because of stress and exposure to intoxicating radiations, giving you the impression of being transported into a bizarre world with extraordinary situations. You saw it as a grand turn of events where you and your son helped save the world from disaster. This visual fantasy went on until you passed out and were woken up by Viren in the morning when the toxic effect of radiations had subsided.

"When I analyze the pattern carefully, this person, Jack, acted in accordance with your desire. You had a desperate desire to see Viren and Reva again, and Jack gave you the solution. You also have a strong desire to see your son come out of his shell and make you proud. So, Jack created a universe where Ryan acted like a superhero, saving the world."

"What's your point, Doc?"

"My point is that Jack is just a creation of your mind, an agent that placates your desires."

"Well, first, I have never desired to see Ryan as a superhero. I just wanted a normal childhood for him. So, seeing him perform an extraordinary feat is a discovery, not a desire. Besides, I can recall every fine detail of this experience, and it makes sense to me. What proof do you have to claim that this is fake, just a hallucination or delusion, whatever you call it?"

Seeing that he perhaps had rubbed me the wrong way, Bob said in a mellow tone, "Mandira, I did not mean to offend you. Ryan certainly has potential like any other child. My son Ben is very fond of him and talks a lot about him. Let's focus on your experience. You think it makes sense to you, but I see several inconsistencies. Jack tells you about this head of a super organization who is managing our world and some other unknown worlds. Did he introduce you to this chief?"

"No, the chief could not see me because he is bound by the order."

"Exactly, he did not see you. Now, according to your story, there is another person, the chief's son, who is trying to destroy the world. Did you see him?"

"No."

"Why? Is he also bound by the order?"

"No. I don't know. He is secretly trying to destroy the world. How could he turn up openly in front of Jack?"

"I see. So, you did not see the son either. Think about it. Doesn't this experience feel like a Hollywood movie? You were accompanied by your son and dog and interacting with a person—the only person—who showed you stunning visuals like CGI from a big budget movie?"

"But I did see hundreds of thousands of humans and animals."

"As you do in the movies. There are many characters, but you do not meet or interact with them all. You did not interact with anyone other than Jack. Before you ask again what my point is, let me say this. What you experienced is a condition called 'delusion of grandeur' aided by visual hallucinations. In the delusion of grandeur, one may believe that they have a special relationship with some supernatural entity, with whom they can communicate and perform some extraordinary tasks.

"In schizophrenia, hallucinations and delusions often go together. Many times, hallucinations reinforce delusions, like in your case. The good news is that your commitment to the hallucinations and false beliefs is not rigid like in some other cases. You possess the cognitive skills to challenge your delusional beliefs when presented with evidence or reasoning."

To prove my point to Bob, I could further argue about how I addressed sleeping Viru from the misty border of Jantar, and he remembered it. But when I had not shared my entire experience with Viru, citing him in a small part of it did not feel right. Moreover, Bob would perhaps attribute it to the delusion of knowing something in advance that my husband had told me. I realized I didn't have to prove anything to Bob more than I needed to myself.

Chapter Two

I came out of Dr. Bob's clinic in a state of unsureness. My perception of having played a phenomenal role in an otherworldly scenario that decided the future of life on earth had taken a massive hit during the last hour of counseling. He had challenged with his humanly logic what felt like my experience of heavenly magic.

Bob did not believe in the slightest possibility of my experience being true. In fact, according to him, the belief that I had been harboring for the last few months was a false belief, a wild creation of my mind. It was hard to ignore him in the light of the reasoning he had given for every event.

Moreover, he was no regular minner of Loka, but an expert psychiatrist, and I wondered if terms like "minner" and "Loka" that nowadays sounded familiar in my head could also be a creation of my mind.

Sitting on a bench at the Summerhill Metro Station, waiting for the metro, I remembered how the past few months had gone. There was big chaos around the world for two or three weeks after those fateful days (or nights) following the C-cat. Patients flooded hospitals with ill health, anxiety, stress, and other mental and emotional conditions. People recovering from the fatigue, excruciating body aches, and health ailments were horrified. There was a general terror of sleep as people feared they might never wake up again.

The media throughout the world went berserk. Several theories of global destruction, mass extinction, alien attack, and divine intervention cropped up every day, sending chills down the spines of the general public. The general harmony amongst people during this period grew stronger globally. The undying spirit of humans was vastly appreciated.

It was not long until scientists discovered a supernova explosion somewhere far, far away in the galaxy that sent out a new kind of radiation called J-rays along with the usual ultraviolet, gamma rays, and subatomic particles. This discovery, followed by evidence and reasoning produced by prominent scientists worldwide, put all the other scary theories to rest. Not to say that this was not scary enough, but better than the theory of mass extinction, as people were expecting the worst.

Scientists reassured the public that it was a one in a thousand years scenario in which those rays could make their way through to the earth's protective shield. Another reassuring thing about the rays was that they did not last in the earth's atmosphere for long, though they were highly intoxicating. Although these rays had proved to be extremely hazardous to health, fatalities were not significant.

Viru was glued to the TV for a day or two, trying to figure out the whole C-cat event, but when he could not, he got back to his job hunt. The long sleep had a surprisingly positive effect on him as he dropped the serious demeanor he'd had since his job loss and became the nonchalant Viru of old times.

I did not share my extraordinary escapade of conscious sleep with Viru, as it was something beyond his comprehension. How could he, or anyone, for that matter, believe in the mere idea of such a thing when I still had doubts about its possibility after experiencing the whole thing?

Viru was in good spirits, and I did not want to distract him or make him think I was going crazy. Moreover, telling him that Ryan and I played a role in saving the world was a perfect recipe to invite his unfunny jokes for weeks, let alone days. Though he had been empathetic towards me lately, I knew the man could not stay away from his jokes for long.

About a month later, he found a job as a project director for a multinational company and got busy with work.

I had noticed an improvement in Ryan's speech and social interaction since the C-cat, but I could not tell if it was him who had changed or just my outlook towards him.

I had lied to Bob today when he asked if Ryan could confirm the events, and I said that I had never brought the topic to his attention. I had broached the subject many times, hoping he would say something, light up, smile, nod approvingly, or give me any other clue about his awareness. But he did nothing. On the contrary, he would gaze at me as if he had no idea of what I talked about, like he was tongue-tied.

I had indeed started seeing Ryan as a superhero, as Bob mentioned, but that was because I witnessed him performing an extraordinary feat and not because I just desired to see him become an extraordinary boy.

When he did not seem to be on board with the mind-blowing experience that we mutually experienced, an element of doubt started to seep into the thin walls of my fragile mind. How could Ryan be indifferent about a defining experience of his life? That was also a big reason for not telling Viru, because I feared Ryan would keep mum and not support my claim.

I had developed a new respect for Caesar after our visit to Shloka (when Jack had declared him a keeper deputed to protect Ryan), but honestly, he did not do anything special to keep up the reputation. He continued to be like before, a mischievous dog who played with my son all the time and irritated Viru with his antics while on morning walks.

Reva had debated the possible causes of C-cat with her father for a few days, and soon, like her father, got back to her routine. A month later, she entered her first teenage year and a new chapter of her life.

A new family had recently moved into the neighborhood. While the social and outgoing Mr. and Mrs. King had spread warmth in a short time by throwing barbecue parties on Sunday afternoons, their two young boys were spreading their charm among the girls of the neighborhood.

The older boy, fourteen-year-old Timothy King, was fond of Reva and looked for every opportunity to talk to her. Tim was an exceptionally handsome boy with brown, silky hair and a chiseled, oval face. His infectious smile cut deep dimples into both his cheeks. Ignoring him initially, followed by hesitating to talk to him, Reva could not avoid his charisma and magnetism for long and finally made friends with Tim. She also started taking more walks in the neighborhood than usual.

Reva maintained that he was just a friend, but with the way she blushed upon the mention of Tim's name, it was clear that she regarded him as more than that.

Viru appeared to be cool about their curious friendship, but he set some ground rules. He made it clear that there could be no hanging out outside the house, and if Tim wanted, he could only meet her in our house in my presence.

The youngest member of the King family and the brother of Timothy was nine-year-old Theodore. The green-eyed, good-looking boy Theodore—or Ted—was naughty and super talkative. It was no surprise that he made good friends with Britney Hayden. Every evening they played in her yard and talked all the time, as if playing a game called "who talks the most." Sometimes Britney and Ted talked simultaneously, and I wondered if they listened to each other at all.

After finishing with Bob, it took me an hour's journey on the metro from Summerhill—the last stop on the green line—all the way back to my home stop in Abbynton. As the metro stopped at Saint Thomas Station, so did my train of thought upon being greeted by a familiar face.

"Mandira! Good to see you. What a great day to be alive!" said Sebastian enthusiastically.

"Oh, Seb. You and your great days. Why is every day great for you?"

"Why not? Autumn is the best season of the year. Haven't you seen it outside? Those beautiful trees with colorful leaves look like the splendid ladies dressed in red, orange, and pink gowns, celebrating life."

"Yes, and you know autumn is also called fall, the trees shedding leaves. Those ladies will drop their gowns and stand in the cold, naked in a week or two. What would they have to celebrate then?"

"Ha ha, you are funny, Mandira. Another way to look at it is that those trees, after bravely bearing a healthy lifecycle of leaves and fruits, will shed their burdens and prepare to embrace the next chapter of their life."

"Such heavy analogies. You should've been my philosophy professor. Even he could not have compared the trees with the ladies dressed in colorful gowns."

"If I were your professor, you would sleep through my lectures. I am better off being a homeless old man with no filter. I can talk whatever rubbish I want."

"You call it rubbish? Your rubbish is so much better than that of others. I wish I could talk like that. You are so full of positive energy. Give me some tips, Professor Sebastian. I want to be carefree and happy like you."

"Well, if I tell you that happiness is a state of mind, you will laugh at me and call me a professor again. So, here's your tip: Do something that gives you pleasure and makes you forget all your worries."

"Like what? I don't know any such thing."

"Are you kidding me? Do you need a hint from me? Cook, good woman, cook."

"Oh, cooking! I do that every day."

"Not regular cooking. Cook one of those best dishes that you love, those Mandira specials that only you can make. And bring some over for me to taste. When are you making those delicious sugar balls? It has been almost a year."

"Oh, that sugar ball is called gulab jamun. I will make it

for Diwali. I will make a lot of sweets. You just need to wait for a month."

The little chitchat and friendly bantering with Sebastian always cheered me up.

Back home, I found the children in the front yard. It had been about an hour since they had returned from school. Standing at the half-opened gate, Reva was multitasking by watching Ryan and Britney in the yard (in my and Elena's absence) and talking to her friend Tim, who was leaning on the gate from the other side. Technically, Reva was following the protocol that Daddy had laid out by not inviting Tim in the house without me and not hanging out with him outside the house.

On her side of the yard, Britney was riding her bike with Ted walking by her side. Both were talking and barely listening to each other.

While Britney was busy playing "who talks the most" with Ted, Ryan settled for his usual dumb charades with Caesar. Ryan, as usual, was sitting on the doorstep of his house with his only buddy Caesar trying to please him. He was looking over at Britney with his keen eyes. Though he rarely expressed anything through his eyes or actions, I could make out that he was not pleased with the presence of Britney's new friend.

Britney had always been fond of Ryan, but nowadays, she rarely talked to him. She had persistently tried to impress Ryan for years, but now it seemed that the threshold of her patience had been crossed. Perhaps, she had accepted that Ryan was incapable of paying attention to her, let alone reciprocating her liking towards him. She believed that Ryan did not care for anyone other than his dog, and certainly not her, but I could see in those envious eyes that she was all he cared for.

Britney did not realize how much it hurt Ryan to see her play with Ted, or perhaps she did, and that was what she really wanted.

And who could be better than Ted, a boy who had the

gift of nonstop talking, to make the mute Ryan jealous? Forget in real life, Ryan could not compete with that talker in his dreams! The thought of dreams suddenly reminded me of the trip to Shloka, and I felt the irony of my opinion about Ryan.

Shortly afterwards, Elena returned from work, and the Haydens, the Kings, and the Sharmas went back to their abodes.

In the evening, while at the dinner table, Viru shared anecdotes of his day at work. He was having a good time with his new job and had had something funny to share every evening.

On this occasion, he spoke about his boss, who often prefixed his sentences with a catchphrase, "To be honest...." Viru said how in a conference call with a customer, his boss used the phrase six times. After the fifth time he said, "To be honest," their Vice President returned, "Jeff, we really appreciate your honesty, but where are the results?" To which he replied, "We are working on it, Peter. It's our top priority for this quarter, to be honest." And the catchphrase, used for the sixth time, only changed place from prefix to suffix in the last sentence.

Viru then gave a demo of how he almost fell off his chair after listening to Jeff's response, which made Reva, who had been giggling all this time, burst out with laughter. Repeating the best line of the joke over and over and becoming more animated each time was something that Viru had learned from his friend Sylvain, and it worked well with his cheerleader daughter Reva.

I never understood his work jokes and how he found them funny. The PAT story was one of his jokes that I had heard many times, as Viru would make it a point to tell it during every party or gathering.

PAT, as Viru explained, was a term used for business results, a short form of Profit After Tax. After hearing the term multiple times, a confused guy in one of those conference calls asked the host to spell out PAT. Perhaps he heard something like "Phad" or "Padh" that sounded alien to him.

Instead of simply giving the abbreviation as "profit after tax," the guy on the other side spelled out PAT like this: "P as in papa, A as in asking, and T as in T." Either he could not think of any word for the letter T, or the word was "tea." So, the PAT became "papa asking tea."

It was a running joke at Viru's office and at home for days. Reva would sometimes come to me as a messenger of Daddy and say, "Mom, PAT."

Viru made fun of the King junior, Timothy, trying to tease Reva. He would never call the boys by their names. He referred to them as "the grooms." Timothy was groom number one, and Theodore was groom number two. Lately, he had simply called them Number One and Number Two.

It all started with one of our dinner table conversations a few months ago, when I remarked that the boys were well-groomed. Like a comedian craving for content, Viru picked up the word "groom" out of context, and the rest is history.

Reva would not get offended by Daddy's bantering and always took his jokes sportingly. Over the years, my clever girl had learned that reaction would tempt Daddy to build upon his jokes, making it a never-ending cycle. However, when she played along, Daddy would lose the fun in the bantering and move on to another topic. Moreover, Reva was his only cheerleader in the house, so Viru would not push her.

I told Viru that it was not cool to make jokes about children, but then Viru's jokes were never guided by moral principles.

While Viru joked and Reva chuckled at the dinner table, Ryan and Caesar, as usual, were the silent spectators. Ryan, my boy of few words, would listen to all the dinner table conversations quietly without reacting to anything. His replies to general questions about the food, school, et cetera would be monosyllabic and could not lead to a conversation, and I did not press him.

If our extraordinary feat of Shloka had not done the trick, I hoped at least Estelle's work with Ryan on his speech and social interaction skills over the past few months would produce the desired results to some extent. A feedback session with his schoolteachers was scheduled for the next week's parent-teacher meeting, and I hoped to hear something positive for a change this time.

Only Ryan brought out the sensitive side of the otherwise flamboyant and nonchalant Viru. He would always treat Ryan with care and affection and spared him from his jokes.

In bed, next to me, Viru snored like a satisfied peasant who had ploughed the farmland all day under the scorching sun, whereas sleep was miles away from my eyes. The meeting with Bob today had left some serious doubts in my mind about my experience during the time of the celestial catastrophe.

This had been my second appointment with Bob since the C-cat, and today he'd had a good explanation to prove the experience as a delusion of grandeur and hallucinations.

Initially, I was reluctant to visit Dr. Bob as I figured that the concept of getting transported to a mystical world in your sleep and returning with no memory of it was beyond anyone's comprehension. Moreover, if I told anyone that Ryan had fixed the order and prevented the catastrophe, I would certainly become a laughingstock.

But then Ryan's indifference, Caesar's stupidity, scientific explanations of C-cat, and Jack's sudden disappearance and no show afterwards made me curious. The secret was killing me, and I felt the pressing need to share it with someone who could hear me out without judging and provide some guidance. So, I could not blame it entirely on Bob's insistence, as I had decided to see him.

Viru made an effort to show he cared by offering to accompany me to the clinic, but I told him that they were just routine appointments as I did not hallucinate anymore, like I initially told him.

I would be adamant had Bob simply brushed aside my

account as some wild fantasy. But he gave me a patient hearing as if he believed in everything I said at first, and then pointed out several inconsistencies and flaws in my description, and I found it difficult to counter his arguments. His detailed account of what he thought happened in my case was equally believable, if not more so, and he backed it with explanation using terms like "conscious," "subconscious," "hallucinations," "delusions," et cetera, which I could not comprehend fully, but they sounded convincing.

Despite Bob's excellent arguments, it was hard to believe that I had one long episode of hallucination or delusion, whatever he called it. Not for a few minutes or hours, but for a day or two days, and only on the fateful day of disaster.

How could hallucinations transport me to a fairytale-ish world that felt impossible but also real at the same time? And what were the odds of Ryan and Caesar being unaffected by the so-called radiations when everything else around us was falling apart?

Though Bob had good reason to blame it on the amount of exposure, I still wondered how people in different geographies responded differently to the radiations. And what about the sleep coma and wake-up syndrome that had perplexed the scientists and health experts long before the C-cat?

The more I thought about it, the harder it became to come to a logical conclusion, and to get some sleep. I was determined to find out the truth and had made up my mind on something, the thought of which made me nervous.

The following two weeks before I met Bob again for my next appointment were going to bring an alarming revelation into my life.

Chapter Three

After my appointment with Bob, I was confused. The surreal experience of the journey to Shloka was ingrained in my mind, but then Bob had pointed out flaws in it and a convincing argument that it was nothing but a complex combination of hallucinations and delusions.

I was up all night trying to solve this crazy riddle. Since my sleep was not kind to me and often evaded me, I researched how it worked (well, according to humans, or should I say the minners of Loka).

There are four stages of sleep involving two main types: non-rapid eye movement (NREM), also known as quiet sleep, and rapid eye movement (REM), also called active sleep. Our body cycles through NREM and REM sleep. Stage one NREM is the transition period between wakefulness and sleep, while NREM stages two and three bring deep sleep. Finally, we transition into stage four, known as REM. Most of our dreams occur during this stage.

When I thought about it, my magical journey of sleep accompanied by Jack, Ryan, and Caesar, was also comprised of four legs, or stops—Antar, Jantar, Mantar, and Shloka.

Antar was the transition from the world that we knew to that unknown place. Jantar and Mantar felt like we were digging deeper into the world to understand how it worked, and, finally, Shloka was a series of bizarre, unconnected, and unrelated visuals, much like dreams.

On some level, I felt that the process of sleep correlated with this magical journey. The four stages of brain activity that we experience regularly and refer to as sleep could be mapped to a continuous passage cutting through four perceived regions. After all, the brain is the ultimate control center, a window to our perception of the world. If a set of brain activities while being awake can bring awareness to the world we know, why can't another set of brain activities introduce us to a distinctive world while we sleep?

But then another part of my brain activity cautioned me not to swim in the deep sea of science fiction and urged me to return to the surface of practicality. It pointed towards a practical explanation that my knowledge of the four stages of sleep perhaps contrived an imaginary world of four regions. After all, as per Bob, visual hallucinations are often inspired by what we know or think.

I could not continue to sit on an unsolved puzzle and let uncertainty guide my future and ruin my sleep. I was desperate to take the path of action and cease to sit at the edge of indecision. That night I hit upon an idea. I made a plan and hoped that its success would help to clear the cloud of confusion.

The very next day, I got the opportunity to execute my plan. It was the Labor Day holiday. Viru took a flight in the morning for a business trip to attend a management meeting in Vancouver the next day, the location of his new company's headquarters.

Reva had plans to visit Abbynton with her friends, including her best pal Timothy, and she would not return until late in the evening. Viru had already granted her permission to go before he left.

So, the three musketeers were left in the house. I was nervous. I could either make some headway or completely fool of myself, and the probability of the latter seemed to be higher. But I knew I had to try the experiment.

After lunch, I told Ryan that we would take a nap together, and he gave his tacit concurrence like he always did. We went to Ryan's room. Caesar, as usual, did not need an invitation to join us, and the three of us huddled and cuddled together somewhat uncomfortably on the little bed.

One minute, two minutes, five minutes, and ten minutes passed. Ryan, by now, was breathing heavier, and Caesar, lying on the edge of the bed, had ceased to move.

I realized that it was a stupid idea. I was about to get off the bed when I noticed that I had missed a step of the process. So, I lay on my side, facing Ryan, slipped my right arm under his head like an extra layer of a pillow, clasped his hand with my left hand, and closed my eyes.

Within a minute, I felt like I was falling off the bed, but did not open my eyes. Then, the great fall happened, and I knew that the transition from wakefulness to sleep, or in other words, from Loka to Antar, had begun. After a considerable amount of time, I landed on the bed of warm, snow-like white sand.

I was on the magnificent island of Jantar. With a smile of accomplishment, I rose from the glittering sand and walked around the majestic, all-seasons trees and twinkling, colorful gem rocks. I did not watch after Ryan and Caesar, as I was positive that they would be around. My eyes were searching for somebody else, and I was not disappointed.

"Hello, Mandira!"

I looked over my shoulder in the direction of the familiar voice and found Jack emerging from behind a huge tree (or from the tree, I wasn't sure), holding a small turtle in his hands.

"I knew you would come back here to see me. It's never safe to tell my tricks to a smart lady like you," he said with a smile.

"You left me no other option, did you?"

"Ok, if you say so. But you should only use my trick for an emergency. You know, you have used administrator access to get here?"

"Administrator access?"

"Yes, the access with more privileges, only meant for

keepers. Minners make their journey through normal user access with fewer privileges," said Jack, placing the turtle on a rock and patting its shiny back gently.

"You sound like an IT guy," I chuckled.

"Oh, we do have an IT and security department here. They maintain the database of all minner user accounts. So, every time you use administrator access, it's a violation of security policy, and I need to get an exception approval from the head, Dr. Lockman Keyhole."

"Let me get this straight. So, when the minners sleep, they get access to the journey with less privilege, something you call 'user access.' Is that why they don't know anything about this world?"

"Yes, with user access, minners can make the journey but cannot retain any memory of the experience. Anyways, all of that is for our IT keepers to take care of. Tell me, what brings you here?"

"What brings me here? Well, the countless questions popping in my head brought me here, Jack. Those questions have been begging for answers since you disappeared. And that brings me to my first question. Why did you disappear suddenly after the big day and never come to see me again?"

"What else do you expect, Mandira? I am a small employee of Kendram. I can pay a visit for business, not for pleasure. I am not allowed to bond with clients. I must be professional, and that's how it works here. I was with you on a mission and had to get back as soon as it finished."

"I see. So, your business is to take me on a mission and turn my life upside down. But what about the confusion and mental agony that resulted from the mission, that's not your business?"

"I apologize for the distress caused to you, Mandira. I will try to clear up your confusion. Tell me, what is bothering you?"

"This is bothering me—talking to you, a weird alien who nobody knows. I close my eyes and arrive at this magical place. I cannot wrap my head around all this. I don't know if this is true!"

"Do you still need proof after using my trick and coming here without my help, Mandira? If you keep doubting it, you will never be content."

"What do you expect, Jack, if you suddenly vanish and don't show up again? I need to see the magic frequently to assure myself that all this is true. When you suddenly take away all these weird experiences and make my life mundane again, you automatically create space for doubt in my mind."

"I can see why you feel that way. You live in Loka, the place of minners who have no knowledge of this. They don't know that invisible forces are controlling and managing the ecosystem without directly interfering in their lives. But you have seen everything. You must believe it," returned Jack.

I noticed that he had added fancy words like "ecosystem" into his vocabulary since our last meeting. And I had no idea why I only noticed that, of all things, in this situation.

Jack pointed towards a distant, large tree with a broad trunk. I squinted my eyes and nodded upon finding Ryan and Caesar sitting on one of the branches that almost touched the ground. I had forgotten about them.

"Ryan was here with us last time, just like he is now," I said. "He opened the gate to Shloka and saved the minners. Then why doesn't he say anything or seem to know about it when I ask him?"

"Let me ask you something in the way that minners of Loka can understand. When you see a dream in your sleep, do you expect Viren saw it too? No. Because that is your dream, only you see it. Similarly, this is your journey because you have initiated it. Only you can have a partial or complete memory of it.

"It was a tricky situation last time. Only Monsieur Ryan could save Loka, and I needed to convince you to permit him to do so, so, I had to tag him on your journey. He saved Loka in your journey but has no memory of it. Today you used my trick to tag him again. You will remember it when you get back to Loka, but he won't, as it is your conscious journey, not his, and he is simply tagging along. My trick is for special cases. You should not use it often."

"So, he doesn't know anything about this place?"

"He does. As I told you before, he knows everything. He can see all the keepers. He remembers every route of Jantar and Mantar by heart. Minners only remember some snapshots of Shloka that they call 'dreams.' But Ryan has the power to explore and remember every part of his daily journey. *His* journey. Not yours or anyone else's."

"Give me one reason why he doesn't give me any clue of all that he sees or knows."

"You asked for one; I will give you many. One, he was born that way. He is present in Loka but also detached from it. It is hard for him to say much. The Supreme made him like that. Perhaps he had some motive behind it. Maybe he will change, or your love will change him.

"Two, you have dedicated all your life to protecting Ryan and worrying about him. He understands that. Perhaps he does not want to bother you more by exposing you to another side of his life that he knows is beyond the comprehension of minners.

"Three, you do not trust his potential, despite witnessing how he saved your Loka. Monsieur Ryan derives power from your confidence and trust in him. Unfortunately, your faith in your son's capabilities keeps shaking, and so does your belief in the existence of the world outside Loka. How can he confide in you or anyone when he thinks they will not believe him?"

I became thoughtful.

"Mandira, we must keep moving while we talk," said Jack, then he shouted, "Hello Monsieur Ryan and mon cher Caesar, come over here! Time to move."

Ryan and Caesar jumped off the tree and came running. I noticed the locket sitting on Ryan's neck.

"Are we going to walk on water now?" I asked, pointing towards the blue sea.

"No, Miss Mandira. New day, new way," returned Jack as

he stomped his foot on the ground. Suddenly, the white sand underneath his boots scattered, like a bed of dry leaves distributed by a leaf blower, and a white, granite-like floor appeared. In a moment, the granite floor cut into halves and slid open, making way for underground steps.

As I walked down the countless steps in the dark, holding hands with Ryan, I could only spot Caesar and Jack—walking one and two steps ahead of us, respectively—thanks to the slight beams of light emerging from the steps that would glow brighter as we stepped our feet and faded back to their original state upon removing them. It felt like we were walking on a piano with light-up keys.

At last, we arrived at what looked like a well-lit subway station platform that was sparsely populated by men and women. They were all wearing black cloaks and hats, just like Jack.

"Where are we, Jack? Who are these people?" I asked.

"We are at the station, waiting for the metro. These are keepers like me, the employees of Kendram, who work in various departments. Some of them work at the branch office of Jantar, and others work at the local offices of Mantar and Shloka. This underground way connects to all the offices. It is a shortcut to go to any of the sites. Only keepers are authorized to use it."

The keepers were exchanging glances at each other and seemed to be smiling at me. In the next moment, I realized it was not me they were looking at; they were all smiling at Ryan. Their excitement at seeing Ryan was like that of children delighted upon seeing their favorite toy.

Just then, the metro arrived at the platform. Living up to the standard of this magical place, it did not look anything like a conventional metro. It was a moving unit of many spherical glass balls connected in a sequence, looking like a giant chain of glass beads strung together that flew about a foot above the white granite floor.

The metro halted, and the glass compartments touched the ground. Jack walked towards the nearest compartment, and so did other keepers.

I was waiting for the doors of the glass balls to slide open, but nothing of that sort happened. Jack simply got sucked into the ball. I followed him, along with Ryan and Caesar, into the ball with slight hesitation. The metro rose from the ground, attained its previous height, and started to move.

Like Ryan, I could have spent some time being awestruck by the amazing ride, but I had resolved to clear my doubts and spare no time for distractions.

"So, these keepers are the employees of Kendram who work here, right?" I asked, glancing at the passengers in the adjoining glass chambers.

"Yes, but not all. The head office is in Parloka. All the big shots, including chief Joseph, sit there."

"I saw one like them in Loka."

"Yes, and you know the reason why you saw me."

"Oh, no, not you. I saw one man with a similar hat and cloak back in the springtime. We were heading back home from the tulip gardens when out of nowhere, this person suddenly appeared in front of my car, and I stopped."

"Really? What did he look like?"

"Don't remember exactly. He disappeared after a few seconds. He was tall and strong. His eyes looked furious. It looks like only I could see him. Or perhaps Caesar also, as he was barking incessantly. Just before that, we saw a wild-looking bear that blocked the narrow road and zig-zagged ahead of my car. Everything was weird."

"I think I can explain. The person you saw was probably Hogdon, and the bear was Duma."

"What? Hogdon?" I was shocked. "That evil son of the chief you talked about? The one who closed the gate of Shloka, causing havoc in Loka? That Hogdon?"

"Yes, Mandira, that Hogdon."

"But why? Why did he show up? Oh my God! Was he there to kill us? Is he after Ryan?"

"Relax, Mandira," returned Jack, sensing my panic, "he

will not do such a foolish thing. He was trying to scare you with that bear, Duma."

"How do you know? If he can show up to scare us, why can't he kill us?"

"Because Monsieur Ryan is famous in Parloka. All the keepers know about him. Did you say this incident happened in springtime?"

"Yes," I nodded.

"So, it happened before the big event when Monsieur Ryan saved Loka. After that big accomplishment, he is now a prime contender for the next chief. Hogdon, also a contender, is his opponent. As per the rules, the contenders cannot see each other before the Meet. Hogdon cannot risk losing his chance to contest for the chief's role."

"What is the Meet?"

"The Meet is the official selection process of the next chief. Joseph and the board of Kendram will conduct it. It will happen after Monsieur Ryan turns twelve. Before that period, contenders are not allowed to see each other. If they do, they will lose their eligibility for the Meet. Hogdon or any other contender cannot see Ryan, let alone harm him or his family."

I was in a state of mind in which processing the information seemed as abstract as believing it. I wondered if my son was becoming a victim of the grand designs of these otherworldly forces. I could not help thinking that that devil had made a threatening appearance along with his bear. When he could attempt to wipe out the entire Loka for no apparent reason, what rules would stop him from eliminating my son, his prime enemy?

"Jack, what you say is not helping. Your argument of relying on the judgment of an eccentric dagger, who does not care for the rules of the selection process, does not inspire confidence for my son's safety. I am scared for my boy. Clearly, we are surrounded by the enemy. How can we feel safe? Hogdon could have killed us that day. Who could have saved us had he attempted to?"

"Er, you forget something. Your prime savior lives with you."

"Who? Ryan?"

"Well, Monsieur Ryan is the ultimate guardian. But the one who protects you from danger is mon cher Caesar."

"Caesar!" I exclaimed, glancing at the dog, who was busy licking Ryan's hand. "This Caesar? Really?"

"Yes, this Caesar. I think it's time for me to tell his story, which I did not finish last time," replied Jack. He did what looked like a typing action with his fingers in the air, and the metro stopped.

"Let's go to the lounge, and I will tell you."

We got off the metro—or should I say our large, round, bubble-like compartment. The bubble did not burst with our contact at its wall, but temporarily altered in shape at the place we exited.

Next, a blinding flash of white light appeared before my eyes, and we found ourselves in a large, round hall. It was all white; the floor, the round walls, and the ceiling. It felt like we were inside a giant white capsule. There was no furniture in this lounge, but several keepers in their black attire were sitting comfortably, as if on invisible chairs or couches. All eyes in the lounge rested on us as we walked in, and smiles were directed at Ryan.

"You can take a seat, Mandira," said Jack.

"Take a seat? But where and how?" I asked.

"Anywhere you like. See, like this," Jack dropped his body backward and was supported midway by something that made a gentle crushing sound. He then comfortably rested in the air. After some hesitation, I let myself fall, hoping that I didn't break my back, and landed safely on an invisible beanbag.

This was the perfect play area for Ryan and Caesar, and they were having much fun. They jumped high in the air and landed on invisible cushions without hitting the ground.

"How do you like this underground place? There's a city here called Keeperton that I'll show you some other time. It was designed by Sir Doug Downunder. The keepers run most of their operations down here."

I wondered if Jack purposely made up funny names, or if those experts were christened after their accomplished tasks, like Sir Doug Downunder for digging under the ground and Sir Lockman Keyhole for displaying prowess with locks and keys.

It was fascinating to learn about this place, but my prime goal was to know about the things concerned directly with my family. Before Jack's thoughts could wander into the city of Keeperton, I redirected him back to the topic of Caesar. What followed was a startling revelation.

Chapter Four

Jack told me that Caesar was a keeper. In fact, an important one. He explained that Kendram, a central governing body (or the parent organization) headquartered in Parloka, managed the operations of Shloka and Loka with the help of local entities, the child organizations. While the city of Keeperton, located in Jantar, managed the order of Shloka, another child organization called Rudram was responsible for managing Loka.

Jack did not divulge details but seemed to suggest that Loka was always at the edge of danger from unknown forces or events, and Rudram had protected it. Keepers of Loka ran Rudram.

The keepers of Loka had neither distinct appearance nor donned unique attire that would distinguish them from the minners, like those of Jack and his buddies. They largely led a regular life, mingling perfectly with humans (and animals) who would never realize their true identity.

The keepers of Loka were represented by a head keeper, the leader of Rudram. Though anyone backed by the majority could lay claim over the title position, the contenders for the top job mostly came from the three key political parties.

The parties were headed by the keeper-bears, the keeper-dogs, and the keeper-humans. Most of the keepers of Loka joined one of these parties or switched between them according to their choice.

Historically, Rudram was dominated by the keeper-bears for the longest time until the arrival of Meena, a feisty female dog, who led the keeper-dogs to victory through a selection process to become the first female to head Rudram. She defeated Duma, her opponent, an aggressive keeper-bear.

The humiliating defeat from a female dog did not go down well with Duma, who murdered the pregnant dog in a cold-blooded rage. Dying Meena delivered three puppies, out of which only one survived. This puppy later went on to become the head of Rudram.

The incident caused a widespread furor, in Rudram and Kendram alike. The keepers were known to be peaceful watchdogs, and they had no history of crime. Duma was tried in the highest court of Kendram. Hogdon had always had a soft spot for bears, and Duma enjoyed his tacit support.

Hogdon used bears to keep his influence in Loka, and a few wise keepers wondered if he had incited Duma to eliminate Meena.

Duma was set for harsh punishment, but his lawyers—supported by Hogdon—argued that eliminating Duma would start a never-ending animosity between the keeper dogs and bears, as many bears still quietly supported Duma.

Anyways, Duma was not eliminated but instead exiled to the wilderness. He was thrown out of the keeper clan and barred from seeing or meeting anyone forever.

Presently he wandered in wild, secluded, and deserted areas away from the places inhabited by minners and keepers. A few believed that he still enjoyed the support of some wicked keeper-bears and, of course, the blessing of Hogdon.

"No wonder you found Hogdon and Duma on that lonely road. Daggers normally operate in secluded places, hiding away from the secure keeper zones," added Jack.

"So, Mandira. No prize for guessing who's the head of

Rudram?"

"It's Caesar. My Caesar," I returned, gazing affectionately at Caesar, who was busy playing with Ryan. They were jumping high in the air and landing on invisible cushions without hitting the ground. All the keepers in the lounge were delighted to see them having fun.

"Well, then why worry about safety when the leader of Rudram lives with you? Not only that, some of our best keeper soldiers of Loka have been deployed for your security."

"Really? We have security?"

"Yes, you do. It's called Watch Force. This job is usually done in invisible mode by the keepers, so you don't see them. Keepers have the power to become invisible to any minner. Monsieur Ryan is the only minner who can see all the keepers. Keepers cannot hide from him. Now that I think of it, you often see one of your keeper soldiers."

"Oh, I see them? Who?"

"Samantha."

"Samantha?"

"Yes, the girl you see in the morning running up to Mount Mary Hills."

Of course, I thought, *No wonder why I see her every single morning. I always thought there was something with that girl, something peculiar about that disciplined running, the punctuality, unfazed by the harshest weather conditions.* I remembered talking to her one time when I was walking Caesar in the morning, and she stopped by to admire him.

Jack's many revelations in quick succession had ceased to produce a shocking effect on me. Hereupon nothing would seem impossible to me. The word "practical" would no longer hold any meaning to me. The line between real and imaginary would be blurred forever. I would not have been surprised if Jack told me next that he could turn me into a cat.

All I cared about was trying to absorb as much information as possible, and gladly my threshold to absorb abstract information had acquired new levels hitherto unknown to me.

"Mandira, I have shared a good deal of information with you. I urge you to stop suspecting and start believing. You will not help your son if you continue to doubt his potential. Look at these keepers, how they adore Monsieur Ryan, their future chief. He's the only minner who will one day lead Kendram, the greatest organization ever. Remember, he's like no one, and no one's like him."

I looked around at the eyes admiring Ryan as I repeated Jack's words in my head, *He's like no one, and no one's like him.*

"Jack, does Ryan know that you people are rooting for him to be the next chief?"

"He doesn't. He knows that he is different than other minners of Loka. He also realizes that he can see and perceive things that a regular minner cannot. Unlike minners, he makes a conscious journey to Shloka every day and retains the memory of it. But he doesn't know he is special and meant to do things that no minner can comprehend. Chief wants to keep him innocent until he turns twelve and becomes ready for the Meet. We need your help here, Mandira. Only you can instill the belief in him about his true potential," said Jack. Then, with a long sigh, he continued, "Well, my job here is done. Let's go. It is time for you to head to Shloka. I will not be able to accompany you there."

"Wait, tell me more about Shloka. Last time you left me there, dazed and confused."

"I think you already know what Shloka is. Shloka is a place where your thoughts, beliefs, and perceptions take the form of an experience. You sometimes retain bits of these experiences in your memory and call them dreams. This visual experience is the real hallucination, not the one you thought you had after seeing me in Loka. These dreams guide you and give you the wings to fly. They are the reason why you feel relaxed every morning when you return to Loka, or wake up in Loka, whatever you call that."

"Does it mean that whatever I see in my dreams, or in

Shloka, so to speak, is not real?"

"Yes, that's exactly what it means. The beauty is, every minner has an experience unique to them in Shloka. Other minners can be part of it but do not share your experience. Shloka is like a galaxy of a billion stars where each star is distinct from the other, much like the experience of each minner."

I was not sure why, but I felt something missing in Jack's answer, so I said, "I want to know more. Last time you said it was a confluence of two rivers, and I saw strange visuals after that. What did you mean by that?"

"Oh, I said that? I was just using fancy words for the real thing. What do you call them? Meta four or five, or something?"

"You mean 'metaphor'?"

"Exactly. Meta-four it is. I was speaking meta-four-i-cally."

Jack had a hard time pronouncing the word. How he knew "confluence," a way more advanced word for his limited vocabulary, was beyond me.

"Sometimes I become philosophical," continued Jack, "I like that side of myself, but I don't get to meet it often. I think my intelligence and work do not go hand in hand. When I retire, I will take literature lessons from Professor Tolstoy of Parloka and write a book on the history of Kendram. That way, I can put my intelligence to good use."

"Intellect."

"What?"

"I think the better word is 'intellect.' You can put your intellect to good use. Anyways, what about that metaphor, the confluence of two rivers?"

"Oh yes, the meta-four. See, using your intellect is not always great. Now I have to tell you another secret about Shloka. Shloka is a symbol of unity that connects Loka and Parloka, like a confluence of two rivers into the ocean. It is the only place where the minners of Loka meet those of Parloka. In simple minner words, it is the place where the dead meet the alive. So, when you see dead minners in your dreams, that's a real meeting taking place in Shloka and no hallucination."

"Wait, what? Do you mean seeing my Grandma last time was the real deal?"

"Absolutely. Only the minners of Parloka have the code that lets them enter your dream and play along. They participate in your dream like a character of a play, but that meeting is real.

"Such a gentle lady, your grandmother is. She lives in Parloka with your grandfather. Every day she travels to Shloka, hoping to see one of her folks from Loka. Sometimes, she brings the grandfather along. Sometimes, she meets her daughter—your mother—sometimes your brothers, and sometimes you. When she's lucky, she meets all of you, and when she's not, she sees none. But that does not stop her from visiting. I hope you get to see her today. You are her best girl."

Tears trickled down from my eyes at the mention of the sweet devotion of Grandma, and I longed to see her in Shloka. I was no longer skeptical about Jack's ambition of becoming a writer. He indeed possessed the art of storytelling and did not require the aid of metaphors, which he called the "fancy words for the real thing."

"We better get going, Mandira, I have other things to finish before I call it one day. See, I used fancy words again. I tell you, Mandira, I have a great future in writing," said Jack as he rose from his invisible beanbag.

"Call it *a* day."

"A what?"

"The correct usage of the idiom is 'call it a day,' but you are certainly getting better, Jack," I returned, unable to curb my instinct of correcting people.

Jack tapped the white floor gently with his right foot and then moved his fingers in the air as if typing some code on an invisible touch screen.

A sphere-shaped bubble appeared in front of us. It

looked like one of the compartments of the metro that we had boarded earlier had detached from it and wandered off the track down to our lounge.

Ryan and Caesar dropped their fun jumping game at the sight of the familiar bubble and ran excitedly towards it. We were sucked into the bubble one by one as soon as we came into contact with its outer wall. The bubble rose from the ground, and we were gently transported out of the lounge amidst a standing ovation from the keepers, directed towards Ryan.

The bubble moved in what looked like a dimly lit tunnel before it arrived close to a metro in motion in a well-lit space. The bubble attached itself to a slot missing a compartment on the metro, and the giant necklace carried on with all the bubble beads.

The metro halted at a stop. We disembarked, walked up the dimly lit steps, and arrived at the ground level. The small opening of the ground that had facilitated our exit slid shut behind us.

We stood at the side of the main road that led to the entrance of Shloka. A large number of minners were going in, and roughly the same number of them were coming out. I also spotted the road that branched off to Parloka, the less trodden path. The gate to Parloka was not closed anymore.

"Jack, what happened there? Didn't Ryan shut the gate to Parloka?" I asked.

"There are no gates now. All the gates of Shloka and Parloka have been removed permanently. The old security system has been discarded. Dr. Keyhole has designed a new system in which access is granted on an individual level.

"Times have changed, Mandira. There are some daggers among the keepers who cannot be trusted. The chief is serious and has reviewed the security system himself. All the minners have open access, but the chief has implemented access policies for the keepers of Kendram. The access is recorded for the keepers who work here. If keepers of Parloka need to visit Shloka for work, they must get approval from the chief himself. Invisible walls will block anyone trying to get unauthorized access."

Jack left us at the entrance of Shloka, and we headed to the dreamland.

Chapter Five

There are times when life brings us to the end of a road that branches off into two directions, and we do not know which one to pick. But we must choose one of the paths, or else we will be stuck at the end forever.

Some people believe that we should listen to our mind, whereas others say to follow your heart, and it all seems like shooting in the dark.

Like many others, I don't know the answer. Perhaps listening to the mind is good sometimes, and following the heart works well other times. But I know one thing. Sitting on the stack of an unsolved puzzle is not a solution, and we must act even if that means taking the wrong path just to realize it midway and correct it.

Two weeks ago, I was sitting at the edge of indecision, unable to spot the ray of truth through the clouds of falsehood. My heart wished every bit of my experience to be real, even if nobody else knew, understood, or believed. It wanted to believe that I had caught a glimpse of an unknown and unexplored universe in which my son was a remarkable force.

On the other hand, my brain questioned its existence, as it did for anything supernatural that humans could not explain. What could be explained by humans was the existence of a mental disorder of illusions and delusions that make us see and perceive things.

Sitting in Bob's clinic today, I was no more in a quandary. My heart and brain were in perfect sync, and for the first time in months, I felt in complete control.

"So, Mandira, how were the last two weeks?" asked Bob, relaxing in his easy chair, "I hope you've had ample time to ponder over your situation. I would like to know where you stand now?"

"Well, Dr. Bob, the last two weeks have been incredible. I did get some time to reflect on our discussion, and, I must say, the more I think, the harder it becomes to ignore the merits of your analysis. Your conclusion seems practical and more likely than the possibility of truth in my otherworldly experience."

"You think so? I am glad to hear that," returned Bob, smiling on being given credit to his judgement for the first time.

"Yes, I do. But a few things happened last week that made me rethink and question your arguments."

"Hmm…Like what?" asked Bob with the fading smile of a person who realized that he had been too quick to celebrate.

"For instance, you asked me if Ryan had given any clue about his knowledge of my supposed experience, since he was part of it."

"Ok, did he?"

"Not really, but I found something that will interest you. Remember the time when Ryan was hurt at school and got bruises on his chest?"

"I do. I apologized to you for Ben's actions. Believe me, he regrets his behavior towards Ryan. He has changed since then."

"No, no, you don't need to apologize for that. Your son is not responsible for the scratches on Ryan's chest."

"He isn't?"

"No, he only pushed him down the stairs, and that did not cause any injury."

"Oh."

"Yes, I am sure it wasn't him. Also, Ben admitted to pushing. He never agreed that he inflicted injuries on Ryan's chest. Don't you remember?"

"Oh, yes. I do now. It's just that I am so busy with work and keep hearing complaints about him. I am not able to keep track of them all. So, you were saying…"

"Yes, I also thought for a long time that it was Ben, but I am sure now that it was not him."

"Oh, ok. How do you know? Was it some other kid?"

"Not a kid. Kids cannot cause such marks. Those were the marks of claws."

"Claws? Like animal claws?"

"Like bear claws."

"Bear claws? Do you mean a bear attacked him?"

"Yes."

"Wait, you said it was at school," said Bob with a bewildered look on his face, "Are you saying that a bear attacked Ryan in the school?"

"Yes."

"That's strange. How? How did a bear enter the school premises?"

"I have no idea. But that's not the worst part. Only Ryan saw the bear and nobody else."

"What? Only Ryan saw it? Where was he?"

"At school, I told you."

"I mean, where exactly was Ryan when the bear attacked him?"

"In the building, I suppose. Could be in the classroom, the corridor, or the toilet, I don't know. But it's impossible in such a busy building that not a single pair of eyes caught sight of a bear that attacked Ryan."

"Ok, I'm not sure I'm getting this. How did you find out about the bear? Did Ryan tell you?"

"Yes."

"What exactly did he say?"

"That a bear scratched him at school."

"But didn't you tell me that Ryan cannot speak?"

"He can speak, very little though. He has a hard time expressing emotions. I asked who scratched him, and he said a bear."

"Hmm. And he did not tell you this back then? He told you now?"

"Yes, he told me last week. But what difference does it make?"

"Well, don't you think children can make up such stories?"

"I could think that about any other child, but not Ryan. He is incapable of making up stories. Even if I assume that he can make up stories, how can he make bloody marks on his chest?"

"Could it be some other boy who injured him?"

"I don't think so. And why would he say it was a bear?"

"I don't know. Is it possible that he scratched himself?"

"Not possible. Ryan does not harm anyone and certainly not himself."

Bob became thoughtful and said after a long pause, "Well, Mandira, this is an old incident, and I don't have first-hand information and all the details to come to a conclusion. Bear attacks are fatal and cause deep cuts and bruises all over. Why would a bear lightly brush its claws against Ryan's chest and leave him unharmed?"

"That's a valid point. But don't forget that it was no ordinary bear attacking an ordinary boy. That bear is only visible to Ryan, and we don't know the motive behind that appearance. I also saw a bear, perhaps the same one, in my supernatural experience that you call my hallucinations."

"What's your point, Mandira?"

"My point is, it's not only me. Ryan can also see things as I do, and others cannot. So, I guess my experience cannot entirely be attributed to episodes of hallucinations. And it would be a hell of a coincidence if you tell me that Ryan is also hallucinating or being delusional."

"Well, I do not think Ryan has schizophrenia. It is uncommon in children younger than twelve. I also don't see a correlation here. You have based your hypothesis on what seems to be a child's whim about an isolated incident that occurred a few months ago. Think of this. You are saying your boy saw a bear, who nobody else could see, who attacked him, left scratches on his chest, and left in the hustle and bustle of the school without being spotted. What is the likelihood of such a crazy event being true?

"Now consider an alternate theory. A boy with difficulty in expressing himself gets injured at school. Perhaps he came into contact with a sharp object either by accident or by an inadvertent mistake of another boy. Now he finds it hard to explain how he got hurt. He has a natural fascination for animals. He spends most of his time in the company of his dog. He gets obsessed with a bear that he perhaps saw on TV on the National Geographic Channel.

"To get away from the constant pressing of his mother about the scratching incident, he finds it easier to blame it on that bear on the National Geographic Channel who attacked an innocent animal in one of the scenes. Doesn't that make more sense?"

"Well, that does make more sense, Doc. But there is one thing that makes much more sense to me now."

"And what is that?"

"Remember last time when you said there were inconsistencies in my extraordinary experience during C-cat? You said that Jack told me about this organization, Kendram, run by Chief Joseph and his son Hogdon, but I did not see any of them, and hence they did not exist."

"Yes, I remember."

"Well, you cannot say that anymore. I have seen Hogdon. In fact, I have met him many times."

Bob squinted his eyes as if in disbelief and then smiled, "Oh, you did? That evil son you talked about, who according to you, created troubles on Earth? Where did you meet him? Did you have another long episode like the last one?"

"I don't think it's an episode unless you call my meeting you an episode."

"Come again?"

"That evil son Hogdon is sitting right in front of me. It's you, Bob. You are Hogdon."

Bob looked at me blankly for a moment and then burst into laughter, "That's a good one, Mandira. Must say, I admire your sense of humor."

I stood up, and my face reddened in anger, "But I do not admire your manipulation, Hogdon. Drop this disguise, you chameleon. You are no psychiatrist. You are a wicked tyrant who is after my son's life and wants to destroy Loka."

"Calm down, ma'am! You are not making any sense. Please sit down and talk to me."

"There's nothing to talk about now, Hogdon. You cannot fool me anymore."

Bob returned with composure, "Please sit, Mandira. Don't be agitated. Let me help you. It seems you're having a fresh episode."

"Oh really, another episode? What now? Am I hallucinating? Aren't you sitting in that chair? Are you an illusion? Enough of your lies, Doctor Hogdon. You're a bully, trying to harm my son, and I am not scared of you. A mother can stand up to any bully, no matter how dangerous, who is after her son's life," I said, angrily walking towards the door.

"C'mon, Mandira. You are in a state of delusion. Where are you going? Don't just leave like that, please. I can explain your outburst."

"You can explain my outburst?" I said, opening the door, "Well, explain it to him."

I pulled an arm into the room. It was Ryan, accompanied by Caesar. Bob jumped out of his seat at the sight of Ryan looking right into his eyes, and Caesar growling at him.

The tables had been turned. It was his turn to get agitated, and he did. The calm demeanor of the firm young man that had inspired confidence was now replaced by nervous jitters, confirming his treacherous designs.

"Why didn't you tell me he was here?" uttered Bob

nervously. "Why'd you bring him here? That's no good, Mandira. That's terrible."

"Why, tell him about your theory of delusions."

Never in my life had I seen anyone rattled in front of my harmless child. People would barely notice him, let alone get intimidated. But here he was, one of the most dreaded and evil things, standing in front of us, looking bewildered.

Finally, shedding the thick wool of morality, the devil retorted, "Oh, Mandira. You are trying to mess with me! Do you think I can be scared by this vegetable? I can destroy all of you right now. You don't know who I am."

"Everyone knows exactly who you are, Hogdon!" returned Jack, appearing from nowhere.

"Jack! So, it is you, trying to help these minners!" said Hogdon, as if he had anticipated him. "You trying to lay a trap for me? Who do you think you are? Chief Joseph? You, a lowly servant of Kendram barking at the master?"

Suddenly, the medieval garb of a long black cloak and hat (the same style as Jack's) appeared on his body, and the clean-shaven, dapper-looking psychiatrist turned into a rugged-faced, furious-eyed devil within a flash of a second.

I recognized him from the time he appeared right in front of my car, and I had braked abruptly when we, along with the Hayden's, were on our way back from the tulip gardens during the springtime.

Unlike his gentlemanly disguise of slim Bob, Hogdon was a tall, strongly built, scary-looking dagger, and his angry eyes increased the palpitations of my heart. I did not feel safe in the company of the pointed-nosed, old Jack, who seemed no match in front of him.

Trying to put up a brave front, I stood right in front of Ryan, in anticipation of danger to his life, though I knew that in any such event, the protective shield of my body and arms would be like a thin wall of glass panel blocking the hurricane.

"You trying to cross my path? You think you can get away with this, Jack?" growled Hogdon.

"I don't care what you think about me, Hogdon. I am an honest keeper following the order of Kendram," returned Jack calmly to Hogdon's angry barb. "But how will you get away with this? You know you are forbidden to see Monsieur Ryan or his family before the Meet. But you are still trying to brainwash the lady. You broke the order, and I caught you red-handed. How will you face the council now?"

Jack's reminder made Hogdon check himself in one moment and furious in the very next, "To hell with the order! I make the order! And I am the council! I am Hogdon, the supreme force! Your order and council cannot touch a single strand of my hair. You will pay for this. You will pay for this, Jack!"

Jack did not reply.

Hogdon turned to me with fuming eyes, and I shuddered with fear.

"You little woman! You think you're clever? You think your dumb boy can beat me and become the Chief of Kendram? Ha. You will pay," he said, pointing his long finger at me. "All of you disgusting minners will pay for this audacity. You cannot save this boy from Hogdon's fury...Duma, *Duma*!"

Suddenly, Hogdon disappeared, and the room was filled with dead silence. Before I could breathe a sigh of relief about Hogdon's departure, the door on the right wall of the room next to the bookshelf swung open, and Duma entered with heavy steps.

A chill went down my spine.

He stopped right at the place where Hogdon had stood previously, facing us with unusual wrath vivid in his eyes.

Duma was the bear. The bear that had taken my breath away during springtime by zigzagging ahead of my car on the way back from the tulip gardens. It was the same red-eyed, large black bear that I had momentarily encountered sitting on a rock in one of those bewildering visuals in Shloka.

My other close encounters with bears were limited to zoos or wildlife sanctuaries. I did not doubt that facing any bear would scare the hell out of me. But facing Duma was nowhere near to an ordinary bear.

That tremendous figure exuded boundless power. Those fiery red eyes staring at me were deeply unsettling, as if sucking every ounce of life out of my flesh and bones. Being in the same room and facing him felt like standing on the threshold of certain death.

Duma fixed his eyes on Ryan, who was peeking out from beneath my arm. My protective instincts got the better of me as I tried my best to block Duma's view of Ryan by hiding him behind my body.

The bear roared fiercely with his jaws wide open, exposing the sharp, protruding canines that could crush rocks. In the next moment, he pounced on us, leaping with his hands and legs spread wide open. I shrank back in fear, holding on to Ryan with all my might.

I heard a loud bang and opened my eyes that had closed momentarily in reflex, realizing that we had narrowly averted the horrible strike, and we were still in one piece.

Before he could knock us down on the ground, Duma was blocked mid-air in a violent clash by a furiously growling Caesar. They both landed on the wooden table, breaking it into two.

If loyalty had a face, I could not think of anybody other than Caesar to qualify for it. I had not expected Caesar to go to the extent of throwing himself into the jaws of death to protect his family. Caesar was half the size but twice as courageous as the beast he took head-on.

The attack made Duma furious, and a wild rage took over the bear as he grabbed Caesar with both paws. He opened his jaws, and those sharp canines pierced the back of Caesar's neck, deep into the flesh, making him growl with excruciating pain.

Watching Caesar become seized under the powerful grip of the beast who was lacerating his back with those ugly pointed teeth, my heart skipped several beats, thinking it was all over. An impulse took over me to thrust at the bear with my bare, weak hands to protect my helpless dog, who I had raised and loved like my third child.

Before I could attempt anything foolish in a fit of panic and get killed, I saw four dogs appear from nowhere to encircle Ryan and me.

Two of them, which looked like twins, each with a brown coat, positioned themselves by our sides. One with a black coat went behind us, and one that looked like a leopard with a white coat and black spots stood right at the front. They were larger than the average sized dog, with broad, athletic bodies and long, strong limbs. I had not seen a dog of that breed before.

The dog army made no attempts to save Caesar, and I quickly realized why. My love for Caesar, like that of a child, had temporarily blinded me to his other side, the real side. He was no ordinary dog and was looking for an opportunity to prove that, and he did.

While Duma was digging into his back, Caesar, in one swift move, turned his head over his shoulder, reached out to one of Duma's ears, and bit it. Duma groaned in pain.

Taken aback by the brisk movement of Caesar, he loosened his grip and jerked him off. But now, it was Caesar's turn to tighten his grip. He would not let that ear go, clenching his teeth firmly, cutting into the flesh, despite the exasperated Duma jerking him around.

The table, the chairs, the shelves, the walls, and every other article that came into contact with their violent struggle either broke or cracked.

It had not occurred to me before that mischievous and playful Caesar could instantly transform himself into a ferocious warrior in the wake of danger to his master. Caesar did not leave the ear until it had detached from Duma's head, and he almost collapsed with unbearable pain.

While fine streams of blood oozed out of the remaining portion of the ear still attached to Duma's head, Caesar spat the piece of a blood-stained ear out of his mouth in sheer disgust.

Separated from each other for the first time since the struggle had commenced, the two stood face-to-face again, and Caesar did not look like a mismatch before Duma anymore.

Duma almost went berserk in anger and jumped on Caesar, but Caesar was careful and savage this time. He aimed for the exposed wound at the right side of Duma's head, crushing the remains of the ear further, causing irreparable damage and inflicting insufferable pain.

Duma shoved him. That was it. Not only had Duma lost his ear, but also the will to fight anymore. The dog, initially the underdog, had managed to turn the tide against the beast twice his size. At that moment, he looked like a formidable force who could make any opponent bite the dust.

Duma perhaps realized this and reached for the door that he had knocked open a few minutes ago to enter the room. Caesar leaped on his back, trying to pin him down, but Duma thrust him violently down to the ground and escaped through the door.

Furious Caesar ran after him but banged into the door that had closed behind Duma. Caesar banged the door many times and growled loudly. He had turned savage with a blood-stained mouth, battered back, and horrifying rage in his eyes. For the first time in my life, I feared him.

Jack, who had silently watched the events unfold, was still dumbfounded, and even the dogs surrounding us seemed nervous.

Caesar was growling incessantly. He had turned into a mad, wild creature that could kill anyone. Nobody would dare to go close to him, except one.

It was Ryan.

He walked towards Caesar without hesitation, and it made me nervous. I wanted to stop Ryan, but there was something about his calm assuredness that made me let him carry on.

Caesar growled loudly at him, but I didn't see a sign of the slightest fear in Ryan. He pressed his hand gently on

Caesar's forehead and spoke—a rare occasion for him, "Caesar, come. Let's go home."

Caesar stopped growling. His eyes became wet, and the rage disappeared as if washed away by the tears. The beast inside him had died down, and the old Caesar was back, licking Ryan's hand.

Chapter Six

How did I discover that Bob was indeed Hogdon? After meeting Jack in Jantar, I was smitten by every bit of my visual experience and every piece of the information acquired from him. There was a strange sense of power in the thought that I saw the impossible and knew the unknown. I knew something that humans could not comprehend, let alone believe. In the light of this new knowledge, I saw myself as a proud, fearless mother of a legend.

I knew that I had acquired a treasure of information to which no other human had the access (except, of course, Ryan), let alone the capacity to comprehend. I was convinced that these experiences were not the episodes of delusion as Dr. Bob believed they were.

I realized that Ryan was destined for greatness, and my family would be at the center stage of significant developments in the near future. I had gone past the stage of self-doubt where Bob could convince me I was wrong.

Still, I could not underestimate his capability to confuse me. If I told him of my thoughts in our appointment the next week, I knew he would again cast aspersions and site inconsistencies in my experience. I even considered canceling my appointment with Bob.

Rising from the bed, I drew back the curtains to let morning twilight enter the dark bedroom. Viru and Caesar had not yet returned from their walk, the walk that was a refreshing activity for Caesar, and a mundane duty for Viru.

But I was not thinking of them. I was looking for someone else through the window. Someone who inspired confidence in me without any effort. Someone whose mere glimpse would light up my morning and start my day.

Then, I saw her. I saw Samantha running along the sidewalk across the street. It was hard to tell with the distance, but I got the feeling that she looked up and smiled at me.

The morning progressed at its usual pace. Viru left for the office. It was a parent-teacher meeting day, and I was to accompany Reva and Ryan to their school. Reva was one of the top students in her class, and for the first time, I was not worried about Ryan's feedback from his teachers that had tormented me every year in the past. In fact, I looked forward to their comments about Ryan's slow progress and weaknesses, as it would amuse rather than distress me, for a change.

We left for the school around ten, leaving Caesar alone at home. It did not bother me anymore to leave Caesar by himself as I believed the head of Rudram had better things to do, though I had no idea what they were and how and when he did them. Who knew he would simply accompany us in an invisible mode?

We started with the lighter part of the day in school by meeting Reva's teachers one by one in the allotted rooms. As expected, all the teachers were fond of Reva and had positive things to say about her. She was showered with praise for academic distinction and extracurricular laurels.

Mr. Marco said that Reva was a self-starter, and I was pleased to hear that. Miss Tina observed that she was always ready to lend a helping hand to others, and I could not agree more. Miss Holly talked about her impressive academic performance and shining grades, and I was all ears. While I beamed with pride and Reva blushed with humility, Ryan waited patiently and watched silently, sitting on one of the side chairs.

After finishing with Reva's teachers, we walked into the

other building to endure the next part of the day. Though I was relaxed and felt less stressed than I had in the previous years, I still hoped to finish Ryan's meetings amicably.

In the corridor on the second floor, we met Harry.

"Hello, Miss Mandira! How are you? Hey, buddy!" said Harry, addressing Ryan and me in one breath.

"Hey, Harry. Good to see you after a long time. We are doing fine. How are you?"

Harry was one of the members of the support staff who had worked with Ryan until last year, helping him through the daily transitions at the school. A thorough gentleman, he was fond of Ryan.

"How is the little prankster doing? Does he pull pranks on you?"

"Pranks? What do you mean?"

"Oh, so it's only me? Didn't he tell you? He scared the hell out of me that day."

"What day? Harry, not sure if I am following. What did Ryan do?"

"Well, I think it was a few months ago, morning time, I reckon. I was walking down this corridor when I saw him running out of the toilet. Do you see the toilet? That one. He looked scared, so I stopped him. I tell you, a fine actor, he is. I asked him, 'Kid, what's up, why are you running?' and he goes, 'Bear.' I go, 'What?' and he goes, '*bear!*' pointing at the toilet."

"Did he see a bear in the toilet?"

"That's what I thought. I almost peed my pants. Then I thought, how could a bear enter the school in the middle of the day and hide in a toilet? So, I went in carefully, and you know what? Forget a bear, there wasn't even a bee! The toilet was empty, not a thing in there. Man, I was about to call backup. Thank God I didn't. My coworkers would have made fun of me for weeks, saying that a little boy fooled me."

Rather than being amused by this account, as he had expected me to be, Harry noticed the horrified reaction on my face and added in a reassuring tone, "Kids do such things all the time. It's no big deal. You ok, Miss Mandira?"

I nodded half-heartedly but couldn't utter an appropriate word in response. Following an awkward silence, Harry excused himself, perhaps thinking that I lacked a sense of humor. Among all the senses that I lacked at that moment, a sense of humor was the least of my worries.

"Mom, what's wrong? Are you ok?" asked Reva.

I don't know what I said to her. I also don't remember how the meetings with Ryan's teachers progressed. I cannot recall the concerns that were raised and my absent-minded response to them.

I could not follow Miss Jannat when she talked about Ryan's social skills. I did not pay attention to Miss Stella when she mentioned his grades. I failed to gather the gist of Mr. Marjory's speech. All I remembered from his feedback was the frequent mention of attention span. How could he expect me to discuss Ryan's attention span when Mr. Marjory had barely managed to gather mine?

It was Duma, I thought, and that's all I could think about. Yes, that wild bear who killed Caesar's pregnant mother had been hiding in that toilet, waiting for Ryan. He had attacked Ryan. *Oh my God, that mad bear tried to kill my son! The bruises on Ryan's chest were inflicted by Duma, by his hideous claws.*

I could see now why Ryan wouldn't eat or drink in the school—so that he didn't have to go to the toilet. He feared that Duma might be hiding in there. That's why he only emptied his bladder at home upon returning from school.

My God, why hadn't Ryan told me? Had he thought that I would not believe him and take it as a joke, like Harry had? Well, he would have been right. I probably wouldn't have believed him at the time.

How had Duma got in there? Jack had told me that he wandered in deserted and unpopulated places. Could toilets have been one of them? Why not. After all, a toilet was probably the least occupied place in the school, useful as a hideout.

But wasn't Duma barred from inhabited places? He was, Jack said so. But then, why would a barbaric bear care for the rules?

What had happened to the Watch Force, that, per Jack, had got everything covered? Did Duma manage to breach their security cover? Well, of course he had.

Had the Watch Force protected Ryan from Duma? Perhaps it had. How else would Ryan have escaped from certain death? Now I understood why Caesar was anxious that day, running back and forth down the street, looking for the school bus.

I was juggling between the questions popping in my head and unknowingly trying to satiate my curiosity with probable answers.

After finishing the feedback session with the teachers, I picked Reva and Ryan up from the common room where they were waiting, and we started to leave.

As we walked along the corridor, an unfamiliar voice called my name, and I stopped, and so did my train of thought.

"Miss Mandira? Hello, are you Miss Mandira?" asked the lady with a boy next to her, who was about Ryan's age.

"Yes, I'm Mandira."

"Good to finally meet you, Mandira. I'm Laurie. This is my son, Ben."

I nodded with a slight smile.

"I didn't get a chance to apologize to you for Ben. Last spring, when Principal Elizabeth informed me that he misbehaved with your son, I was so ashamed and gave him a bitter scolding. This is not the way I raised—"

"Wait, is he Ben?" I asked, cutting her short, and continued without waiting for an answer, "Did you say you're his mom?"

"Yes."

My mind was suddenly awake and confused.

"But how can you be his mom? Ben's mom is dead."

"Well, I am quite sure, Mandira, that I am his mom,"

returned Laurie with an awkward smile, "and as far as I can tell, I am not dead."

"I am sorry, but his Dad told me that was the case."

"His Dad? He does not have one. I'm a single mom."

"Single mom?"

"Yes, I am raising Ben all by myself."

"I am confused. Don't you know Bob? I mean, the psychiatrist Dr. Robert Sutherland?"

"Nope, I don't know any guy named Bob. I have never dated a psychiatrist. Wait a minute. Is there a psychiatrist guy claiming that he is Ben's Dad? Did he tell you that I, his mother, is dead?

"Umm…"

"How do you know this person? Did you meet him here, at the school, Mandira?"

No thoughts that could be worded into an appropriate response crossed my mind. Seeing me dumbstruck, Laurie broke the awkward silence.

"Well, Mandira, this doesn't seem to be the right time. I will see you around. Let's go, Ben." Taking Ben's hand, Laurie took off hurriedly as if she had just encountered a lunatic.

"Mom, why did you talk to Ben's mom like that?" asked Reva, visibly unsettled, "I have seen her before with Ben. She is the only one who comes to school every time. There's no Dad."

My mind was numb. Bob had told me that he was Ben's father, but I had never seen them together.

"And who is this psychiatrist guy? Bob, is it? How do you know him? What did he tell you?"

Reva did not know that I was consulting a psychiatrist. Viru and I had decided to keep my situation under wraps from the kids. I did not know what to tell Reva about Bob, who I thought I knew, but not anymore.

"Umm…I think I got confused. I am sorry, Revu."

"Confused? With whom, Mom?"

"Well, here's the thing, umm…" I said, trying hard to

make something up. "It was Elena. Yes, Elena knows a psychiatrist named Bob, whose son's name is also Ben. She told me about him. So I confused that Ben with this one. That Ben's mom is dead."

"That does not make any sense. Why would you confuse this Ben with any other? This Ben pushed Ryan down the stairs. I have told you many times about him. I don't know, Ma, but sometimes you act weird. That was so embarrassing," returned Reva, trying to suppress her vexation.

I made no further effort to justify my cooked-up story to Reva, for I had a more important thing to figure out—who was Bob? Why had he lied about Ben?

Did he lie about Ben to make my acquaintance? I wondered. *But why would he do that? How did I meet him? Did I see him in the school? No, not even once.*

Oh yeah, I saw him the first time in Summerhill when I was walking down the shortcut to the main road. He stopped me. But what was I doing in Summerhill? That place is far away from the city.

I remember, I went to buy spices for Ryan. He had stopped eating at school, and I decided to step up my cooking to increase his appetite and make up for the nutrition at home.

Bob had introduced himself to me as Ben's Dad and apologized for his son's behavior towards Ryan. But he was not his Dad. How had he known Ben in the first place? Not only that, but how had he known that Ben had bullied Ryan?

I had believed that Ben had inflicted those bruises on Ryan's chest, but it was now clear that that was an act of the hideous bear Duma. How had Bob known that I was disturbed by that incident and blamed Ben for it?

He'd said that Ben's mom had died in an accident, and that he had raised him by himself. Why? For sympathy? But why did he want my sympathy?

This doesn't make any sense.

How had I ended up consulting him? Yes, he had given me his visiting card in that first meeting, and I approached him later.

I flashbacked to all my meetings with Bob and analyzed them one by one. The more I dug into my memories, the more I realized how apparent the inconsistencies were.

Perhaps the motive behind the pretense of Ben's noble single Dad was to gain my trust. Giving away his visiting card could have been a ploy to disclose his occupation and indirectly encourage me to consult him. Perhaps that first, seemingly chance meeting was a prelude to a larger plot.

He knew that I was disturbed and would seek help. How? I could not say. But then, I could not say how he knew so many other things about me, either. He had declared me schizophrenic and attributed my encounters with Jack to hallucinations and delusions.

Damn, why didn't I think of getting a second opinion?

Ok, let's be honest, no other psychiatrist would believe my story either, and I get that.

But it occurred to me that no other psychiatrist would go as far in pushing their logic as Bob did, leaving no room for the element of mystery.

He seemed eager to obliterate the foundation on which any point of view other than his could be built, as if it were a necessity rather than just rational thinking. He made my accounts look like incoherent senseless delusions. He explained the C-cat event with such aplomb that I wondered if he was a scientist masquerading as a psychiatrist. But now, it seemed to me that he was an imposter masquerading as a psychiatrist.

Why would a psychiatrist open a clinic in a remote place far away from the city where hardly anyone came? And that in the basement of a seemingly abandoned building?

That last thought startled me.

Oh my God. He is a dagger! I realized.

Jack had told me that daggers operated in secluded places. Those appointments in that remote place were a trap to lead me into sharing the intricate details of my experience, dissecting it from the lens of a psychiatrist so that its veracity could be cunningly dismissed. He had been trying to brainwash me.

He desired to stop me from interacting with Jack. He advised me to ignore him if he ever showed up, citing the consequences of hallucinations. In fact, he had warned me against talking even if Jack insisted. This person had been persistently trying to keep this unknown world hidden from me, as opposed to Jack, who had uncovered it.

This enemy of Jack could very well be the enemy of Ryan and, in turn, the enemy of Loka. It will be no wonder if this wicked, manipulative person is none other than Hogdon.

A chill went down my spine at the thought of Hogdon. It was not an arbitrary thought, considering he had once abruptly shown up on a deserted road in front of my car.

I didn't send Ryan to school the following day as he (and Caesar, of course) were to join me for yet another conscious trip to Shloka to see Jack.

After hearing about the whole account, Jack was convinced that Dr. Bob was indeed Hogdon. According to him, only a high-rank member of Kendram could successfully evade the impenetrable security cover of the Watch Force of Rudram.

Hogdon would go to any length to stop the rise of Ryan, and what better way to do this other than to influence his mother's thoughts? He knew that only I could keep him away from following his destiny by continuing to protect him.

Jack also told me that the D-force, deputed by Caesar, must have protected Ryan from Duma's deadly attack in the toilet. The D-force was an army of four feisty dogs, led by Tormon, the dog with a white coat and black spots. In the absence of Caesar, they followed Ryan everywhere like a shadow, in an invisible mode.

Jack had a plan in his mind for my next appointment, the final face-off with Dr. Bob, aka, Hogdon. The only way to expose Hogdon before Kendram was to catch him red-handed, and we did.

Chapter Seven

It was Diwali, the festival of lights. Diwali symbolizes the victory of light over darkness, good over evil, and knowledge over ignorance. According to Indian mythology, God Rama returned to his kingdom, Ayodhya, on this day with his wife Sita after defeating the evil Ravana in an epic battle. People celebrated the homecoming of the victorious God by illuminating the entire kingdom with lamps.

The word Diwali originated from the Sanskrit word Deepavali. "Deepa" is a word for a lamp and, "vali" means "rows." So, Diwali (or Deepavali) literally translates to "rows of lighted lamps."

It was 12:30 p.m. and Viru had not yet finished installing the outdoor lights, the project that he had been working on since early morning. I had asked him to do it yesterday, but Mr. Procrastinator's answer was, "But honey, Diwali is tomorrow, not today." Then he bragged about his job as project director meaning that he was an expert in managing complex projects, and that installing lights was a simple task.

Reva was busy making rangoli on the doorstep and entertaining the endless questions about the colorful powders from the two talking machines—Britney and Theodore. Rangoli is an art form, a decoration drawn generally in front of the house as a mark of welcoming God to the household.

I had finished making the sweets—three types of them,

as my family could not for once settle with a common choice. Viru requested laddu, Reva wanted barfi and Ryan and Caesar…well, they did not put forth any demand, but I knew Ryan loved gulab jamun.

Next, I needed to cook for the Diwali party that we were hosting that evening for our neighbors: the Haydens, the Kings, and a few of Viru's colleagues, including his best friend, Sylvain. So, I needed to step up my cooking and scale up the preparation with the support of my assistant chef, Reva.

It was a busy Sunday for the family except for two members, Ryan and Caesar, who were doing what they did best —nothing.

It had been fifteen days since the final encounter with Bob, aka Hogdon. I still wondered how I got the courage to stand up to that wicked, treacherous devil. If it was not for Ryan, I would not have become the warrior I had that day.

Ever wondered what melts like wax for the suffering of her children and hardens like granite to protect them? The heart of a mother.

Though I had the reassuring support of Jack and Caesar (and D-force, the four dogs, which I discovered were there for the first time), and they certainly did not disappoint, going into the pit to confront the snake was utterly unsettling. Those revengeful eyes of Hogdon gave me nightmares.

I couldn't believe how Caesar had risked his life to fight a raging bear twice his size. Not only was he protecting his family from getting destroyed, but he was also avenging the one destroyed already. He was settling the personal score with Duma for the cold-blooded murder of his mother and siblings. That coward bear without an ear will never forget that Caesar, in a fit of rage, could have torn much more than his ear into pieces, had he not run away.

Since that day, I had noticed a transformation in Ryan, as if, in me, he had found a confidante who shared his secret world. I felt closer to him. I wasn't sure if only I felt that way, but my otherwise nervous boy was beaming with confidence these days.

Though he would not express it in words, Ryan had always reciprocated my love to him through his beautiful eyes. I did not doubt in my mind that he loved me more than anyone in this world.

But I always felt that there was a corner deep down in his heart hidden from everyone, and no matter how hard I tried, it would not open to me. Ryan's camaraderie with Caesar sometimes gave me the impression that only he knew the mystery of the corner, and that thought made me jealous.

Now, as I had stepped into the uncharted territory unknown to humans, Ryan knew that Caesar was no longer his only companion, and the door to the corner of trust in his heart had now opened for me.

Viru was always last to notice any change in the general affairs of the household or the conduct of its members, but he also pointed out that Ryan was talking and observing more than he usually did. However, he (and Reva) had no idea about the series of mind-boggling events that had led to this slight but noticeable progress.

I finished cooking around 3 p.m., with the help of my efficient assistant. Reva left for a walk, her excuse to see Tim.

Viru was still grappling with his three big meshes of strings with countless LEDs attached to them. His only accomplishment so far (if it indeed qualified for one) was that he had been on the rooftop all morning and on the tree in the front yard since noon.

At first, he had struggled to suspend the rows of strings of the first mesh from the rooftop. Then, he'd had a tough time with the second mesh wrapping around the shrub fence in the backyard. And his final challenge was to cover the tree in the front yard with the third mesh.

But that was not all. When he had finished laying the three meshes, another problem cropped up. Viru had spent the entire time laying the meshes individually and did not realize that they were supposed to be connected together. The cords of the tail-plugs of the meshes fell short of the length to connect, and the whole exercise became futile. An alternate option would not work as there were not enough extension cords to connect each of the meshes individually to the power point.

So, now Viru was refurbishing his entire project, this time keeping in mind the adequate length of the cords to connect the meshes. I wondered if our project director really got anything done in his company.

I was not worried, though, as, with Viru, you always needed a backup plan, and I had one. I had enough stock of oil lamps and candles to light around the house in the evening. On such occasions, I always gave Viru those low-priority assignments that we could live without in the event of him messing up. In other words, I only trusted him with the kind of work that added value to the occasion but would not be an absolute necessity for its success.

That morning, Britney and Ted had been excited to see Mr. Viren in action on the rooftop and were still hopeful when he was working on the shrub fence. But by the time he climbed the tree, they had lost all faith in his project and got busy with Reva's mesmerizing designs of rangoli, and finally with their usual play.

Ryan was sitting on the front doorstep, in his favorite spot, staying clear of the boundary marked by Reva with white chalk around her rangoli design before she left for a walk. Caesar, his permanent companion, was stretched on the floor beside him.

As always, Ryan silently watched Britney playing with Ted in her front yard. They were digging a hole in the ground to plant a tree and, as usual, talking simultaneously, neither listening to the other. Britney, who was once fond of Ryan, had lost interest in him, partially for a few months, and completely after making friends with Ted.

Though Ryan never spoke to her or engaged in play, I could always see in his eyes that he enjoyed her attention.

Initially, I'd had the impression that Britney was trying to make Ryan jealous, as she sounded more enthusiastic to talk to Ted in front of him. But I soon realized that that was not the case. Britney had forgotten Ryan. After all, she had found a friend who talked as much as her, if not more. What was the point of wasting time with Ryan, who would not even care for one-word replies, let alone engage in playing?

After watching Britney and Ted play for some time, Ryan came up to me in the kitchen, where I was garnishing my fresh cooked food items with coriander, cream, and spring onions. Caesar followed him.

"What is it, dear? You want something?"

Ryan made no reply.

I stopped garnishing and looked at him. He was struggling to say something that he wanted to, like other times.

"Tell me, Ryan. Are you hungry?"

Ryan replied with great difficulty, "Mommy…can I play?"

"Of course you can play, my child. Who do you want to play with? Caesar?"

"Britney. Mommy…can I play with Britney?"

My eyes welled up with tears. This was big. For any other mom, it would be just another question from her child, but to me, it was a significant milestone, as if a speechless boy had suddenly found his voice. Ryan had made an effort to initiate a conversation for the first time by coming to me and expressing a desire other than the usual food or water, something that had not happened in the past nine years.

"Yes, you can certainly play with Britney," I said, fighting my tears. "You need to ask her. Are you going to ask her, my dear?"

Ryan became thoughtful for some time and then nodded his head.

"Go, son, and ask her."

Ryan sheepishly walked over to the side, where he had a good view of Britney's front yard, still careful not to spoil

Reva's rangoli. Dropping the garnish work, my favorite part of cooking, I stood close to the entrance door, such that I could see all of them, but so Britney and Ted could not see me.

Ryan stood there for a few seconds and said, "Britney."

Britney did not see or hear Ryan. Her back was facing him, and Ryan's soft voice was muffled by the loud talking of Ted.

Ryan watched quietly for about a minute and tried again, "Britney!"

Ryan was louder this time. His voice broke into a mild shrill, just like somebody incapable of using a high pitch, giving it a shot for the first time. Britney heard him this time and turned around.

"Ryan? Did you just call my name?" said Britney, taken aback to hear her name from Ryan's mouth for the first time.

"Britney."

"Sshhhh. Hey, drop it," uttered Britney promptly, shushing Ted, who was still talking nonstop about the plant, oblivious of the fact that she was not paying attention anymore.

Ted stopped talking, and there was absolute silence for the first time in the last few minutes.

"Yes, Ryan? Are you saying something?"

"Britney, will you play with me?" returned Ryan softly, with some hesitation.

Britney could not believe her ears. It was a rare moment when Britney was speechless. Not only had Ryan called her by her name, but he had also expressed the desire to play with her.

My heart was beating. I was as eager as Ryan, if not more, to see her reaction. I was hoping and praying that Britney did not shut him off after all these years of silent treatment from Ryan.

Suddenly, Ted broke the silence with abrupt laughter. "Bwahahaha! Hey look, this dumbo is talking!" said Ted mockingly, and he mimicked Ryan, taking a soft tone,

"Britney! Will you play with me? Ha ha."

"Hey! Don't you do that!" Britney snapped angrily at Ted. "And don't call him a dumbo. Ryan is my friend."

"But he is dumb——"

"No but! You are mean to my friend. I am not playing with you. Go home."

"But why you upset? You never talk to him."

"So what? It's none of your business. Ryan is my best friend."

"So, you're not playing with me anymore?"

"No. I will play with my best friend."

"Oh, *this* best friend? He can't even talk. What will you play with him? Dumb charades?"

"Go home, you idiot. Now!"

"Alright. I am going. I don't need you. Play with your stupid friend. I will not plant your tree, anymore. You do it yourself. I have so many other friends. Rocky always asks me, 'Why do you play with that gal? She's no good.' I didn't listen to him. But he is right. Tony says..." Ted kept muttering to himself as he left.

Forgetting her tree plantation fun, Britney left the three half-dug holes and the scattered plants in her yard and came up to Ryan.

As she arrived near our entrance, she saw me behind the half-opened door and said, "Mrs. Sharma, Ryan invited me to play with him. Did you see?"

"Really? That's nice, Britney," I returned, pretending to be ignorant.

"Yes, he did. He said, 'Britney will you play with me?' He said my name! Did you see that?" asked Britney, visibly thrilled, and she continued without waiting for an answer, "Imagine! He's never called me Britney before. That is so cool."

"Yes, that's cool, dear. Carry on, you two. Come inside if you want."

"Na, we will sit here on the steps," came her prompt reply, and she continued (already forgetting me), "Come,

Ryan, sit here. What do you want to play? I know a lot of games."

I watched them for some time with blurred vision, thanks to my wet eyes. Britney, as usual, talked nonstop, but took short pauses in between for Ryan, lest he struggled to keep up. Ryan barely talked but took keen interest and even nodded when she took those pauses.

Caesar, for a change, did not seem to mind Britney hogging all his master's attention. On the contrary, he seemed to like her company and looked excited for both of them.

I went back to the kitchen and finished my garnishing work. I was happy and felt like sharing the development with Viru, who was still wrestling with the decoration lights somewhere on the roof, but then changed my mind. I decided I would rather not distract the project director from his project that had already slipped way past its deadline. Reva was also out on her walk, so there was no one else.

I craved sweets. I took a warm piece of gulab jamun soaked in the sugar syrup and gulped it down my throat. It tasted like the best dessert I had ever made.

A thought of Sebastian crossed my mind. He was fond of gulab jamun. I had promised to save him some for Diwali. I looked at the wall clock. There was still an hour and a half before the evening prayer before the party.

Why wait until tomorrow when I still have time? I thought.

There is no better joy than to serve the ardent fan of your cookery skills. I quickly packed a nice box stuffed with gulab jamun, barfi, and laddu and hit the street.

In a few minutes, I was at the Saint Thomas Subway Station, going down the escalator.

Sebastian greeted me with a smile at the other end of the escalator. "Hi! What a pleasant surprise, Mandira. I thought you would be busy with your Diwali celebrations today."

"Oh, I have been occupied since this morning, Seb. Then I remembered, I had promised you something. So, here you go." I handed the box to Sebastian.

"I think I know what it is," said Seb, as he peeked in, slightly opening the lid. "Gulab jamun! I knew it. And laddu, and what's this called?"

"That is barfi."

"Barfi!" he said, now taking off the lid. "They smell so good." Sebastian took a piece of gulab jamun, gulped it down his throat, and savored the taste. "This tastes like heaven!" he said with half-closed eyes, "You have made my day, Mandira."

"I think only my son loves gulab jamun as much as you do."

"Why wouldn't he? After all, there are only two of us. You see, Mandira, every great person must love gulab jamun."

"Well, for now, he just loves them. I don't think he has turned as great as you are yet." I returned as we broke into laughter.

"I bet he has, Mandira."

"That he turns out to be a good human is all I hope for him. I don't want great."

"Well, Mandira, goodness is a choice anyone can make, but greatness is destiny; not everyone can choose."

"My God, you and your philosophy sometimes goes over and above my head. Anyways, he is just a kid, not even ten yet."

"So what if he's a kid? Mandira, it takes nothing to find the right age but takes ages to find the right one."

"That's deep. You are on fire today, Seb. That is why you are great. I better get going. They must be waiting for me. Happy Diwali, Seb."

"Happy Diwali, Mandira. May the Supreme bless you."

As I came out of the subway station, I recalled something unusual about my conversation with Sebastian. *Something was odd,* I thought as I attempted to break down our brief conversation in my head.

Sebastian had been in good spirits as always. He liked the sweets and complimented me as expected. But when I mentioned Ryan, his reaction seemed a bit odd.

He spoke as if he knew Ryan very well. I rarely spoke about Ryan in front of him, but it seemed that he was implying by his "goodness versus greatness" remark that Ryan was destined to be great; "It takes nothing to find the right age but takes ages to find the right one." What did that mean? That Ryan was the right one? Did he know something about Ryan? Did he know the secret?

I didn't think so. No human other than Ryan and I knew about it. Even Ryan did not know his own destiny. Perhaps he was making a casual remark about Ryan to cheer me like he always did, and I was trying to find meaning in his smart lines. But why did I feel that I had heard that line before?

It takes nothing to find the right age, but takes ages to find the right one, I repeated in my head. *It takes nothing...*

"Oh my God! I heard that line from Jack!" I said aloud.

A quick memory flashback from my conscious trip to Shloka left an unsettling feeling. Jack had told me that the chief used this line in reference to Ryan to convince the board members of Kendram.

How does Seb know this line? Could it be a coincidence? How can it be? Is Seb a keeper like Jack?

He had said, "May the Supreme bless you." The only other person who had used that term for God was Jack. Sebastian certainly was a keeper.

What else had he said? He'd said, "All greats must like gulab jamun," and I'd found it funny. He'd also said, "After all, there are only two of us."

Two of us? Ryan and Sebastian? Was he the one who had used that line originally?

Oh, God. Does that mean that Sebastian is none other than...

The last thought rattled me. I ran back into the subway station and hurried down the escalator. Sebastian was not present on the other side.

I looked around at every corner of the station. I punched my card and hastened to the steps leading down to the platform, hoping to find him sitting on one of those waiting chairs or benches, perhaps waiting for the metro, but no luck. Sebastian was nowhere to be seen.

I looked at the board for the metro schedule. The next metro was scheduled to arrive in one minute, which meant the last one had left around nine minutes ago, as the metro frequency was every ten minutes. He could not have taken the last metro as I had been talking to him around that time. Moreover, he spent most of his time at the station and rarely took the metro. This assumption was based on the notion of how well I thought I knew him, but did I really?

I left the platform and stopped at the candy shop on the corner.

"Hey! How are you?" I asked the middle-aged owner of the shop.

"I am doing good, young lady. Tell me."

"Did you see Sebastian? I can't find him."

"Sebastian? Who?"

"Sebastian. The homeless man who lives around here. Have you seen him?"

"There is no homeless man around here, young lady."

"Oh, there is one. He stands over there, near the escalator. An old, bearded man. Perhaps you haven't noticed. I talk to him every day."

"Well, miss, I have been sitting here in this shop for the past five years. Most of my time is passed by watching people going up and down that escalator. I have never seen any old, bearded, homeless man. I *have* seen you many times. I thought you had a habit of talking to yourself. Do you see…I mean, have you…"

The candy shop owner did not complete his sentence, but his expression clearly conveyed his thoughts.

I excused myself and joined the flock of people who had just deboarded the metro, heading up the escalator.

I was not surprised to hear that the shop owner had never seen Sebastian. In fact, I would not have been surprised if nobody had ever seen him, except for me. Why would they? After all, he did not show up for them. He showed up for me. The top leader of the paramount organization unknown to humankind would not have been there in the first place if it were not for me.

Jack had told me that Chief Joseph could not meet me as the order bound him. Jack was right. He hadn't. He had not met me in the capacity of the Chief of Kendram. He did not say or do anything in the capacity of the Chief of Kendram. But he did see me.

He watched me in the disguise of an old homeless man called Sebastian. Sebastian who amazed me with his wit and wisdom alike. He guided me without giving me any advice. He inspired me without making any rousing speeches. He taught me so much without preaching.

Just seeing him every day, gushing over my food, appreciating his precious life, and laughing at his problems reassured me that everything would be ok. He instilled the belief in me that if a homeless man with no material possessions whatsoever could pull it off, so could I.

Before, I had not known the true identity of Sebastian, but I knew that I could see him every day if I wanted to. Now that I knew him, I did not know if I would see him again.

I wondered which one was better—knowing, or not knowing. Was the wisdom acquired from knowing better than the contentment from not knowing? Or the other way around?

*

The guests started arriving soon after we finished offering prayers to Lakshmi, the goddess of wealth and prosperity.

Elena came early and joined me in the kitchen to help me with last-minute arrangements. She expressed her amazement about the bonding of Britney and Ryan.

Britney had not left Ryan alone since that afternoon after his request to play had taken her by surprise. She was teaching him every game known to her that she had perhaps wished to play with him for all these years. As a faithful student of an expert coach, Ryan showed keen interest in all her games and their rules.

After the Haydens, the Kings arrived, followed by the Bergenzas (the lady famous in the neighborhood for her cats, also known as "Cat Woman", and her husband). Then came Viru's colleagues (from his former and present company), Sylvain, Daniel, and Emmanuel, accompanied by their spouses.

The guests were received and welcomed at the entrance by Viru and the beautiful rangoli design. It had a border made of colorful powders with "Happy Diwali" written, with the petals of rose and marigold at the center. Reva had embellished her rangoli by lighting oil lamps around it, and her whole effort was received with curiosity and commendation.

Timothy, the biggest fan of Reva's art, spent a long time sitting beside her rangoli, carefully observing the design and tacitly admiring her effort.

Elena and Reva helped me with serving welcome drinks, the jaljira, and juice. While some of the guests made themselves comfortable in the living room, others walked through the open sliding glass door, out to the back yard, either taking a casual stroll or relaxing on the wooden chairs.

Suddenly the entire house, including the backyard and the front yard, became illuminated by colorful LED lights. I looked at Viru, who had just turned on the switch on the extension board, and he winked at me.

In my absentmindedness since that afternoon, it had not occurred to me that he had accomplished his lighting project and had saved it for last. Full marks to our project director who had done an impressive job "meeting the deliverables," as he would like to say in his project management terminology. Extra points were given for decorating the welcome banner with the dancing lights at the far end of the backyard where he had arranged the counter for beverages.

Soon the party was in full bloom. My sweets were a big hit. The guests who knew the others made conversation, and those who didn't make their acquaintance.

Sylvain told an account of his recent trekking expedition to some of the guests gathered around him, making them laugh with his action-packed storytelling.

Viru enjoyed an animated conversation with colleagues and was busy at the counter, serving people with beverages like gin, wine, and vodka, and making cocktails out of them.

Sylvain's wife Molly entertained the ladies in the living room. It turned out she was no less gifted than her husband in the art of storytelling.

Reva had joined Tim at the entrance, sitting near him around the rangoli.

After apologizing for his behavior that afternoon, Ted joined Ryan and Britney in the backyard to light sparklers. Both were now talking simultaneously, explaining to Ryan how to swing the sparkler in the air.

Caesar relaxed on the ground near Ryan, sprawling his legs on the trimmed grass. The scars on his neck from his fight with Duma were still visible.

He did not seem to mind the lack of attention from the companion he cared about the most. When his eyes met mine, he seemed to say, "Don't worry, Mom. I've got his back."

I recalled my dream of the previous night when I had met my Grandma. According to Jack, seeing minners of Parloka in dreams was an actual meeting with them, and that goldmine of information made my dreams special for me.

Grandma had been a frequent visitor in my dreams since my conscious visit to Shloka. Jack had mentioned that finding me in Shloka among millions of dreaming minners was, for Grandma, like finding a needle in a haystack. But that dedicated woman still set forth to Shloka from Parloka every day, and my eyes welled up with tears at the thought of it.

In the dream, I was sitting on the couch in the living room, holding a two or three-month-old Ryan in my arms. I was busy engaging in baby talk and Ryan was laughing hard when I heard a gentle knock and looked at the half-opened door.

It was Grandma standing at the door with a very handsome man.

"What a pleasant surprise, Grandma, come on in," I said excitedly.

Grandma came in and joined in my baby talk with Ryan. The man stayed at the door.

"Who is that man, Grandma?"

"You don't know, Munni?"

"Know what?"

"Know him? He is your Grandpa, Munni."

"He is Grandpa? For real?" I asked in disbelief, and she nodded, smiling.

"Why doesn't he come inside?"

"He will not come inside. That's the way he is. A shy man."

I went up to him and greeted him, instead. "Hi, Grandpa. I am so happy to see you."

Grandpa smiled and nodded approvingly. An awkward silence followed. He was indeed a shy man.

"Would you like to come in, Grandpa?"

Grandpa gestured with his hands that he was ok standing at the door.

"Look, Grandpa, this is Ryan," I said, holding up Ryan.

Grandpa gazed at Ryan for a long time with a twinkle in his eye, then spoke for the first time, "How beautiful. The guardian is born."

******

About the Author

Rohit is fond of writing. To him, writing is like constructing a house of imagination, with the bricks being the words.

Rohit grew up in Shimla, India. His work took him to Montreal, Canada, where he moved in 2015 with his wife Richa and son Aahan.

He spends his pastime reading and taking pictures of Richa. While he reads out of his love for books, the photography is simply out of duty.

Rohit likes to read both fiction and non-fiction, his choice being the literary classics. His favorite books include *Anna Karenina* and *War and Peace* by Leo Tolstoy, *A Tale of Two Cities* by Charles Dickens, *To Kill a Mockingbird* by Harper Lee, and *The Great Gatsby* by F. Scott Fitzgerald.

Rohit considers *Anna Karenina* to be a masterpiece. He believes that the book touches upon many topics like love, relationships, philosophy, science, agriculture, politics, success, and failure, leaving an indelible impression of Tolstoy's skillful craftsmanship.

Thanks for reading. If you enjoyed this book, please consider leaving an honest review on Amazon or your store of choice.